BESTSELLING AUTHOR

# CAYCE POPONEA

© 2017 by Cayce Poponea @Write Hand Publications

**ISBN-13: 978-1542983983**
**ISBN-10: 1542983983**

Cover design by Jada Delee
Editing by Elizabeth Simonton

WRITE HAND
PUBLICATIONS

# CHAPTER ONE

*Zach*

"KNOW WHAT I MISS most about back home?" The whizzing sound of stray bullets buzzed in the air beside us. Nudging Reaper with my left elbow, I tipped my head in the direction of the two Boots sitting against the hill below us. These boys are so new; I can smell their fear from a mile away. Hell, if I looked hard enough, I'd bet they still had a price tag on them somewhere.

"Not getting shot at as the sun comes up?"

The pair hadn't noticed the six of us sitting not five feet behind them. They were too busy ducking down the second they heard the sound of stray bullets ricocheting off the rocks around them. Too green to realize by the time you hear the ping, it's too late.

"Nah," the guy on the right says, leaning back as he pulls a cigarette out of his pocket, trying to act as if he isn't about to shit his pants. His hands are shaking as he flicks the lighter several times before the cherry red ember forms on the end of the white stick. So far he's my favorite of the pair and I need a good name for him, one to tease him with once he realizes what is sitting behind him.

"The smell of warm pussy first thing in the morning." He admits, taking in a big breath of air and crossing his boots at the ankle. Reaper grunts, furrowing his brow as we both listen to the Boot trying hard to sound like a man. Another bullet whizzes past, maneuvering between the thin trees and embedding in the rock beside his head. The falling pebbles catch the attention of the kids below us; wide eyes do a double take, as the reality of where we are sinks in. Another bullet sings by, this time giving me a taste of the dirt on the back of my neck.

"Motherfucker," the darkness surrounding us does nothing to hide my anger. "Reaper, you wanna do something about the chicken shit who's shooting at us?" My words are a day late and a dollar short as he methodically points his gun at the ridge across the way. Matthew Parish, known to the five of us as Reaper, holds more records associated with firearms than any man I know. Too bad he can't claim the majority of them, his SEAL status forbids it.

He licks his thumb, sliding the wet digit along the side of his riffle, something he has done since I met him during Hell Week. Hailing from West Virginia, he's the third son of a pig farmer and only member of his family to ever leave the state. Two shots from his rifle and the spent casings eject to the side, followed by a wad of spit mixed with tobacco into the dirt. The Army kids below jump and cover their heads, as if it will do any good. We all watch and wait for return fire, when there is none, the morning rays of sunshine are allowed to come up in silence.

"Mornin', boys." Havoc, Alex Nakos, fresh out of medical after a gunshot wound from our last mission, tips his helmet at the wide-eyed men below. Havoc can turn anything into an explosive, and I do mean anything, messing up our enemy's world in the process. Havoc comes from a huge Greek family, complete with endless stories of his mother's obsession with marrying him off to a good Greek girl. Every week she sends him a care package, it's filled with some of the best sweets I've ever tasted. Fuck, I'd marry anyone she wanted me to if it meant I could eat the shit she sends.

"Sir," they say in unison, their hands twitching in an automatic attempt to salute him. For weeks these kids are taught how to hold their hands in a straight line against their eyebrow, only to be threatened if they do it out here in the desert.

"No, Sirs around here," he corrects. "I'm Havoc, this guy to my left is Viper." He introduced, sending a back handed slap to my left arm. I'd been given the call sign when I was able to crawl through a narrow gap during Hell Week, sneaking up on the team we were competing against. I managed to silently infiltrate their six and take the flag they were protecting. The leader of the team called me a viper, since I was able to maneuver into tight spaces and strike without a sound.

"This ugly fuck here is Doc." Logan Forbes is more than just your standard issue Corpsman; he is a man of incredible honor and integrity. When he was about to head off to med school, his family discovered an uncle was embezzling from their company, leaving it on the edge of bankruptcy. He refused to give up on becoming a doctor, so after making a few phone calls to some lawmakers in Washington, he signed up for the military in exchange for tuition. A year into his training, his family was able to regain the company's holdings. He could have gotten out of his contract with the Navy, but he didn't. On the final day of his internship, the Twin Towers fell in New York City and he was on an airplane by dinnertime the same day to the Middle East.

"On his left, is Chief." Aiden Sawyer, had found the girl he was gonna propose to on a porn web page one evening. When he confronted her about it, she brushed him off saying it was better than stripping on a stage. He returned the ring to the jewelers and joined the military the next day. Chief is the oldest of our group and by far the wisest. Which is why he's our operations guy; he has skills, which would make MacGyver scratch his head.

"On the very end, is Ghost," Ryan Biggs, the sixth of seven brothers, his family owned a remote ranch in Montana. His grandfather had been an avid HAM radio user and passed his skills on to Ghost. His dreams for the future didn't include herding cattle and mending fences, so as soon as he graduated from school he enlisted in the Marines. We all swear he can make the sand of the desert carry a message for him.

"Last but not least, the man who just lit up your asses with hot rounds, killing the piece of shit taking pot shots, is the infamous Reaper.

Skilled marksman and expert bullshit detector." The Boots turned to each of my team as Havoc introduces everyone. I watched their peach fuzzed faces as they begin to deduce who and what we are. Our hair is longer than the regs allow and we've all grown a beard. Every one of us carries a better gun, and has some kick ass toys the general public has no idea are made. Our uniforms are different as well; no marking, no name badges, not a single insignia to identify us as SEALs.

"His radar is accurate as usual. You, Correra..." Havoc reaches out tapping his gloved finger against the nametag of the cocky Boot. "...Are full of it. The last piece of pussy you had was when your momma brought you into the world, kicking and screaming and pissing down your leg." Leaning in his direction, Havoc takes a deep and dramatic sniff through his nose. "Not much has changed, still pissing yourself." His buddy snorts, smacking him in the chest, capturing his attention and blank stare as the rest of us laugh at Havoc's teasing.

"Fuck you." Correra retorts, clambering to his feet and stomping away. "Awe, don't go away mad," Havoc calls to his retreating and angry steps. "Just fucking go away." Shaking his head back and forth, silently judging the thin skinned boy. If Correra was going to survive his time in this place, and the military, he would need to grow a set of balls and be prepared to dish out his own brand of insults. Life out here is tough; being isolated from your family and friends, waiting days, sometimes weeks, for the next supply truck to bring a letter from home. You learn to rely on your team for more than just watching your back, and you learn the value of life and how quickly it can all change.

"Wow, never thought I'd see flowers in the middle of the desert." The sun fills the valley revealing beautiful poppy fields, as the remaining Boot stands with his hands wrapped around his rifle, staring off in awe of the valley of bright pink and white flowers below. Korengal Valley is known for two things: it's the most dangerous enemy stronghold in Afghanistan and it's the largest poppy producing area in the Middle East.

"You will see and do shit here you may or may not be able to forget. Drugs and dust storms will fill your dreams and star in your nightmares." I tell him, shifting my ass into a new position, the numbness had begun to

6

settle in hours ago. The Boot looks over his shoulder, a single line of sweat sliding down his pale face and into his still clean looking uniform.

"Those flowers," Reaper breaks in, while whittling a stick with the edge of his knife, the shavings arching out and into the dirt. "Are fucking poison." Boot looks back towards the valley, "Seriously?" he says, disbelieving.

Reaper stops his destruction of the piece of wood and raises his head as he rests an arm on his knee. "Yes, *really*. Every spring and summer, that field, and a number of others you can't see from this ridgeline, produce a poppy flower. The plant itself is attractive, not just with the beauty it gives, but the wealth it brings to the fucker who owns this land. Or at least thinks he does." Turning to the side, Reaper spits the wad of chew he had in his mouth to the ground.

"Why is that, sir?" Boot lowers himself onto bended knee, tipping his helmet back and removing his sunglasses.

"Where you from…" Reaper leans in to get a closer look at his nametag, "…Moore?"

I should've held in the snicker I let slide into the conversation. As the leader of this team and this Boots' superior officer, I have a duty to keep control, yet I know what is about to come. Reaper may appear to be this hillbilly from the Ozarks, but he is one smart motherfucker with a photographic memory.

"Colorado, sir." Moore responds proudly.

"Well, Colorado, I need you to listen to me and listen good." Moore nods his head in agreement like a three year old wanting a second scoop of ice cream. "There are things you have to know about this place if you want to survive it. First, Aarash Konar the cold hearted prick who is the reason y'all are here, instead of back in the fucking air conditioning. Aarash has his hands in many deep pockets, including Al- Qaeda and ISIS. Being the largest supplier of heroin in the world, he is able to get anything he wants and right now, that's more land to grow his crops. Which is why you're here, to push back the lines he holds along the ridge where the sniper was shooting from this morning."

Moore listened with interest, his face contorting like most who hear this shit for the first time. The pink of his cheeks reflecting his youth and ignorance of what was happening in the world around him.

"Then why not just send in a few fighter jets and bomb the shit out of the ridge? Instead of wasting our time and money?" Moore isn't the first to question this, and he won't be the last. United forces are labeled as being the grand authority with the biggest dick and fiercest warfare.

"Russia tried that shit in the eighties when they occupied this space. They came in with delusions of kicking the shit out of the goat farmers. Ten years later, they marched back to the motherland with their whipped asses in hand, leaving behind hundreds of blonde haired children and the brand of loser."

The rumbling of heavy truck tires against the dirt road ends all conversations, necks crane in an attempt to catch a glimpse of the vehicle approaching. As the first truck rounds the bend, the anticipation of this being the medical convoy we have been assigned to escort across the valley increases. Reaper was telling the truth when he said what our purpose here was. Our team however, needs to get a medical group to the other side of this valley as the insurgents have a nasty habit of firing at our evac helicopters, making it near impossible to get our wounded men out and back to base for treatment.

"Moore, you keep your head down and your mouth shut. Trust no one and suspect every person you meet is out to kill you." Reaper resumed his whittling, not concerned with the cargo of the truck, which has now stopped along the makeshift road. Moore thanks him and turns to leave, sliding his sunglasses back on his face.

"Hey, Colorado," Reaper calls, having beaten me in creating a nickname for the kid. Moore turns around, shifting his gun to his other shoulder. "Get your name tags off your uniform and tell your buddies to do the same. Don't think for a second the bastards in the village won't rat you out to the enemy just for showing up in their business."

Reaching up, Moore pulls several times before the letters of his last name come away from his uniform. Nodding his head, he wadded up the piece of cloth in his clenched fist, turns and continues his path.

"Any word on the arrival of the truck?" Doc inquires as we watch Moore disappear into the mess tent.

"Only that they left late last night and the GPS shows them still moving in this direction." News of this particular mission had not been a welcomed one. We were all dog-tired from back to back assignments. Plans to hunker down, either under a palm tree or a tall oak, preferably with a nameless girl to help pass the time, were now on permanent hold until we could get this medical team past the insurgents and into their new home.

"Looks like supplies have arrived." Ghost stands from his crouched position, dusting off the pebbles, which were most likely causing him the same discomfort as all of us. "I'm gonna see if I can lend a hand."

He wasn't foolin anyone. Ghost has a high profile girlfriend back in the states, a national news reporter looking to make a name for herself by landing an anchor position. We've been silent for nearly two months, no email or phone calls. Our families know to send letters when they don't hear from us in a few days. Last time we went this long without contact, she got squirrely and did something she shouldn't have with an old friend of hers. Ghost forgave her, even took all the blame for not being around to warm her bed every night.

No one says a word as we watch Ghost walk over to the edge of the truck. A line of junior enlisted pass the unloaded contents to the center of the camp where two officers with clip boards point out instructions. Mailbags are usually the last to be unloaded, giving the workers an incentive to get the job done quick. Ghost may be an officer, a seasoned and lethal killer branded as a SEAL, but he is also an honorable man. He is willing to stand beside the fresh-faced kids who have, by now, figured out why his uniform is different and his face is sporting a full beard.

As the last box is tossed from the truck, the line breaks and forms a semicircle around three canvas bags; the black, block lettering on the side causes a hush to spread over the crowd. Ghost bends over, pulling the cords of one bag open, a job normally reserved for the commander of the unit. Nothing will be said to him for breaking the rules, not when they don't really apply to us.

9

With a black satchel under his arm, Ghost returns to our group, a slow smile forming on his face. "Viper, can I get the key?" I could play with him, tell him I left it back in base camp, but I want to see if I have any news from back home. My brother Zane and his wife Meghan were buying a house the last I heard from him. My sister Savannah had just opened a bakery, specializing in cupcakes. She had some trouble passing a city inspection and I hoped my father didn't have to step in to help her.

Ghost takes the key from me, jamming it into the coppery metal of the satchel and twists several times to open the lock. He reaches in, pulling out a multitude of letters and small packages, a few fall from the force he is using, landing on the dirt below.

Doc bends over, picking up the wayward letters. He glances at each one, shifting each pieces of parchment to read the face of the next. "LT, all of these babies are for you." Extending his hand out for me to take them.

My focus remains on Ghost as he hands out the letters in his hand. With each one he gives away, I can see his reserve falling just a little more as the stack gets shorter. My heartbeat quickens, I can feel my teeth sinking further into the soft flesh of my tongue. With the last letter coming up quick, a hush came over all of us as we watched the anguish turn to delight. We didn't need to ask who the letter was from or if the last two were for him, the tucking of paper into his pocket and whistle as he took his place against the rocky ledge said it all.

"Hey, LT," Reaper breaking the silence news from home created. "Remember the property I was looking into buying?" Last time we had been at base camp, he had perused the Internet looking for property to purchase. The group of us had an average of thirteen months left on our enlistments. Reaper wanted to buy a little strip of land, and live peaceful and alone once his time was up. After his fiancée Carrie, learned of the scar hidden behind his beard, she mailed him his ring and ended their engagement. Now, he had it in his head all women are evil and none of them would give him, or his deformed face, the time of day.

"The one in Montana or Oregon?" I teased. Being from Georgia myself, nothing north or west of the Mason-Dixon line mattered much to me. "Very funny, fucktard." Kicking my boot as he handed me the piece of paper he had in his hand. "This little beauty is bank owned and my realtor says they are eager to sell." I will admit, being born and raised in Atlanta, I am a big city boy through and through. Yet seeing the beauty in the land he wanted to purchase, the small house nestled in the tall trees of South Carolina, I could see the appeal. "How close to Charleston is this place?"

During the time we spent in Afghanistan, our team took on a Marine, Chase Morgan. Reaper and Havoc took a shining to him and began teaching him everything they knew. Pretty soon, he earned himself a call sign for his ability to make water catch fire. It was after he showed us this skill, his name was born; Diesel. Granted he did catch flak for his movie star good looks, and I've no doubt it helped to steer the men along in giving him the name. Diesel would share stories of his brothers back in Charleston; he made the historic city sound almost magical.

"Two hours, I wouldn't want to crowd Diesel or his kin." Taking back the flyer, he tucks it safely inside his shirt pocket. "When we get done with this shit, I'm gonna call her and have her start the paperwork." He picks up his whittling from before, Reaper's way of ending a conversation.

"Hey, anyone know if Kincaid has a sister or a wife?" Doc asks the group, a white sheet of paper dangling from his fingers, while his eyes flicker over the words on the page.

"Both. Why do you ask?" Havoc looks up from his own letter as he answers.

"Cause I got a letter from one of them."

Kincaid was a fellow SEAL we met when we did a joint mission with the 53rd Marine division. He ended up staying with us for about four months while Havoc recovered from his injuries.

Chief jumps to his feet, snatching the letter out of Doc's hands. "You lucky, motherfucker." He laughs as he scans the letter. "Harper Kincaid is the sister and one of the sweetest ladies to walk the planet." Chief tosses the paper back to Doc. "She works with the USO and Navy League to make sure single soldiers aren't forgotten during the holidays." Doc continues to read and reread the letter, turning the page around and checking the back. Chief has a Cheshire grin on his face, keeping the rest of the story to himself.

"Good news, Ladies," Havoc adds, turning the postcard we all know had to be from his Mother. "I was too slow in letting Athenia Pantel know I was looking for a good Greek girl to marry and she accepted the proposal of George Kalavesis instead." Havoc would be hard pressed to find a career in Hollywood, as his acting skills suck.

"Awe, don't fret, son. Your sweet momma will have a new girl lined up before you know it." Havoc turns the post card sideways, flinging it at my head. I laugh as I catch it with ease, enjoying the photo of the Isle of Cyprus on the front.

"What about you, LT? Any news from home?" Chief asks, his own letter folded in his hands. I knew better than to think I could wait until I had a moment alone, as a team, we shared practically everything. I pull the four envelopes from my pocket, peering at the return addresses and logos. "Well, First Mortgage can offer me a free evaluation on my current rates." Chuckling, I toss the junk mail into the dirt at my right. "Next, we have an offer to make the grass of my lawn greener." Reaper snickered at that one as it joined the pile. "A letter from my baby sister, no doubt telling me about the new guy in her life I'll need to kick the shit out of for breaking her heart." I shove the letter back into my pocket. Savannah was in love with the idea of being in love. She hopped like a fucking bunny from one obsession to the next; tossing everything she had into the relationship, being used for her name and her bank account.

"Finally, we have an airmail letter from Kennedy Forrester." The red, white, and blue stripes along the border of the envelope, lightweight, almost tissue paper texture. Years ago this paper was common when sending mail overseas, when the price was dictated by the weight of the post. Sliding my callused finger under the seal, I separated the flap from the glued edge, taking care not to rip the fragile paper as I removed the thin letter.

*Zack,*

*I hate the way we left things. I know I said I would be there for you no matter what happened, but it scared me when you started asking for information I wasn't comfortable giving you. I want to help...*

I stopped reading the letter the second I realized it wasn't intended for me. My name is Zach, not Zack. Picking up the discarded envelope, I noticed the last name is wrong as well. Zack Michels, instead of Michaels, the only thing correct was the APO address. "Which was delivered to the wrong Zach." I add, as I know my team is waiting to know who Kennedy is. "I'll look up the poor bastard when we get back and give him his letter."

The rumbling of tires starts at the same time sniper fire resumes. I look to Reaper who has already lined up his rifle to the ridge to the West of us. Two shots ring out, one additional from the sniper and the second from the barrel of Reaper's gun. We all collectively stand as the convoy stops in a swirl of dust behind us. We have a job to do, regardless of wrongly delivered mail, surprise packages, land purchases, and good Greek girls.

Reaper hesitates, his gun still raised to the ridge, finger remaining on the trigger. "The kid was right, you know?" Remaining still a second longer before lowering his gun and standing beside me. His green eyes flash to mine, a knowing smile framing his face. "I do miss the smell of warm pussy in the morning.

# CHAPTER TWO

*Kennedy*

"THAT'S IT, MR. GREEN, LET SUGAR do her magic."
Clenching the bridle in hand, my eyes bouncing back and forth between our patient, John Green an injured veteran from California, and Sugar our four year old Gelding. It had taken me three visits to convince him he wouldn't fall off the horse, injuring himself further. His wife contacted us almost a year ago when he came out of surgery unable to move his legs. Navy doctors gave him a less than five percent chance of ever walking again after his accident involving an IED explosion.
"I need you to focus on the movement of her hind legs." Equestrian therapy was once considered nothing more than voodoo to the medical community. All that changed when a celebrity or two showed marked improvements after attending this very facility.

"Memorize how she sways back and forth." Mr. Green closes his eyes while holding the horn with one hand and the reins with the other; his knuckles are white from the intensity of his grip. "Remember to breathe, Mr. Green." I add with humor.

Most of the patients start out in much the same way, scared to death of climbing on a horse, and trusting a spit of a girl to keep them from falling. Sabrina Hall, the owner and my boss, tells me it's the charm of my southern accent that wraps them around my finger and helps them feel at ease.

"Looking good, John." Speaking of Sabrina, she is perched by the gate, her salt and pepper hair pulled back in a low ponytail, tan corduroy shirt hanging over the top of her jeans, the legs tucked into her boots. "Keep this up and you'll be walking by Christmas." I appreciated her optimism, always believing everyone would be a success story, and while I have seen quite a few patients take those steps doctors said would never happen, Mr. Green would not be one of them. Unfortunately, my time here in Colorado was up and I was expected back in Atlanta by the end of next month.

I would miss everything about Colorado, the fresh air which filtered through the mountains, the snow as it piles high in the dead of winter, and the majestic mountains peaks, stretching with effort to touch the sky. Mostly, I would miss the freedom of doing what I love without fear of disappointing my family, specifically my mother, with my dirty boots and worn out blue jeans.

When I first arrived in Colorado Springs, I called my parents to share the delights I'd found here. Mother reminded me the altitude was much too high and would result in unbearable headaches for her, inhibiting any travel plans I would allude to. Somehow she managed to deal with the discomfort when her bridge club gathered in Aspen for a weekend retreat. My being three hours from her provided no reason for her to make a stop to say hello, not that I expected any less from her.

Growing up as a child of John and Claudia Forrester came with certain privileges, and even greater expectations. According to my mother, women of my upbringing were to be well versed in languages, culture, and design. All the necessary skills I would need in order to land a proper husband, one with deep pockets lined with old family money and southern society holdings.

I wanted to stand on my own, pave the way to my future with hard work and dedication, not by dropping my last name or asking for favors. I'd always wanted to work with horses, since the first pony my daddy ever bought me, a deep love was born. As I grew older, I learned of different ways horses were used in the modern world. A documentary on paraplegics gave me the passion to help those injured in an accident by way of horses.

When I graduated high school, my mother tried to force me to attend the same college she and my sister did. I begged my father to let me attend the University of Colorado and then allow me to stay an additional two years to fellowship train with Sabrina. He was hesitant, upsetting my mother wasn't something either of us enjoyed, but he allowed it, with stipulations of course. I loved working here; the smell of hay, the sounds of the horses as they woke in the morning, even cleaning out the stalls gave me a smile, which lasted the whole day.

Sabrina had offered me a full time position, but I couldn't accept it. I would keep my word I gave to my family and return to Atlanta. My mother had called daily with updates of teas and charity events scheduled in the next few months after my return. I was surprised she didn't have a list of men she wished me to entertain as well. While I would do as she asked and return to Atlanta, I wouldn't be following in her footsteps and joining any society groups. I had my heart set on something much bigger than chairing an event.

"Heard you come in early last night." Sabrina, my best friend as well as boss, maintains her view of Mr. Green as he passes by us. "Date not go well?" She's trying to hold back a smile, the lines around her mouth giving her amusement away.

"You know as well as I do Ethan and I have nothing in common."

I didn't have the heart, or perhaps courage, to say no to the young man who came to the center three months ago to take photos for the reporter doing a story on Sabrina. Ethan Porter, a freelance photographer from Denver, is everything I don't particularly find appealing in the opposite sex. His blonde hair, brown eyes, and pale skin were not on the list of attributes I wanted in the man I chose to date.

Ethan had been sweet and considerate with his compliments and openly flirting, returning virtually every weekend to see if I would grant him the honor of taking me to dinner. I tried to explain to him my time here was quite limited, but he remained persistent, continuing to drive the hour each way on the chance I would say yes.

"Yes, but does he know this?" Unable to control the laughter bubbling up inside, a chortle leaves her throat, quickly evolving into a belly laugh. Sabrina had enjoyed more laughs when it came to Ethan and his affection for me than what I would consider appropriate. At first, she—as many friends do to one another—teased me for having captured his attention. When he wouldn't stop his pursuit, her teasing took on a life of its own.

"Go ahead and laugh, but I'm fairly certain we have seen the last of Mr. Porter." Shifting the humor to reflect the odd sense of accomplishment I felt after the conversation I had with Ethan. Sabrina accused me of being far too polite to ever intentionally hurting anyone's feelings. Too bad she had never been the recipient of a backhanded compliment served with a glass of freshly brewed sweet tea.

"Oh, this should be good," her laughter ceasing, eyes narrowing in disbelief. "What, did you pull out the stern face and then bless his heart?" Shaking her head as her focus returned to observing me work. "Your southern anecdotes only work on the locals who understand them. Men like Ethan find them to be like foreplay, always diving in for more."

She was right, from the first moment I arrived in Colorado, I had one person after another asking me to say a plethora of words, repeating them mockingly at the slowness of how I spoke. "Actually, I used something I learned in a movie I watched a few years ago." Sugar had begun to slow her footing, slacking off when she thought I was too busy talking to Sabrina. Clicking my tongue, I let her know I was still watching her.

"You doing all right, Mr. Green?" His knuckles were no longer white from the death grip he had earlier, still grasping the horn and the reins, it was now in a more relaxed fashion.

"Yep, but she's right, it's the sound of your accent keeping me on this horse." Even I couldn't avoid joining in the laughter at Mr. Green's honesty.

"Careful, Mr. Green, next time I'll put you on Loco." A once explosive smile was now a line of concern, and I had to work hard to keep my game face on.

"What kind of name is that for a horse?"

Sabrina chose this moment to disappear into the stables, her way of hiding her face and ruining my teasing. Loco is a rescue horse we found abandoned on a farm the owners lost to the bank. Extremely malnourished and skittish as hell, but I managed to get him to trust me enough to get in the horse trailer. It took a lot of work, sleepless nights and a few prayers, but now Loco is one of the best horses we have around here. When it came time to give him a name, José the handyman around here said we were crazy for keeping an animal who could snap at any moment. The name and the horse are working out just fine.

"Keep working hard and watch yourself, and you'll never have to find out."

\* \* \*

I brushed the dirt and shedding hair from Sugar, a mindless task I have always enjoyed. It's a good time to let your mind wonder, ponder over the events of the day. I refused to think of the day when I would no longer have this escape; too busy keeping up the facade of being the daughter my mother needs me to be.

"You were about to tell me how you got rid of stalker boy with your movie knowledge." Startled from my musings of doom and gloom, a gasp leaves my mouth and Sugar pushes back two steps. "Whoa, there." I croon, trying to calm her, swallowing my fear, as it isn't good for her.

"Easy girl." Sabrina makes her way around to the front of Sugar, talking to her in hushed tones.

"Go ahead, Kennedy. Sugar wants to know why her favorite snack giver won't be coming by anymore." Huffing, I know she will keep after me if I don't tell her the whole story.

"Ethan wanted to pick me up, as you are well aware." Stepping back from the horse and tucking the brush into my back pocket, I remove the carrot I have as a reward, placing it under Sugar's nose "We both know how well that idea went."

My dating experience was sadly limited. Friends told me I was too picky and should take a guy home just to get a release. I never bought into the casual sex thing; I had been the girl all those public service announcements had reached. I never touched drugs, never cheated on a test or skipped class. Never once did I give my number to a boy I didn't know or let a guy pick me up from my house.

"So we agreed to meet at Simone's, over by the hospital." I watch Sugar eat the carrot, her lips curling away from her teeth as she enjoyed the well-deserved treat.

"When I arrived, he was already there with a glass of red wine waiting for me." Sabrina quirked an eyebrow at me, knowing how much I hated red wine. "When the waiter came by asking what I would like, I took the opportunity to set things straight."

Following Sabrina out the door of the stall, I rubbed my hand down the nose of Sugar one last time. "Doesn't sound too scandalous, kind of boring really." She shrugs, continuing down the hall toward her office.

"Hey! Do you want to hear this, or would you rather pick fun at me?" A slow glance over her shoulder briefly shows me her unamused eyes before turning back around.

"As the waiter told us of the chef's specials, I slid the glass of wine in his direction, ordered the lamb chops and politely asked him to remove the wine and bring me a glass of water with lemon instead."

As we turned out of the stables, I caught the incredible aroma of Martha's, famous chicken and noodles. Her food was legendary, and a nice bonus for working here. A far cry better than the food I had back in my room last night.

"As soon as the waiter excused himself, Ethan asked if there was something wrong with the wine. I leaned forward, checked to see if anyone was listening, and excitedly told him I had used an ovulation kit earlier in the day and if everything went well with the date, we could be parents before the first snowfall."

For the first time in a long while, Sabrina didn't have a witty comeback. No carefully crafted words to make me cringe or shake my head. "As the waiter set our plates down, Ethan received an urgent phone call and had to leave, begging for my forgiveness and a rain check." I was taking far too much amusement in my accomplishment than I should; boasting about deception was not a good character building exercise.

"So you pulled the almost pregnancy card and sent him packing?"

"I know, I know. It was dishonest and I shouldn't have done it, but you have to admit he was becoming a pest." I argued, why I'm not sure.

"Oh, Kennedy, you're not the first girl to toss that particular card and you won't be the last." Her tone was the same Lucia, our cook back home, would use when I did something she didn't approve of.

"Listen, you are a pretty girl with your whole life ahead of you and there is a blank canvas before you, just waiting for bad decisions and regrettable boyfriends. As you get older, you will learn the art of seduction and how to tell a good lie."

Several of the ranch hands already stood in line, no one wanted to miss Martha's Sunday dinner. Sabrina picked up a plate, holding it out for me to take. "But until you can perfect the lying part, you might want to knock off the politeness and soak up some pure bitch." My mouth dropped open in surprise, eyes wide no doubt.

"Ethan called you on your poker face," she nodded to the table behind me. I found myself turning around slowly, terrified at what I would find.

"Those came for you after Mr. Green's wife picked him up. Peach roses, at least a dozen in total, sat out of place on the wooden table beside the military picture of Sabrina's son. While their beauty was unquestionable, the rationale was, Ethan knew I was leaving in less than a month, moving halfway across the country to disappoint my mother even more than I currently do.

"My advice to you is be straight with the boy, or call that lawyer father of yours and get a restraining order on him."

# CHAPTER THREE

*Zach*

"CO WANTS TO MEET WITH US AT 1300." Havoc muttered as he adjusted the straps of his rifle, giving me a look of amusement we both knew I shared. As the leader of this team, it was my job to keep my men informed and out of trouble, placing my life in front of theirs. This particular CO hadn't stepped outside of his tent to do more than take a piss. He had no clue what dangers surrounded him out here, or maybe he did and didn't have big enough balls to face them. Either way, this meeting he wanted to have, was pointless.

"Make sure you wear your shortest skirt so he can appreciate your sexy legs." Doc butted in, his sense of humor one of our favorite qualities about him. Even if you were taking your last breath, Doc was going to help you make it count.

"Fuck him, I'm saving that shit for you." Havoc pulls Doc in close, dramatically kissing his cheek. Doc pushes him off, wiping the residue of the teasing on his sleeve.

"All right y'all huddle in and let's have a real meeting."

Walking over to where the trucks would pull in, we formed a semicircle under a pitiful excuse for a tree. Ghost waited while the truck, which had brought the mail in earlier, loaded up to head back out. Bags of mail were the last to go on, as the men here did not have access to computers, and cell service was intermittent with the mountain range.

"We have two areas where they have experienced heavy fire, one of which is reported to be a new hotspot for IEDs." IEDs were nasty bombs buried under the dirt just waiting for an unsuspecting victim. Didn't matter if it was a two hundred pound soldier or a fifty pound child, the result was the same.

"I can radio for a sweep, but we might as well hire a band to announce our arrival." Ghost was right, we would travel under the cover of night, using night vision goggles to navigate in order to avoid being noticed as much as possible.

"No to the sweep." I instructed as everyone nodded their heads in agreement. "We put Havoc in the lead truck and Reaper bringing up the rear. We need fire power from both angles." I looked into the eyes of the men I trust most in this world, knowing each would follow me into the depths of hell if I asked them and, in reality, I was about to ask just that.

"One more piece of information y'all need to know. This caravan is different from the others we've done." Clearing the dust from my throat as the rumblings of newly arriving trucks sounded in the distance. "We have four civilian nurses this time." I have high expectations of my men, but at the end of the day, we are all trained individuals who are overgrown boys deep inside.

"Do we know if any of them are single?" Case in point as proven by Doc.

"Won't matter to you, Doc." Chief cautions. "You're about to get all the girl you need once you open the box from Harper Kincaid." The letter from Kennedy is still fresh in my pocket and a strange feeling is brewing in my chest.

Doc could talk a big game, but we all knew he wanted a family like the rest of us. One could argue he was a handsome guy, but logically every man managed to shine in this uniform. What we did know, Doc had dated every man's wet dream in the form of Victoria's Secret model, Lisa James.

Out of the corner of my eye, I noticed Senior Chief Fuller, Captain Reynolds' right hand man. While many of the kids around here gave him the respect his rank required, our Chief would rather spit in his face than address him properly. Reaching the rank of Senior before he turned thirty was a feat unheard of.

"Pecker Gnat at three o'clock." Havoc warned, he too hated Fuller with a passion, a direct result of the respect he held for Chief.

"Gentleman." Fuller called to us, making his way in our direction. His hands tucked behind his back, his gait looked as if a broom handle was lodged up his ass. "Captain Reynolds is ready to see you." Rocking back and forth on the balls of his feet, waiting for us to jump to attention and scurry across the camp.

"Roger that, Senior." I say and return to talking with my team. Pecker Gnat continues to wait like an expectant father, standing closer to my left shoulder than I'm comfortable with.

"LT, you did hear me say the *Captain* is waiting?" As a Lieutenant, I out rank him and his attitude toward me is out of line. With his lips permanently planted around the cock of the CO, he assumed he could speak to me as he feels. But he is wrong, very fucking wrong.

Adjusting my stance, the top of his baldhead does not reach my shoulder. He may have sucked a few dicks on his climb to the top, but my dick was reserved for the girl I chose to be with. "Senior, need I remind you, my team is not attached to this unit? We are here on the orders of Admiral Coin, who, correct me if I'm wrong, could shit down Captain's throat in the middle of the afternoon and he would have to open wide, taking every bit of it." Keeping less than an inch of space between our chests, remaining well within the regulations I know Reaper could spout off at a moment's notice. "Now, until the United States military decides a chief of any level will out rank a Lieutenant, I recommend you scurry on back and let the Captain know we will be there in a minute."

* * *

Captain Reynolds sat behind his mahogany desk, a photo of an older woman placed at a forty-five degree angle to his left. An open, and abandoned, laptop took up space in the center of the desk. Everyone knew he had been sent here as a show piece, never with any intentions of stepping foot outside of this camp until it was time to go back to the States. For twenty-three minutes, he lectured us about how critical this mission was to the progression of our troops gaining foot on this war on terror. The man sat in his matching chair, not a single drop of sweat trickling down his clean-shaven face, the rumored ice packs he sat on were doing their job. He reminded us of how the military has adapted a no tolerance policy when it came to sexual harassment involving active duty. I wanted so badly to say it was men like him who women considered sex as a harassment, not men like those standing before him who know how to make a woman swoon, without the uniform.

As we left his tent, the bright sun in the afternoon sky nearly blinded us from the four trucks, which had finally arrived. Four women, dressed in jeans and hiking boots stood under the same sorry excuse of a tree we had half an hour earlier. Five feet away stood another half dozen active duty, all laughing while a couple smoked a cigarette.

"Fuck me, that was a half hour of my life I'll never get back." Doc complained as soon as we were out of earshot.

"Chin up, Doc." Reaper wrapped his arm around him, pulling him close to his side. "He has to talk as much as he does to keep that fucking desk from turning to dust." I looked to Reaper through perplexed eyes. "Come on Viper, you ever known a patio chair made out of wood to last long in the summer heat without treating it every year?"

Hurried introductions are made as the sun begins its descent behind the mountain range. Four nurses all a little green with an average of less than three years out of school between them. Not a single one of them having ever left the States before this. "You four stick with one of us, I don't care who you choose, but when the bullets start flying, you better do exactly as we say."

One of the nurses, the only blonde in the bunch, shifted her hips and looked me up and down. "Don't you mean *if* the bullets start flying and not when, Captain America?"

Stepping closer to her, leaving no room for bullshit. "No, Barbie, I mean when. Now get in one of those trucks so we can get the fuck out of here."

24

My team waited until the ladies were inside the trucks before they let their laughter fly. "Captain America? You got a wild one on your hands there." Doc teased, checking his bag one last time.

"Bitches like that gonna..." Reaper's words are cut short as something reflective crosses his face. He looks behind me with squinted eyes at the ridge where I assume the light is coming from, but sees nothing.

"Ghost get me an update on any activity." Before he can respond, the flash comes from the left, along the side closest to us. "Havoc get an ID on who the fuck they're signaling." Using mirrors to communicate is a practice as old as time. If I were a gambling man, I would wager the first was a mistake, never meant to hit Reaper's face.

"If something's going down, they aren't talking about it.' Ghost voices in frustration.

"Three points," Reaper reports. "First one on the west ridge, second in the north and the third on the valley floor. My suspicion is they either know we're about to move or they're moving some product. Either way, this is about to be a long fucking night." Reaper spoke what we all were thinking. Lucky for me, or maybe her, Barbie chose the last truck with Reaper. He was a hard faced man who didn't warm up to easily. With his face the way it was, he had begun to avoid people he didn't know at all. As the last of the daylight turned her head from the desert, I caught another flash of light from the North side.

"I got it, Viper." Havoc whispered into his microphone. "No doubt this shit is about us." The edge of nervousness began to creep into my chest, something I'd grown to rely on when trouble was brewing. When a SEAL became complacent and cocky, it was time to retire or move on as cocky will get you killed. "Everyone watch your surroundings and keep communications to a minimum."

Our decent down the hill was filled with maneuvering over small trenches and over several dried out bushes. The motion of tackling these small hills jostled us around and with the rough terrain, the progress is brain numbing slow. Just after midnight, when I assumed our cargo would be fast asleep, the most annoying voice came over my earpiece. "Captain, can we please pull over? Some of us can't hold our bladders for an eternity." How one tiny woman made me want to rip off Reaper's head and spit down his throat is beyond me.

"First of all, there are no Captain's in this or any vehicle near us. Second, use the bags I told you about before we started and third, hand that earpiece back to Reaper."

"Now you listen to me, we have been stuck inside this..."

"Reaper, you better shut her the fuck up or I will!" I barked through clenched teeth. Our job was difficult enough without this loud mouthed bitch telling anyone who was listening we were on the move.

"Viper, something just came off the back tire of your truck, stop where you are." This was the last thing I needed. The more we stopped, the longer it would take us to cross, increasing the likelihood of an ambush by leaps and bounds.

"Ma'am, I'm coming back to get you. Don't you say a fucking word do you understand?" We traveled with navigation lights only, a small red light which gave you enough to see the person next to you and not much else, avoiding turning on the headlight to try and stay hidden. If Barbie opened her mouth, the mountains would carry the sound all the way to the people with the mirrors. A woman in their eyes was only good for one purpose.

Jumping out of my seat, I ran to the last truck, as Ghost got out of the second truck, passing him on my way. The temperatures had dropped to the thirties, making my heavy uniform less sweltering.

As I came up to the door of the final truck, Reaper was already out scanning the area. I jumped into the bed of the truck as Blondie jumps out, her finger raised as if to argue.

"Shut the fuck up," I whispered as loud and harsh as I could.

"But..."

Slapping my hand over her mouth, her eyes widening in surprise. "I said shut up," enunciating each word. "You and your bitching is going to get one of us killed."

Blondie reaches up; pulling my gloved hand at the same time she turns her head. "Don't you threaten me!" She speaks in a raised voice, eyes flicking up and down my body, causing my irritation to break through its boiling point.

Just as I'm about to lay into her, loud voices are heard in the distance followed by rapid gun fire. Muzzle flashes announce the arrival of the people we've been trying to avoid. Several bullets ricochet off the edge of the road as the blonde starts to panic, screaming at the top of her lungs. I quickly shove her to the dirt, scooting her under the cover of the truck.

"Don't you move, do you understand me?" She nods her head, tears flowing freely mixed with the dirt of the ground below. "Not a word, not a single scream, no matter what the fuck you see or hear." Not waiting for her decision, I crawl to the side of the truck to get an assessment of what was going on.

"Viper, we got eight up top, and four on our six."

"They ain't here to offer us scotch and Cuban cigars, take 'em down, take 'em down." Another benefit to being a SEAL, there was no calling back to base and asking permission to engage. This mission would never make the headlines or appear on CNN. None of us would earn a medal for bravery or be interviewed for a documentary.

My orders are carried out and the night is lit up with tracer rounds coming from Reaper's favorite toy, a modified M16. The sounds of wounded men, crying out their agony and firing the last of their ammo into the sky, draw a map for the others who were still coming at us. Firing off my rifle, I take down the two men charging at us. Just as quickly as it began, the quiet sounds of the desert night returned.

"Hold your positions." This wasn't over, not this easily.

"Viper, we got three coming up on your left. You're not gonna like this."

Keeping my rifle drawn, the three images grew clearer in my night vision goggles. Ghost is correct as usual, my back teeth clenched as I recognize the smug bastard in the middle; Aarash Konar.

"No shoot, my friends." His accent is heavy and humor filled. This cocksucker fears nothing and feels he can do whatever he wants. "I am unarmed and want only to talk to this Captain you have." I avoid shooting a death glare to the loud-mouthed bitch under the truck. Standing not ten feet from me is the man responsible for the entire illegal drug trafficking in the region. We are imposing on his ability to continue to ship his product by occupying and destroying the fields and plants he has.

"That's far enough." I command, our eyes locking in the moonlight. Aarash and I have met on several occasions, one of those resulting in the scar I have along the side of my hip. He has a fondness for American girls, feeding them a line of bullshit about living like a princess back at his palace. Two years ago, he found one who saw through his bullshit and told him to fuck off. Aarash took her crassness as foreplay, kidnapping her from her hotel room. Lucky for her, she was *Skyping* with her father when it happened. We knew the second we saw the recording where to find her. As we were leaving the compound, he took a cheap shot, slicing my side with his knife. I looked him in the eye and told him he had the strength of a newborn baby and to quit playing with the big boy toys.

"Now, turn around and head back where you came from." Six sets of guns pointed in his direction. Chances are there was twice that many pointed at us. "Or don't, and see what happens."

Aarash held up his hands in surrender, "No need for violence, my friend. We came to see what the noise was."

"Aarash, save the bull shit for the cocksuckers you sell your shit to. You and I both know why you are here." Raising my rifle to my shoulder, I have his bushy eyebrows in my sights.

"I won't repeat myself, leave and let us pass, or see what happens." From my left, Reaper licks his thumb; shit is about to get real.

"Lieutenant Zach Michaels, from Atlanta Georgia. Your brother, Zane, threw his knee out and lost me a lot of money. I saw him play when I visit my brother Aaron in US. He attends your Georgetown University." Swallowing hard, uncomfortable with how much he knew about me and my family. If the motherfucker said a word about my mother, I wouldn't hesitate to put a bullet through his head. Remaining stoic, confirming nothing about who he knew me to be. Some hacker living in their parent's basement, snuck into the system, stole records and sold them to dick heads like Aarash.

"Is this not you, Lieutenant?" Before I can tell him where to stick his information, bullets ring out from the right side of the ridge, hitting the men standing on either side of Aarash. Havoc jumps to the side of the middle truck, a rocket launcher on his shoulder. Five more shots ring out before Havoc sets the rocket free, the fucker who killed Aarash's men, also gave away their position.

The blast from the rocket is too much for the blonde under the truck, she bounds out, hands over her ears screaming. "Stop it!"

Face covered in dirt and shed tears, hands scraped and bleeding from my roughness in tossing her to safety. "All of this shooting is ridiculous."

Havoc looks over his shoulder, Ghost is holding what looks like a crowbar in his hand and I'm assuming it was what fell off my truck, or was tossed at it.

"Don't you fucking listen to anything?" Doc is out from the left, marching with purpose in Blonde's direction. Not only is she a loud mouth, but she is quick as hell, diving around Doc and landing eye to eye with Aarash.

Something exchanges between them before Doc can attempt to pull her back. Blondie places her back against Aarash's chest, her arms spread out beside her. "If you want to kill him, you will have to kill me." She is determined as hell it's comical really. She has no idea the kind of monster she is attempting to protect.

"Your funeral." I shrug, lowering my rifle, her foolishness giving me a new idea of how to use him. "Ghost, let's find this man a seat aboard our bus and let these two kids get acquainted." Reaper is less welcoming to my idea, where Doc finds it just as amusing.

"Okay, just got to make sure he isn't carrying anything which would hurt us." Ghost moves to go around Blondie, when she realizes Aarash is about to be searched.

"What do you think you are doing?" Swatting at Ghost with her hands. "This man is defending his land, ask him nicely to use his roads." Placing a tiny hand on Aarash's cloth covered arm. "Sir, please know these men do not represent me. I apologize for the Neanderthal treatment you and your family have received."

Ghost looks to me, silently confirming to continue. Moving around, I hand my rifle to Doc. "Well, since me and my team don't represent you and the facts seem to be getting in the way of your flirting with Aarash here." I reach around, tugging his turban off his head. Blondie jumps back as half a dozen grenades fall to the ground. I look to the dark balls rolling

29

around, and then back to her shocked eyes. "Think I need to look further?" My question is swimming in sarcasm, but Blondie's bottom lip vibrates with a quiver as she turns and crawls back under the truck.

. . .

As the first rays of the new day creep over the top of the ridge, we pull the last of the supplies from the truck. Blondie, whose name I learned ten minutes ago is Vivian, gave no argument as we handed Aarash over to the security team on this side of the valley. She remained silent and worked hard at getting the med station ready to take in wounded.

Ghost radioed for our helicopter ride back to base, a small reprieve awaited us once we landed. Havoc checked the tires of the truck for any damage before thanking the driver for all his help.

"You know, Captain, with the amount of friction between us, the sex would be incredible." Vivian stood in a pose most men would find sexy, legs slightly parted, with her hip jutted out to her left and her bottom lip held prisoner by her teeth.

Walking closer to her, I shortened the distance and the need to raise my voice any louder than necessary. "You know, the Navy has a zero tolerance policy on sexual harassment. With what you just said, I could have your ass before a judge by nightfall." The thundering sounds of the helo blades off the surrounding mountains keep her from defending her proposition. Leaning in, my lips nearly touch the ridge of her ear, "Besides, I wouldn't fuck you for practice."

# CHAPTER FOUR

*Kennedy*

"I SENT YOU THE NEW CHANEL suit Caroline picked up for you in Paris, make sure you wear it with the pearls you received from your father last year. And for heaven's sake, have your hair and makeup professionally done." My mother's instructional phone calls had begun last week, with less than a month left of my time here in Colorado, her planning for my arrival had taken on a new frenzy. Caroline, my sister and a carbon copy of our mother, did everything she said to do, including marrying the man hand picked for her. She would be sitting beside her with a disapproving look of her own.

"Monica Timmons is rumored to have a weekend in New York planned, the last thing we need is for her to see you walking around the airport in some hillbilly attire." She considered anything made of cotton to be the fabric of the poor and underprivileged. Denim was for factory workers and those who had to remain employed at menial jobs in order to provide for themselves. My days of wearing anything comfortable were limited, at least in her eyes.

"Simon will pick you up and bring you back to the house." Simon is her driver, not that she really needs to be driven anywhere as she rarely leaves the house. Choosing instead to hold her social gatherings in the castle she built with my father's money and surrounding herself with the latest find her designer brings her. Every piece has a story and belonged to one former presidential family.

"Your father arranged for a man from the dealership to deliver your new car, make sure you thank him before he leaves for the office. I've also spoken with Barbra Vale, her son William, is interested in having dinner with you as soon as you settle in." A mental shiver ran up my spine, Will Vale was known to have his hand in more vaginas than a gynecologist. He used the pretense of his family's money, and one degree of separation from the Kennedy family, to get what he wanted from desperate women. The last time his name crossed my mother's lips was the day she asked my father to let him work at my father's firm, something to do until he passed the Georgia state bar. "I cannot emphasize to you enough how important a gentleman like William Vale is to our family."

The Vale's skirted around the definition of prosperous, with their bad investments and overspending. Will had failed the bar twice already, an embarrassment his family hid from their circle of friends. Most of the furniture my mother had in her collection came from the back room sales Mrs. Vale used to keep the lights on in their home. Will may want to have a meal with me, but it would be in his favor and not mine, something I wasn't interested in.

"Gloria will be here when you arrive, we agreed your wardrobe will need refreshing." This call ended as all the others I'd received, no bid of farewell or exchange of I love you's to end the conversation. When Claudia Forrester was finished speaking to you she ended the call, never waiting to see if you had a reply, as it never mattered to her.

Ethan had reached out a few times to try and reschedule, I'd used my mother as an excuse, always busy with something she needed from me before I left for Atlanta. He remained steadfast, sending additional flowers and constant text messages. The more he pursued, the further he drove the wedge between us. I tried to remain courteous and polite, but his last few calls had gone to voicemail and eventually in the deleted file.

Sabrina enjoyed the flowers he sent, always setting them beside the framed photo of her son. His impassive face and unwavering eyes atop a crisp uniform, the majestic colors of our American flag behind him. One afternoon, after the deliveryman had left, I asked her how she and her late husband met. Curtis Moore had his own detached face on the long table, the likeness between the two men uncanny.

"My cousin was allowed to have a pool party for her seventeenth birthday. My mother said I had to attend, no matter how much I protested. Being the ripe old age of twenty, I felt a party for kids was beneath me." Sabrina ran a finger along the wooden framed photo of her deceased husband, a content smile gracing her face, memories trapped behind her blue eyes. "I begged my friend Tracy to come along and give me someone to talk to. Aunt Janet, my cousin Becky's mother, hired a band to play as a surprise for her daughter. As I suspected, the backyard was covered in hot pink and neon green, with balloons and party hats all around. When the band came out, Becky jumped up and down, screaming her head off like an idiot. I was about to take a drink and wish Becky a happy birthday, when the deepest voice I'd ever heard spoke through the speakers placed around the yard. I almost choked on the soda as my eyes found the owner of the voice. When our eyes met, I was hopelessly lost." Her voice dips to an almost whisper, her mind lost in her memory.

"Curtis sought me out during the first break they had, asking me to wait around so he could drive me home." Her strained voice was husky with emotion. "That ride home, became a seat in a bar across town two nights later, watching as he played for a slightly older crowd. Later, as we sat on the hood of his car, kissing under the stars, he confessed he was weeks away from leaving for boot camp. He asked me to wear his class ring and keep his car until he came back after training. Months later he came back, hair short and a diamond ring in his hand, asking my father's permission to marry me."

Twisting her ring on her left hand, blinking her eyes rapidly as the present came back to her. "We were married in our family's church and he had orders to come here to Colorado Springs. We were young and in love, with nothing of any value between us, but we managed just fine."

Stepping away from the photo and her memories, her eyes bright with the tears she refuses to shed, finding strength somewhere deep inside. "The call came early one Saturday morning, by Sunday night I stood outside a chain link fence as his plane took off for the desert. A month later when my period failed to show up, I knew our tiny family was about to grow. Curtis came home long enough for me to give birth to our son and take the two of us home from the hospital, before he had to board the plane again. Two weeks later the Chaplain came to my front door, with an apology from the President and sorrow for a man he'd never met. My Curtis had been shot in an ambush not two days after he returned to Iraq."

Sabrina had always presented herself as such a confident and secure woman, listening to her now, I understood why. "My love for Curtis was instant and still lives inside of me. Sometimes, I dream he's in the bed with me, all smiles and playful. No man will ever hold a candle to him, never make me feel the way he did." She reaches out to touch the petals of the flowers, their pinks and greens looking too bridal for her simple dining room. "Kennedy do yourself a favor, find a man you can live with, but more importantly, one you can't live without."

Sabrina leaves the room in silence, her advice and sad story weighing heavy and deep in my soul. She was right; somewhere out there was my one true love. I could either sit back and wait for fate to steer him my way, or I could do everything in my power to find him.

With a clear resolve, and an ounce of borrowed courage, I opened my laptop after the lights from the main house turned off for the night. Searches of dating websites left me with more questions than reassurances this was the path to follow. After nearly two hours of clicking through the smiling faces of men who had signed up with the same purpose, I noticed an advertisement on the left sidebar of my screen. MilitaryConnections.com, the blue and red font stood out against the white background. An animated flag waved as bright yellow script scrolled from right to left, telling me a uniformed man or woman in the service awaited me.

Where the other sites had a multitude of generalized questions about my physical preferences, this site asked questions about me and what I enjoyed doing. Before I knew it, I had a registered account and a response from a handsome man named Zack Michels.

Military Connections MESSAGE: 1

FROM: Zack Michels


*Dear Kennedy,*

*Imagine my surprise as I settled in for what I expected to be a dull Friday night, only to find the new photo of a beautiful girl from back home. Forgive my rudeness, my name is Zack Michels and I am from Liberty, Kansas. Although, for the past several months, I've laid my head down in the middle of Pakistan. I hope I haven't spooked you; the time stamp on your profile says you created this account in the last few hours. Honest to God, I'm a down home guy who lived his entire life on a farm. My parents raised me to be respectful and love my country, by joining the Navy; I feel I'm doing my best. Sadly, my father didn't get to see me wear this uniform, as he died a week before my sixteenth birthday. Now, before you extend your apology for my loss, know he loved us and made sure we all knew it. His death, although a rough period at the time, has made me a stronger person. I'd love to hear from you. See if you think we could be something special.*


*Waiting patiently*
*Lieutenant Zack Michels*


I read his email twice, my heart pounding in my chest as I compared his words to the photo he attached. Sandy blonde hair and hazel eyes half covered by a straw cowboy hat. With a smile as big as the sky, he sat in the seat of a tractor, his knees dirty from what I would assume was hard work. Before I could over think my way out of it, I composed a return letter.


Military Connections REPLY TO MESSAGE: 1

*Zack,*

My cursor blinked as I tried to find the words. It was insane to think an instant attraction could be formed based on a single letter and photo. Sabrina spoke of her and Curtis sharing a single look and what could be described as fireworks. Could I feel this for Zack or should I try and see if I found someone who made my heart drop into my boots?

*Thank you for your letter, it was nice to see a friendly face as my first response. To set your mind at ease, you did not spook me. It would take more than a pleasant letter to accomplish this.*

*My name is indeed Kennedy and I currently live in Colorado Springs, Colorado, where I work with horses and spinal injury patients. I love what I do, in both my involvement with the horses and the men who have served our country.*

Fingers hovering over the keys, my mind blank as to what to say to him. Finally, after looking at the clock, surprised at how the minutes had faded away, I type the lamest nine words ever.

*I look forward to conversing with you as well.*

*Kennedy*

Clicking send, I close my laptop, and then cast a final look at the dark windows of the main house. Maybe tonight will be a night when Curtis fills Sabrina's dreams and soothes her heart.

\* \* \*

My eyes open long before my alarm is scheduled to wake me. Horses don't comprehend sleeping in on the weekends or having a day off. My mother would faint if she knew how deep in horseshit I spent most mornings, taking care of the animals before most of my needs were addressed. Sabrina joins me, her eyes are bright and the smile she is known for back in its rightful place.

"Morning, Kennedy."

"Morning, Sabrina. You look well rested." I offer, not wanting to assume anything. My father says I was born with the ability to read the truth in people's faces, making me an excellent candidate to become a Judge.

"Emotions get the best of me, robbing me of the calm I feel when I think of Curtis. Thank God for the invention of a good sleeping pill." Sliding her hand up and down Loco's nose, the greedy guy eats up the attention, nudging her chest when she attempts to take her hand away. "Although, I did notice you had your lights on for a long while last night. Everything all right?"

I war with myself if I should tell her of the inspiration her story stirred inside of me, but chicken out at the last second. "I did some research on the internet, found an article on the success rates of online dating sites."

Her head turns in my direction, a questioning wrinkle in her brow. "Kennedy, you don't need a dating site to get a date. You have little Ethan tripping all over himself trying to get your attention." The smile from earlier has multiplied, now involving teeth and jostling shoulders.

Being up this early gives me an opportunity to evaluate my thoughts from last night, one thing stands out most in what I need to do about Ethan. "Funny you mention him," baiting her, I watch as she ignores Loco's sucking up and comes to stand beside me. "I realized last night, how unfair I've been to him. Stringing him along with a sliver of hope in a future with me. I plan to call him today and set the record straight and give him the opportunity to find a girl who can return his feelings."


Military Connections MESSAGE: 2
FROM: Zack Michels

*Kennedy,*

*So glad to hear from you!! So you enjoy horses? We have several back home on the farm; I'd love to show them to you someday. You must love living in Colorado Springs, having all that beauty surrounding you. I must tell you, I'm calling you my good luck charm. After I got your letter, the Navy has issued me new orders back stateside. I will get to spend a week with my mother and siblings before heading off to Washington State. So if you don't hear from me for a few days, it's just me traveling and definitely not me ignoring you. I have a feeling about us; something tells me you are going to be someone special in my life.*

*Yours, Zack*

In calling Ethan, I assumed he would arrange to see me in a couple of days, turns out he was a few miles away taking photos of the mountains for a coffee table book he is creating. It's better this way, letting him find the girl he needs to be with. One who will appreciate the attention he wants to give, instead of wasting it on me.

Less than five minutes after I ended the call with him, the dust from his Jeep is swirling in the afternoon breeze. His face is bright with a smile as he raises his hand to wave at me. If he suspected what I was about to tell him, he hid his emotions well.

"Hey," he greets me as he pulled his tall body from the cab of his car, leaning over to place a kiss on my right cheek. "You look beautiful as always."

Looking over my shoulder, Sabrina staying at my request. "Sabrina, good to see you." Where my mother would smile and addressing him with false salutations, Sabrina stands with her arms crossed, a watchful eye saved just for him.

Brushing off her lack of welcome, he wraps an arm around me in an attempt to make our conversation private. I have no desire to be alone with him, encouraging any of the ideas he may have about why I've called him here. Pulling his momentum to a stop, I separate his arm from my shoulders.

"Listen, you're a great guy and one of these days you're going to find a girl who can return your feelings. I'm sorry it can't be me." Ethan turned his head to the left, wrinkling his eyes as he studied my face. "I'm leaving soon to go back home, which is half way across the country. My life there is complicated and full of obligations, things I would never wish on anyone." Ethan continued to watch me, his arms crossed and face serious, "I've enjoyed our friendship, but—"

"You can't get rid of me this easily. I know you're scared when it comes to being around men, but don't worry," he reaches out to run his finger along my face. "I can be patient." Ethan jumps back into his Jeep, backing out of the driveway the same calm way he pulled in.

Sabrina joined me as I stood shocked in my boots, this conversation taking a detour I hadn't prepared for. "Kennedy, mark my words, you haven't seen the last of that young man."

By the time the sun took its daily trek along the horizon, falling into the depths hidden from our eyes, I had finished all my work and settled in to check my email. Jason, my brother, let me know he would be picking me up from the airport instead of Simon. Apparently he had something he wanted to discuss with me, promising it would be life changing for our family. To my surprise, I also received additional emails from Zack.

Military Connections MESSAGE: 2
FROM: Zack Michels

*Kennedy,*

*I wanted to let you know I am about to board a flight back to the states. In less than twenty-four hours I will be closer to you, so close we could travel by car to see one another. I've spoken with my mother about you; telling her I've met a girl who is as pretty as a picture, with a heart I hope to one day win.*

*Yours, Zack*

Military Connections MESSAGE: 3
FROM: Zack Michels

*Kennedy,*

*I'm on my first layover, long enough to eat a quick bite and send an email to a beautiful girl. My plane flew over the mountains and I instantly thought of you. Wondering what you were doing at that precise moment. I hope you are happy, riding your horses or laughing at a funny movie. I'll email again when I land in the states, with only a few hundred miles separating us, instead of an ocean.*

*Yours, Zack*

What should have flattered me sent a different kind of chills up my spine. Zack's wording made it appear as if we were already a couple, instead of two individuals who stumbled upon one another. Perhaps fast is the speed used by these dating websites, acting rapidly before all of the good ones are gone.

Military Connections REPLY TO MESSAGE: 2
FROM: Zack Michels

*Lieutenant Michels,*

*I wish you safe and pleasant travels. Your family must be excited to see you, although I'm not certain of the length of time you have spent away from them. Among the many things we need to learn from one another as our friendship grows. Enjoy your time with them, treasure every moment and do not worry about corresponding with me. I understand all too well the importance of reunions.*

*Sincerely, Kennedy*

# CHAPTER FIVE

*Zach*

A S I CROSSED THE COMPOUND, I took in the sights that had become the norm for all of us here. A group of guys picking up a game of basketball, another cluster with a guitar with a guy strumming passionately, yet singing quite poorly, and some were working out with the wind and sand swirling around them.

"Afternoon, Sir."

Ramsey stood not six paces from me, his eyes bright while I watched in horror as he raised his right hand to salute me. As I clear the distance between us, there are at least a handful of people who had witnessed his deadly error. Twisting his wrist, not giving a shit if I broke every finger he had, my momentum forces him to stumble backward, my intent to get us safely inside of a building.

"Do that shit again and the only salute you will be able to give is when you jack off in the morning!" I seethed, tossing his hand into his chest. Ramsey had been here for about three months and he was the scariest type of soldier. The kind who wanted to see some action and stare the insurgents in the face. Guys like him had imaginary battle scenes they told their buddies about back home. Ones where they took on twelve guys, when in reality they pissed their pants and hid in the fucking sand until the shooting stopped. He boasted he wanted to be a SEAL, be the baddest of the bad, but we all knew he wouldn't make it past the front gate of training.

"Yes, Sir. My mistake, Vi—LT." Fucker knew better than to use my call sign, something reserved for my men. "I heard you ran into some action out there. Took on a hundred men with Aarash leading the pack."

Ramsey reminded me of the bouncing cartoon pup from *Chester and Spike* as he stood in the center of the room, waiting on the details of a battle he had already created in his head. "Don't believe everything you hear, Ramsey. Just keep your eyes open and your fucking hand at your side." I turned to take my leave, a hot shower and the letter inside my pocket requiring my attention.

"Roger that, LT. Hey, I hear you have a younger sister, she dating anybody?" His words stopped me in my tracks. Just before we had gone on patrol this last time, he came into the area where I was *Skyping* with my aunt and sister. He took one look at Savannah and jizzed himself. Once I said goodbye to them, I made it quite clear to him to keep his fucking mind, and hands, off my little sister, the sole of my boot can be very intimidating.

"Ramsey, I told you before, my sister better not cross your mind." It was no secret around here; my sister was pretty yet a little thick in the middle. Her desire to be in love got her heart broken, along with a few noses courtesy of my twin, Zane. While Savannah had enough love to share with the world, she was also a complete pain in the fucking ass. But I loved her, and it was my duty, as her older brother, to protect her. "It's none of your fucking business who she's dating, cause it damn sure ain't gonna be you."

Not waiting to hear another word, lacking confidence in my ability to not add Ramsey's name to the list of bloody knuckles I'd collected over the years. I wince as the bright rays of the desert sun blinded me instantly, even with my cover and sunglasses; the sharpness of the sun was a bitch.

Being an officer, the shower facilities were slightly better than those for the enlisted. Where they had a makeshift room, with showerheads every three feet, we were sectioned off, giving a false sense of privacy. Standing under the lukewarm water, I wash away the stench of the mission. The smell of my shampoo brings back the memory of Chief and the conversation we had on the helicopter ride home. He had been the last to board the bird, rushing to make sure we didn't leave him behind.

"You think this is a limo service now?" I shouted over the noise of the blades. "Nah," he said, no smart assed comment or quick-witted comeback.

"Oh, hell, no." I shoved at him as he donned his headset. Chief always had something to say; no matter if it was a strained, 'fuck you' or a 'shut the fuck up', he always said something.

"What happened to make you late?"

Chief couldn't hold back his smile, shaking his head as he looked out the side of the helicopter. "When the bullets started flying, I had already jumped into the truck with the nurses. After the first shot hit the front glass, the woman with the glasses lost her cool. I had covered her with my body and told her over and over she was safe inside the vehicle, but she was too scared to listen and started screaming how she didn't want to die. I tried to put my hand over her mouth, but she was about to hyperventilate." I knew what he was about to say before the words left his mouth. Chief, like the rest of us, had his fair share of young ladies cross his path. He took a few home with him, but never spoke of having anything serious. "So I did the only thing I could think of to do," he shrugged his shoulders as the knowing grin reappeared. "I kissed her."

After the team razzed him about the timid girl who stood off to the side and never made eye contact, he caught my attention and had me switch to a secure channel on the radio.

"Her name is Rachel Alexander, I didn't plan on kissing her, but Zach..." this was Aiden talking, and not Chief, confiding his joy in a friend, "...something caught in me." Rubbing his chest, his eyes locked with mine.

He confessed how the kiss started out as a way to keep her quiet, ensuring her safety. Combined with the heat of the moment and the sweet smell of her hair, his rules of engagement went right out the window.

He'd gotten her information and gave her his, they promised to keep in touch and kissed again, thus the reason he nearly missed the helo.

As I was about to head to my rack and write a letter to Miss Forrester, my satellite phone sounded from my pack. Snatching it up, I walked back into the heat of the day, knowing the reception would be better outside. The number on the screen was familiar, a friend I hoped to see once I made it back to the states.

"Hey, dickhead, you get married yet?"

"Nah, man, I got rid of her. Sir, I got shit to talk to you about."

Chase Morgan, Diesel, had been one of the finest soldiers I've ever served with. Early on he showed determination and responsibility, confirming my decision to include him in our missions. Late last year, he started exchanging emails with a girl from back home in South Carolina. They seemed to get serious pretty swiftly and he told us of his plans to head home and marry her.

"Sound serious, Diesel."

"I'm gonna put you on speakerphone and let my brother Austin tell you what's going on."

Keeping my eyes on the ridge of the closest mountain, the dead bushes swaying in the wind, I listened as Austin told me of the list he came across and how a number of identities were compromised. Ironically, the girl who Chase had set about to marry was in the center of the theft. My thoughts went back to Aarash and how he knew about my family back in Atlanta. Could this security breach Austin spoke of be some new way the enemy found to get to our core?

"Zach, I can email you what I have if you need any proof of what I'm saying."

"Diesel trusts you, so I trust you as well. But let me know if you have anything else come up."

\* \* \*

*Dear Ms. Forrester,*

*My name is Zach Michaels. I realize you don't know me, but I received your letter by mistake. I apologize, as I didn't pay attention to the name on the envelope before opening it. I read a few lines before I questioned who you were, and it was then I checked the address and noticed you had sent it to someone else. My sad news doesn't end there, I wanted to do the right thing and make sure your Zack got his letter. However, moments ago I learned you, and apparently myself, have been unwillingly involved in an Internet scam. I'm sorry to be the one to tell you this, but your love interest, Zack Michels is a computer-generated scam. Please accept my apologies. I have included my email address if you wish to confirm this Zach Michaels is telling you the truth.*

*Sincerely,*
*Lieutenant Zach Michaels*


I placed Kennedy's letter in an envelope before tossing it in the outgoing mail bin, hating the thought anyone could be so cruel as to lie to a young girl. What benefit would they have in a scam such as this? Was this a webpage decorated with half naked men posing as soldiers, tossing out lines of bullshit found in romance novels to their intended victims? Luring credit card numbers in exchange for a chance at a date with the hot guy they assumed cared for them.

Returning to my tent, deciding to do a little investigating on my own. I would need to email my brother Zane, giving him a heads up to watch out for out little sister Savannah. Last I heard, she and my sister in law, Meghan, were signing her up for online dating websites.


*USA Today Fraud Report: Officials revealed today a major identity theft ring has been uncovered. This organization was spearheaded by Virginia Greyson, 25, of Charleston, South Carolina. A career criminal with a rap sheet listing repeated arrests for prostitution and illegal possession of drugs and paraphernalia.*

*Reports allege that Greyson created a fictitious website, MilitaryConnections.com, targeting single females and males. The reports indicated thousands of unsuspecting young men and women visited the website in the hopes of finding love with a man or woman currently serving in the US Military. Greyson would assign each of them a fictitious soldier, complete with an email and an address in Afghanistan. Several victims reported Greyson sent them an email stating their 'soldier' was being deployed. After a few days, an urgent email would be received stating their soldier's family was in trouble and monetary help was needed. Promises were made for repayment within seventy-two hours. Once the account numbers or actual money transfers had occurred, the email addresses would then become inactive. At the time of her arrest, Greyson was reported to have scammed more than two million dollars. She is currently being held without bond in an undisclosed location. Authorities are asking if anyone has joined this webpage and been given the name, Zack Michels, to contact them at the following number. Studies show that women, ages twenty-two to thirty-five, are prime targets for identity theft.*

To: Zane22@gmail.com
From: Zachory.Michaels.LT.@OPS.MIL
CC:
Subject: Hey, heads up!!!!

*Zane,*

*Hey bro, attached is an article I found while I was looking for some information for a friend. One of my guys knew the girl who has been arrested for this scam. Scary how they chose a name so close to mine, which is how I became aware of this. I managed to receive a letter from one of her victims. I heard Savannah has been trying to find Mr. Right using the Internet and I want you to tell her to be careful. I hope to be home in a few months, so be ready for an ass kicking.*

*Kiss Meghan and the kids for me and tell them I miss them. Also, make sure to tell Mom I'm doing fine and can't wait to see her.*

*Your Brother,*
*Zach*

I hit send and shutdown my laptop. I needed to get in a run, work some of this frustration out of my system. With my boots laced, I joined the other idiots as we circled the tents in the blazing desert sun. It was a mile all the way around if you stuck to the trail and not cut between the tents. You could always spot the new guys with their running shoes and earphones. Chuckling to myself as I start my run, those of us who had been here any length of time knew they didn't stand a chance in the intense heat the sand absorbed. When I first got here, I'd put my ear buds in and tried to listen to music. It wasn't too long before I threw them away from all the goddamn sand collected in them.

Starting out, I could feel the sun's heat as it pelted down on my back and the clink of my dog tags keeping rhythm for me where my music once did. As I ran, my mind wandered to Kennedy. What does she do? Is she a student, a mother, or both? Does she have an older brother to watch over her? From what little I had read of her letter, and the news report, she at least thought she had someone over here.

Movement in the corner of my vision brought me back to the sand and heat, Ramsey trying to pass me on my left, time to school the little fucker. As he ran alongside me, I took a quick left, hurdling over one of the air-conditioning units for the infirmary. When Zane and I were in high school, we would take turns trying to outdo the other while playing football with the neighborhood kids. When Zane went pro, I worked his ass hard before tryouts. Ramsey was no match for me, screaming like a little bitch when his shin hit the cover of the unit. I didn't take the time to stop and see if he was all right, fucker deserved it for thinking about Savannah.

* * *

Things had been quiet for the past two weeks; too quiet if you ask me. Zane had written me back, letting me know he and dad had given Savannah and Meghan a strong talking to. Seems the news report had made its way to my father's desk. If you think I'm protective of Savannah, he's one hundred times worse. As his only daughter, she may have him wrapped around her finger, but he protects that finger with his life. Curiosity had gotten the better of me and I wondered if anything new was out about, Virginia Greyson. As I signed onto my laptop, I was surprised to see I had an email from Kennedy.

To: Zachory..Michaels.LT.@OPS.MIL
From: HorseWhisper@..gmail.com
CC:
Subject: Thank You.

*Dear Lieutenant Michaels,*

*First, let me say thank you for your service. I cannot imagine how difficult it is for you, and your men, to be so far away from your families. I wish you a safe return and if you need anything stateside, it would be my honor to assist you.*

*As for the letter, I'm happy to say you were not the one to deliver the bad news. The day before I received your thoughtful letter, I was visited by someone from the Federal Prosecutor's office. Mr. Hawthorne arrived at the worst possible time, as my mother's bridge club was about to meet, filling me in on all of the ghastly details. Mr. Hawthorne insisted I refer to him as Steven, however, I knew my mother and her friends were listening in the next room. My mother, Claudia, is of the firm belief we address others with respect and reverence, therefore, he remained Mr. Hawthorne. Once he excused himself, leaving behind his business card, she cornered me demanding to know why a man with the government wanted to speak with me and accused me of having a romantic involvement with the gentleman. Lieutenant Michaels, the man was in his fifties, with maturity written in the lines of his skin.*

*It's just...my mother can be such a snob, concerned more with the activities of her friends than the relationships of her daughter. It is so infuriating when all I hear day after day is if only I were more well-rounded like my sister Caroline, I could attract the attention of a fine young man. What my mother doesn't seem to understand is the men around my age aren't interested in what a girl's IQ is, but more her bra size and how quickly he can separate her from her panties. Nothing ever seems good enough for her, regardless of how I dress or how many society chairs I occupy.*

*My brother, Jason, just happened to stop by at the same time Mr. Hawthorne was leaving. He isn't related to me by blood, though. His mother, my father's secretary, died of ovarian cancer when he was three. He came to live with us when his father couldn't be located. My father, who is a prominent attorney here in Georgia, filed all of the paperwork and he's been with us ever since.*

*Jason questioned why I felt the need to contact such a website, taking such drastic measures to find a person of the opposite sex. If I'm being honest, and trust me Lieutenant Michaels, honesty is extremely important to me, I just wanted something,* someone...different. I wanted to talk with someone who has done something they enjoy, not out of obligation or social advantage, but something that makes them truly happy.

When I first began conversing with Mr. Michels, or Miss Greyson, as it now seems, he/she presented themselves as a small town farm boy. His tales of adventure had him joining the Navy in order to see the world, along with finding cultures he had only read about. He was real, he was simple, and he was exactly the type of person I wanted to befriend. He sent me a picture of a sandy-haired young man sitting atop a tractor, complete with a cowboy hat and flannel shirt. I now know it was an image from a Google search. He attempted to lure me further into his trap as he told me he was falling in love with me, asking for my cell number so we could talk. Where I'm certain words such as this may have other women swooning, to me it seemed too Jane Austen to be real. How in the world can you fall in love with a man you've never conversed with outside of email?

My suspicions started when he told me he was shipping out on a secret mission. Three days later, I received an email informing me his mother had been in an accident and the State was stepping in to take his younger siblings into foster care. With his current mission in full progress, he wasn't in the position to come home to take care of them. He needed to get his aunt a plane ticket, but his credit card was expired. He swore he would get the money to me in a few days. I asked for a phone number for the county his family was in, telling him I would go to my father and have him intercede on his behalf. That was the last email I ever received from him. I was worried something had happened, so as you know, I sent a handwritten letter instead.

I told Jason everything, feeling like such an idiot. But you know what? He told me he understood why I did it. He didn't like it of course, but he understood. Jason is being pressured to join my father's firm, but being a lawyer isn't something he wants to do. His real career choice, his dream job, well let's just say it would give our parents massive heart attacks. When he confessed what he wanted to be, and I'm sorry, but I swore to him I wouldn't tell a soul, he also reminded me Hannah, his girlfriend, wouldn't be happy either. Hannah is the daughter of one of my father's partners at the firm. Where Jason is a calm and patient man, Hannah is a brash and, dare I say, bitchy girl? Her parents have given her everything she has ever demanded and now, it seems, she expects the same from Jason.

My sister, Caroline, a woman forged from the shadow of our mother, has always done everything asked of her. When she finished college, she was told to apply for a job in the Governor's office, not to give her a steady income or excellent benefits. No, it was *to gain access to Richard Caldwell, her now husband and new contender for State Senate. With my mother and Caroline, there is always an agenda behind everything they do. Which is probably the reason Jason and I are so close.*

*He confessed Hannah has started to, not so subtly, hint that she is ready for him to propose. I questioned whether this was something he wanted to do. When he failed to respond, I had my answer. Hannah may have my parents believing she is the perfect wife for Jason, but I know my brother doesn't love her. Now, maybe that isn't an issue for her, perhaps I should have introduced Hannah to Virginia, they both seem to have a common goal.*

*Lieutenant Michaels, this letter has given you more information than I think you bargained for, I apologize, but I do tend to ramble which is another personality trait my mother frowns upon. I will understand if you find me a complete lunatic and want no further contact, or if you are happily married, engaged, or in a relationship of any sort—I don't judge— please send my praises to your significant other as you are truly a kind man. They are lucky to have you in their life.*

*With best wishes and gratitude,*
*Kennedy Forrester*

I smiled sitting back against my chair, my hands tucked behind my neck, reading and re-reading her words. In my mind I pictured this young girl with a plaid skirt, knee socks, black-rimmed glasses, and braces. I had no idea how old she was, but by the maturity of her words and the fact her mother was trying desperately to couple her off, she had to be of at least college age. As I clicked the button to reply to her email, I couldn't help but feel relief that this Steven Hawthorn had been of no interest to her.

# CHAPTER SIX

## *Kennedy*

"FORRESTER, TURNER AND WILKINS. This is Lauren, how may I direct your call?" My suitcases had barely been placed in storage when I received the distressful email from Zack. My fear of his poor brothers and sisters being placed in a foster home gave me the courage to seek out the help of the last man on Earth I ever wanted to speak with.

"William Vale, please."

"May I ask who is calling?"

Lauren Wilkins, a bigger busy body than my dear old mother, knew exactly who I was. She had a set of moon eyes for Will since we were in prep school. She was welcome to him for all I care, him and all his deplorable history.

"Kennedy Forrester, he is expecting me."

"Oh, hello, Kennedy. I hadn't heard you were back in town. How have you been?" Lauren was nosy and a liar, she and her mother sent their RSVP for the tea being held tomorrow; she knew good and well I had been back in town.

"Oh, yes. I've been back for a few days. Will made mention of escorting me to dinner, I'm calling to discuss more permanent plans." Of course my intention was to get out of them, but she didn't need to know this.

"Mr. Vale is in a meeting with your father, shall I leave a message for him?"

"No, thank you."

Twenty minutes later, I smiled in greeting to a shocked Lauren as I pushed open the glass doors to my father's office. She was in the middle of a conversation on the phone so I brushed past her with a friendly wave.

Will sat in his corner office, just as I suspected he would be. A stack of papers on his desk, making it look like he was busy with something. "Mr. Vale." Knocking on his door, a smile eating my face, my tone as demure as I could muster. His eyes flashed to mine, the color of surprise lighting up his face as he rises to greet me.

"Kennedy, what a pleasant surprise. Please come in, come in."

Holding on to the Oscar worthy smile, I took the offered seat across from his desk. "I hope I'm not interrupting anything. I know how busy my father must keep you, but I thought it would be nice to talk privately."

"Oh," his face shifted, confusion wrinkling the space between his brows. "Is something wrong?"

"I'm sorry, nothing is wrong per say. My parents have voiced your intentions of seeking my company for dinner in hopes of starting a relationship." I tried to act as innocent and shy as possible, giving him the illusion I was interested in what he had to offer.

"Well, yes, Kennedy, I have expressed an interest to your father. He emphasized the importance of proceeding in an honorable manner. I assured him the last thing I wanted to do would be to make you uncomfortable in any way. A beautiful woman such as yourself deserves to be lavished with gifts and admiration, something I am prepared to do, if you will allow me."

Bowing my head in fake shyness, my fingers fumble at the pearls around my neck. "I'm sorry, did I come across too strong?" *Good Lord, he was making this too easy.*

"No," raising my eyes back in his direction. "It's just I didn't really believe a man like you would ever be interested in me." Fanning my face, adding to the whole overwhelmed and falling hard part I was playing.

"Well, I am. I find you to be one of the most beautiful ladies I have ever met."

"Is it hot in here?" As I pull at the collar of my blouse, Will jumps to his feet and comes around his desk.

"Let me get you a glass of water." He touches my face before he makes a quick exit. Not wasting a second, I scurried around the desk, tapping the spacebar to wake his computer. Clicking on the web browser, a paused video of two women having sex pops up. Of course Will would be watching stuff like this instead of doing what my father was paying him for.

Opening a new browser, I typed in the webpage I knew my father had access to. Familiar with where he kept his passwords, I normally would have steered clear of his private files, but this was important. I had to get in touch with Zack. As I typed in Zack Michels, the program showed the name with a different spelling. I didn't have time to argue with a government database, so I quickly wrote down the address, slipping back out before Will could return.

\* \* \*

Everyday for the month, I waited patiently, but the mail would present with no word from Zack. In a casual conversation I had with my father, I learned the state would look for a family member before placing children in foster care. I prayed his brothers and sisters were with someone they knew and loved, instead of one of the dreadful images I had created in my head.

Mother awaited me at the top of the stairs, a porcelain cup in one hand and her cell phone in the other. Closing the door behind me, I began mentally preparing myself for the brow beating I was sure to receive.

"Henrietta reports you received a letter today."

53

Rolling my eyes internally, Henrietta took tattling to a new level. As children we got away with nothing courtesy of the prying eyes of our housekeeper.

"Oh, must be from one of my friends in Colorado."

"Why would you give away our home address? Next thing we know they will show up at the front door to rob us in the night." She groused, taking a sip of what I assumed, given the time of day, was tea. "At least you are dressed properly."

Sensing this was the end of the interrogation; I began climbing the stairs to my room. As I walked beside her, the hand holding her phone blocked my path.

"Don't forget Kennedy, we are expecting an important guest today"

"Of course, Mother."

She needn't say whom we were expecting. Miss Emma's presence was the equivalent of saying Cher or Prince was about to arrive. Everyone in Atlanta knew who she was and mother needed her in the group of friends she kept, as lots of influential people hung on every word she said.

Meeting my mother's friends, smiling at the surgically altered faces of the women she hand picked to surround herself with, each one meeting the criteria of whatever social ladder she was in need of climbing. Caroline sat with her group of admirers; five women, each with a pedigree they crawled and hurled over mountains to maintain. All five waiting to receive the call they had been selected to join Atlanta's elite social level. Their conversations turned from the heat and humidity, which had already started its assent, to the three open chairs on the hospital board.

"Mrs. Forrester?" Henrietta interrupts, her pressed white apron covering the gray uniform she wore only when these ladies were visiting.

"Yes?" Mother's tone joyful and fake. All conversations stop, and eyes turn in the direction of Henrietta.

"There is a Mr. Hawthorn, who wishes to speak with Miss Kennedy." Mother's eyes flash to mine, pursed lips she masks with a wave of her hand. She is angry and I know I will hear about this for hours after the ladies leave.

"Kennedy, don't make your gentleman wait, sweetheart, it's rude."

Excusing myself to an arena full of giggles and hushed whispers, I notice the card pinched between Henrietta's thumb and index finger. My mother will know every detail about the card, of this I was sure. Refusing to look at the card, I toss her an ugly oath under my breath, something else my mother will no doubt learn as well.

Standing in a dark blue suit, his hair gray and thin. Admiring the massive painting of my mother hanging in the entry. Sensing my presence, he turns in my direction.

"Mr. Hawthorne?"

"Miss Forrester." He crosses the room, his hand outstretched, a warm smile resting on his face. His jacket flutters open with his movement, revealing the handle of a gun. "I'm sorry for interrupting, but it is imperative I speak with you. My name is Stephen Hawthorne, I'm an investigator with the FBI. I'd like to ask you a few questions about a Zack Michels."

Releasing his hand from mine, I chance a quick glance over my shoulder to check for eavesdroppers. Finding the room behind me too quiet for comfort, I motion for Mr. Hawthorne to follow me down the hall. I usher him into my father's office, the one room in this house I know will give me privacy. A few years ago, my father sent my mother off to New York for a shopping weekend with my sister. While she was away, he had a company come in and soundproof his office.

"Please, have a seat." I offered politely as I closed the door behind us.

"Thank you, again sorry to pull you from your party. I'll make this as brief as possible."

"Trust me," waving in the direction of the hall. "You saved me more than anything."

"Right." Pulling out a notepad, he flips open the cover and several white pages. "Miss Forrester, your name was found in a recent seizure of an illegal website, Military Connections. Are you familiar with this name?"

Red flags waved overhead, warning me of the possible implications I may face by answering his question. "Mr. Hawthorne, while I know I have done nothing wrong, perhaps I should contact my father who is an attorney here in Atlanta."

"You're correct, you have done nothing wrong, but it's your choice to involve your attorney. Maybe if I tell you what we know, it may help you in deciding to place a call to his office." His face full of affirmation, wrinkles giving his decades of experience away. "A few weeks ago some files were found in the home of a...Virginia Greyson in Charleston, South Carolina. Located in the basement of the home, was a fictitious dating website which had been created by the owner and a...Kevin Winters. According to our experts, the pair created a program within the site, which used keywords and phrases obtained in the initial profile page to lure in clients. These keywords would be automatically added to an email reply, making it seem as if the subscriber had someone in the military who was interested in a romantic connection. Your name was one of the tens of thousands we found on the client list."

Nausea filled my stomach. All the emails I'd received from Zack were fake; his overzealousness was as false as the ladies in the room down the hall.

"From what we've discovered, Miss Greyson and Mr. Winters have stolen nearly two million dollars from around the world. Now, according to the data in the files, you were one of the few who did not send any additional money when Mr. Michels requested it. With Miss Greyson currently behind bars awaiting transfer to a federal institution, we are actively pursuing evidence to put her in prison for a great many years."

"And what of the other person involved? Winters, I believe you said." Mr. Hawthorne nodded his head, dropping his hands into a relaxed position. "Mr. Winters was killed during a meth lab explosion."

After Mr. Hawthorne listened to my story, taking several notes and confirming selected parts of my version, he assured me he would be in contact with any developments.

Mother stood in the hall, a curious look on her face. I ignored her assumption of any romantic interest I held for the man. As I sat on my bed, I remembered the letter I had received earlier. Assuming it would be from Sabrina, I pulled the envelope from my desk, the return address leaving me stunned and at a loss for words. But as I read the words this kind soldier had for me, I couldn't let this act of kindness go without a proper thank you. While I sat at my computer, the words fell like a summer rain, easy and welcomed. After I hit the send button, I worried he would think me too forward in saying all I had.

* * *

Before I left Colorado, I had composed a list of facilities I would love to work for. At the top of the list sat Hart Stables and Therapy Center. It was considered to be in the top two percent across the country, specializing in children and veterans. According to the webpage, they had one opening and I knew they would have hundreds of applicants. While my chances were slim, they weren't zero.

By the time I had finished the personal profile and taken the online quiz they required, four hours had passed. As I was about to close my computer, a single ping sounded alerting me to a new email.

To: HorseWhisperer
From: Michaels, Zach. LT
CC:
Subject: Re: Thank You

*Dear Kennedy,*

*I hope this letter finds you in better spirits after the crushing news I had the misfortune of rehashing. I feel terrible for introducing myself with such a bitter pill, but felt it must be done. If we are to continue to correspond, and I sincerely hope we do, I ask you to please call me Zach, as my team refers to me as Lieutenant. Since you shared a little about yourself, I feel the need to be honest with you.*

*I noticed your address is Atlanta, Georgia. My family resides in Atlanta, so we're neighbors. You say your father is a lawyer and desires your brother to join his firm? This is something I can relate to. My father is the Chief of Staff at Emory University Hospital. He has made his desire for me to follow in his footsteps quite clear. However, unlike your father, mine is proud of the career choice I made. Perhaps Jason would be surprised by your father's reaction, if he told him what he truly wanted. I must say, Kennedy, your loyalty to your brother is commendable, and yet it had me pondering dozens of job choices ranging from a security guard to a drag queen. Hey, if he does want to be a drag queen...I don't judge either.*

*My mother is a lot like yours; she's a member of a number of boards. Although she doesn't play bridge, she's got a great poker face. She holds a monthly book club supposedly discussing classic literature, but my father says it's an excuse to drink moonshine and gossip.*

*My parents have been happily married for over twenty-five years. I pray someday I will find a girl who will complete me as much as my parents do each other. There, I answered a question you didn't really ask me. I have no wife, no girlfriend or boyfriend. I would like to explore that one-day, but I know with me being here it makes it difficult to date. It's one thing for someone to say they will wait for you, it's entirely another for them to actually do it. So for now, I remain single.*

*Let's see, what can I tell you about me, the regular guy and not the SEAL? And yes, they are different people. I'm twenty-five...speaking of age, I'm assuming you are older than eighteen? Otherwise this Greyson woman has more legal trouble than she can handle.*

*I love music, most every genre, but my appreciation for rap is limited. I'm just your average guy: tall, brown hair and brown eyes. When I'm back in Atlanta, I live with my parents. Sounds pretty lame, huh? Once I joined the military, I had my housing taken care of, no reason to have a house I would never be in.*

*I was around seven when I began to scribble on the corners of discarded envelopes and leftover take out napkins. My mother caught on to my talent and purchased me a case of sketchpads. My drawings have become more and more detailed as I've grown older. When I was fifteen, my brother and I went to a state football championship game. While we were stopped at a roadside diner, I noticed next to it was this little tattoo shop. Our friends dared me and Zane to go inside. We knew we couldn't actually get a tattoo, but from the moment I stepped inside, I knew what I wanted to do.*

*When I get out of the military, I want to open my own tattoo shop, placing my drawings forever on the skin of people and have my art travel around the world. I wanted to put my business degree to good use by opening my own shop, however my brother and I are so competitive, when he was drafted by the Falcons his senior year of college, I spouted off I was going to become a SEAL. Zane laughed at me and said I wouldn't make it past day one of Hell Week. Since I'm writing you from Afghanistan, and you've seen my Special Ops email address, we know who came out on top. I've seen some amazing things and some horrific things, but I wouldn't trade those experiences for anything.*

*Now, let me ask you, what do you want to be when you grow up? A ballerina? A construction worker? The possibilities are endless, don't let your fear of what your parents will think cloud your dreams, unless you want to be a drug dealer.*

*My sister, Savannah, is the baby of the family. She's pretty, and not because her older brother is saying this, she really is. She's one of those people who have so much happiness it seems to pour out of her. She surrounds herself with positive people and brings such joy to those around her. If I could change one thing about her, she falls in, what she calls, "love" far too easily. She's laid her heart on the line time and time again only to get it broken. I envy her in a way. She's at least willing to put herself out there. Most people, myself included, have run away from the L word.*

*My brother is married to a wonderful woman, Meghan. They are polar opposites, but it works for them. Where he is muscular and athletic, as the former defensive end for an NFL team should be, she is a klutz. The girl can trip over air. While he's considered a heartthrob, according to People Magazine, she's the poster child for the girl next door. It took over a year for her to agree to let him take her for a cup of coffee. She worked in the library and he had a term paper due, but the book he needed was checked out at the one by our house. He walked in, and there she was, with her hair in braided pigtails and clothes two sizes too big. He said she had the most beautiful eyes he had ever seen. He went back every day to ask her out and time after time, she turned him down. He went in this one particular afternoon when she was supposed to be working to find she was home sick. The guy, who was working for her, told my brother if he was playing some sick twisted game with Meghan, he would kick the shit out of him. He also told Zane, Meghan was always turning him down because she didn't understand why he was even giving her a second glance. Once my brother told his side of the story, the guy—who walked Meghan down the aisle—helped get Meghan to say yes to him.*

*When Zane was drafted, she broke up with him, worried he would cheat on her with a cheerleader or overzealous fan. When my brother came home that night, he sat in our kitchen and cried. After several weeks of Zane sending flowers and letters, he was out of ideas on how to get her back. Savannah suggested having the people Meghan feared the most talk to her. Taking her advice, Zane loaded up as many cheerleaders as he could find and went to the library where Meghan worked. After she was told what a perfect gentlemen Zane was and how he talked so much about this girl he was in love with, they knew he was off limits. Meghan took him back the next week. Right before he was injured, he proposed to her during halftime on national TV. Now they have three children, whom I never get to see, but am going to spoil rotten when I get back. Zane is now the defensive coach for the Falcons and says he loves his job more than when he played.*

*So, tell me the truth, were there really no sparks between you and Mr. Hawthorne? Come on, I know how those older men can be, throwing money at pretty young girls, making you feel like a million bucks. Just be careful, Kennedy, make sure your dad checks him out good, make sure he isn't hiding dead bodies in the trunk of his car.*

*I think by the sheer size of this email, I'm the rambler now. I did enjoy hearing about your family and I hope you enjoyed hearing about mine. I have a meeting I have to attend in a few minutes, but I look forward to hearing from you again.*

*Sincerely*
*Zach*

# CHAPTER SEVEN

*Zach*

"HEY, LT, YOU AWAKE IN THERE?"
Chief stood in the frame of my door, his hair still wet from his shower. I'd been staring at my laptop, half expecting a new email from Kennedy and knowing I needed to respond to my sister, Savannah.

"Hey, Chief, come on in." I close the lid of my computer as he sits on the edge of my rack.

"Captain Brown asked if we would be willing to tag along with a patrol this afternoon, get a good look at some of the new guys and how they're doing."

"What time do we leave?" The last thing I wanted was to drag my ass back into the heat of the desert with a hundred pound pack on my back. Listening as these boys, pretending to be men, talked shit about what they did back home.

"Sixteen hundred, according to Ghost, it's been quiet for far too long." I hated when the chatter over the radio dropped off, it meant they were waiting for us to do something, or had something planned. Either way, we would need to be on alert.

"Oh, one more thing." Chief had risen to his feet and was halfway to the door, turning to look over his shoulder, his eyes apologetic. "Captain gave Ramsey the green light to come along." Any hope of this being a quiet and uneventful patrol just rolled out the window.

Equipment had been checked, water supplies verified and all relevant questions answered. Ghost had chosen three guys to show them how to communicate without using the radio. Havoc wanted to walk in the lead position, needing to get this over with as soon as possible. Doc and I took the rear; he preferred to monitor the guys, watching for heat exhaustion and anyone being reckless. I liked to watch the locals as we passed, watch them as they waited for us to leave, seeing if they tried to contact anyone.

We hadn't gone half way when one of the guys asked to stop and take a break. Reaper looked to me for direction. I nodded my approval for him to rain hell fire down on the piss ant.

"What the fuck you mean, take a goddamn break? We ain't reached the halfway mark and your poor tootsies already hurting." Reaper had a way of getting your mind off stuff, while making you the butt of his jokes. "Well too fucking bad, you pussy! Should have read the fine motherfucking print before you signed your life away to Uncle Sam." The young man kept his eyes on his boots, trying to avoid the much larger man's taunting.

"Bet you're regretting all those hours you spent in your momma's basement playing fucking *Nintendo*, instead of finding a pretty girl with a tight ass. You wasted too much time pretending you were shooting zombies, when you should have been bending some girl over the back of your couch and pounding her from behind, building up some stamina. Now all you got is your left hand and sweat running down you fucking butt crack." A few snickers can be heard deep in the ranks, followed by the young man telling his friend to shut up.

"I bet your dick is too tiny, huh? Afraid to let the girls know you're working with something shorter than a tampon? That's all right, kid. A few months in this desert, you'll be a walking, talking, fucking machine who can do back flips while wearing full gear." Out of the corner of my eye, I noticed two things. First, Ghost building up his momentum, doing a front flip beside Reaper. Second, a local woman stood beside an animal pen, a rifle in her hand, raising the barrel in our general direction.

"Three o'clock!" I shout as the first shot sounded from the woman's gun. Organized chaos spread among the men, who get as low to the ground as humanly possible, returning fire to sources unknown. Ramsey has his face in the dirt, hands glued to the backside of his neck, curled into the fetal position.

The sounds of gunfire were like dueling banjos between the men surrounding me, and the enemy in the rocks and shadows. Echoes of pinging of shells as they bounce off gear, boots and sides of helmets, surrounds us. A cloud of dust, created by the quick movements of the moment, dissipates revealing several bodies slumped over where the insurgents emerged from their hiding places.

A building, behind where the woman with the gun stood, muffles the sound of several men, yelling something sounding like, "move" or "mortar", it's hard to tell over the noise surrounding me.

"Motherfucker." Havoc swears from my left, a bullet having grazed his right shoulder.

"You hurt?"

"Fuck no, but the asshole tore my shirt."

Havoc tucked himself behind a cluster of rocks, a wide rip in his sleeve and a pissed off look on his face. I know how he feels, having to replace a uniform once you get it broken in, trouble with a new uniform is the material is stiff as a fucking board and not warn in the right places.

"You gonna pick up that fucking gun or cuddle with it?" Reaper kicks at Ramsey, who has yet to open his eyes to the action he so desperately wanted to see. "Put a tampon in that fucking pussy of yours and get in this!" Another bullet buzzes past me as the voices in the shack become more frantic.

"Cock suckers!" Havoc yells as he tosses several grenades into the open doorway of the mud structure. Clanging and more shouted chaos rings out as the tiny balls of destruction bounce around inside. Less than a second later, the first of them detonates; creating a domino effect as whatever they had inside explodes, taking the mud and inhabitants with it.

63

Dust and rocks rain down around us as Ramsey once again finds the ground to be his best friend.

"Everyone okay?" I hear Doc inquire as he jumps to his feet, ready to treat any wounded. I'd had him on nearly every mission, so I know his routine and how to read him. Havoc and Reaper have their guns raised, walking cautiously toward the smoking remnants of the building. Ramsey, finally decided to join the land of the living, watches the backs of the two men inch closer. As he stands, he stumbles and I look to see what had gotten in his way. Nothing catches my eye at first, until he turns around to face me and I notice the area at the top of his thighs. For all the shit Ramsey talks, the reality of real bullets flying at you has hit him square in the face, his fear evident in his wet crotch. Ramsey had pissed himself.

"Viper." Havoc calls into my ear through the radio. I glance up in the direction I last saw him walking, noticing several pieces of wood smoldering with the last ounce of life they have. He and Reaper stand over what looks like a singed wooden crate. But it's the piece of wood Havoc holds in his hand, which makes my blood boil. In block lettering, stenciled in perfectly clear English: C-4.

* * *

Every inch of my body aches as I climb into my bed. The hike back to base had been several degrees more somber, with the exception of Ramsey and the diaper jokes projected at him. Once back behind the barbed wire and illusion of safety, I woke the Captain up with news of the explosives we found. Aarash had managed to get his hands in the pocket of some bottom feeding, pieces of shit, who sold him stolen artillery.

Once upon a time I believed by training as hard as I did, I could help put an end to mad men like Aarash, making the world a safer place for my family and good people like Kennedy. Thinking her name gave me a surge of energy, a desire to know she was okay. Flipping open my laptop, my heart races as I waited for the Internet to connect.

To: Michaels, Zach. LT
From: HorseWhisperer
CC:

Subject: I want to be Barbie

*Dear Zach,*

*To answer your question, completely tongue-in-cheek, I want to be Barbie. She has everything, even two boys who fight for her, Ken and GI Joe. She is pictured and portrayed as the girl who can and will do everything. I envy her courage, always wearing a smile and perfect makeup, taking on every challenge little girls have been giving her for the past forty plus years. She has the latest clothing, which would make my mother happy, and a beautiful horse, which makes me happy. So, yes, I want to be Barbie.*

*But seriously, I'm twenty-three and I have my Master's degree. I know twenty-three and a Master's degree? I've always been an overachiever. In high school, I took as many college level classes as I could so when I graduated, I was considered a sophomore. I also found loopholes in the rules to graduate college. I tested out of as many classes as allowed and took summer classes every year. Last June, I graduated with a degree in design, but my passion is Equestrian Therapy. As a matter of fact, I just sent a resume to one of the country's top centers right here in Atlanta, thanks to you giving me the courage to put myself out there. I haven't told my mother about the job, I know she wouldn't approve.*

*When I applied to college, she insisted I attend Princeton, while I wanted the University of Colorado. My father came to the rescue and made a deal between us. I got to attend U of C, but had to major in design, getting my degree in Equestrian Therapy was on my own time. Thankfully, my father extended his generosity and paid my tuition. For the past year, I've worked with some incredible people, learning what real pain is and adjusting my priorities. My boss offered me a permanent position, but I had to turn it down. I am a person of my word, having sworn to my mother I would return to Georgia and help her in her charity work. I do miss Colorado, the people and especially the horses. Granted, I could spend all of my time with the horse I own here, a rescue my father found through a client, but my mother would frown on the idea. To her, horses are something you brag about owning, not something you care for and treasure. Being seen with the right breed of horse when an important set of eyes are watching is more to her thinking. As much as I would love to get away from my mother, I like the idea of being in Georgia.*

*I love everything about the area we live in. I love the weather, the restaurants, and people...just everything. I'm also taking some liberty here and assuming you and your*

65

brother have the same last name? If this is correct, then I met him while attending classes. He was in a nutrition class I took as an elective. I only knew it was him because all the jocks were talking about him. You're right, he is athletic, and although he may be pleasing to the eye for some, he just didn't do anything for me.

I told my brother what you said about telling my parents about his career choice and he has decided to put his dream into action, so to speak. He is actively searching for a place. I'm sorry, I know I'm being elusive, but I did give my word after all. Your family seems wonderful and easy going. I would love to have a family like that.

As for Mr. Hawthorn, my mother investigated, he's married, much to her dismay. He also has three children, two in college and one who is married and expecting a baby.

I was shopping yesterday and ran into Hannah, who was looking at engagement rings. Can you believe that? Jason hasn't even asked her and she's already picking one out. I mean, every girl looks through bridal magazines dreaming of what her wedding will be like, but isn't it the man's responsibility to pick out a ring she would like? Maybe I'm old fashioned in that respect, but it's how I feel.

So a tattoo artist? Do you have any tattoos yourself? I don't want to assume due to your active duty status you have an anchor on your bicep or a naked lady on your chest. As for you describing yourself, you do seem like a handsome man. I've been described as the girl next door, not strikingly beautiful like my sister, Caroline. I have dark brown hair, brown eyes and skin so pale I get a sunburn from the fluorescent lights in the kitchen. I don't like to dress provocatively or display myself in any questionable ways. I wear glasses when I read, which I do a lot of when I have time to myself. My gosh! I sound like I'm forty-three instead of twenty-three.

I love horses; love isn't really a strong enough word for what I feel around them. I enjoy music, although the boy bands of the 90's are my weakness. I play the cello, at my mother's insistence of course, but it isn't my passion and I stumble my way through it.

I can't believe you went to SEAL training to prove your brother wrong! I watched a documentary after you mentioned it and the training looks grueling. You, Zach, have to be very physically fit. Oh no...that sounded like flirting. Honestly, I'm not. I'm like your sister-in-law Meghan; the cute and available guy would never ask me out. I can see why she avoided your brother's attention. Girls like me know what they see in the mirror every morning and it isn't the stuff they print in Sports Illustrated or Playboy, but more like Martha Stewart Home or Housekeeping Digest. I'm okay with the fact I will never grace the cover of a magazine or walk down a runway, but I have a *passion for making every patient feel hopeful the treatment I help them with will work. With my years of design school, I can make the vision trapped in someone's head, become a reality in their dream bedroom. Let's see Tiffany, Ms. November, who loves beach volley ball and puppies, do that.*

*I won't keep you any longer; I know you have a loving family to communicate with. You left me with questions, and since you admitted you wanted to continue to correspond, I wanted to reply. Tell me, Zach, if you could open a tattoo shop anywhere in the world, where would it be? I send you wishes to remain safe and for a speedy return to our great state of Georgia.*

*You friend,*
*Kennedy*

When Zane and I were growing up, our father would give us, what we coined "life lessons." He would tell us his secrets to successful relationships. Reading Kennedy's latest email reminded me of what he had told us the summer we went off to football camp. "*Boys, girls are going to come in and out of your lives. Some will turn your head, but not your heart. So be careful of the ones that come in pretty little packages. Sometimes they're like those pieces of candy, sweet on the outside, but bitter and awful on the inside. You look for the girl who spends more time filling her brain than stuffing her bra. Looks may come and go, but it's a lot easier to have a conversation when you don't have to use pictures to get your point across.*"

Kennedy was thousands of miles away, through at least four different time zones, and yet she was as open and honest as she could be. She thought of herself as this plain, ordinary girl, but I suspected the reality was completely different.

I had six months left of my tour. Less than a year remained on my contract with Uncle Sam, and until this last mission, I was still riding the fence on staying longer. Diesel and I had several conversations about leaving and hanging out together. Something was pulling me home, back to the roots, which ran deep. Maybe it was the dream of a tattoo shop, or maybe it was this polite, proper, southern lady who has sealed my decision

In today's day and age, it might be odd that my mother doesn't have an email account, yet my eighty year old grandmother not only has email, but two Facebook pages. She's very computer savvy and it drives my mom insane. I haven't had a recent email from her and I was going to have to give her shit for it. I would have to tell Kennedy about the oddity that was my family.

To: CupCakeCutie
From: Michaels. Zach, L.T.
CC:
Subject: How are you?

*Savannah,*

*Hey! I recently came in contact with a young lady who had the misfortune of being caught by a scam artist. I don't know how much of the news you follow, but a new scam has victimized young men and women who are trying to find a little companionship and maybe a chance at love. It specifically involves individuals who are interested in active duty military. This person, Virginia Greyson—the crazy bitch who is now sitting in a jail cell somewhere—sadly attempted to victimize a wonderful girl I have become friends with. Her name is Kennedy and she is from near where you and I live. Please, do your poor brother a favor and stick to dating someone close. Have Zane check them out. I have enough to worry about over here, without you doing something crazy. Mom and dad always told us everyone has someone special out there for them. I know it's hard to wait, hell I've waited longer than you have, but be patient and let it happen. I love you and can't wait to see you.*

*Your brother,*
*Zach*

\* \* \*

I'd been dreaming of a girl dancing in a field of wild flowers, her dark hair splashed with the rays of the sun running down the long strands of her hair and fingertips reaching out to caress the tips of the tall grass surrounding her. Her smile, wide and welcoming, with straight white teeth surrounded by red inviting lips. "Viper," her voice called to me, giggling

68

as she continued to walk backwards, beckoning me with the curl of her index finger. "Viper..." her soft voice changed to a much deeper one, the delicate skin of her face fading into a cloud of white.

"Viper, Captain needs to see us." Ghost's voice replaced the beautiful girl, the dip of my heart forcing my body to jolt up in my bed. "Sorry, Sir. Captain just called a meeting."

Captain Brown was a fair and decent man and a graduate of West Point. When I first arrived, he did his standard meet and greet, letting me know exactly what was expected of me. As I sat in his office that afternoon, I noticed behind him on the wall was a picture of, who I assumed were, his family. Two dark haired, blue-eyed children stood on either side of a beautiful, middle-aged woman. He noticed me looking and pulled the wooden frame off the makeshift shelf. They were his twins, Corey and Carney; they had just turned four in the picture. His wife, Natasha, was from Russia and they had tried for over ten years to have their children. They went to doctor after doctor, trying treatment after treatment. Finally, Natasha came to the decision children were not possible; three months later she became pregnant with the twins.

"Gentlemen, sorry to wake you so soon after the last mission, but this comes from POTUS directly. An American student, Alyssa Nicholson, twenty two, was kidnapped nearly two weeks ago by who we've now confirmed was Aarash Konar. Intel as of two hours ago, has him returning to the area with the kidnapped girl." My thoughts immediately went to Kennedy, even though I knew it wasn't her, it was an instantaneous reaction.

"I'm counting on the best of the best to go in and bring this girl home to her family."

He dismissed us and excused himself, Chief following behind him. I've been on countless missions like this very one, kidnappings and ambushes happened all the time. This girl, this American, was more than just your standard issue college student, she was some Senator or Governor's daughter. More than likely, she was being used to get back at her father for crossing the wrong terrorist in his attempt to get what he wanted.

"You know, Diesel would have loved this one." Ghost commented as he shoved a handful of flash grenades in his pack. "You're right, he would have." I agreed, zipping my own pack.

The building where the girl was being kept was ten klicks away. Using the cover of night, we silently made our way to the target. One thing I appreciated about this place was the clearness of the nighttime sky, the stars shining like tiny twinkling lights above our heads. I wondered if Kennedy could see the same stars, or did clouds cover the sky? With the glow of a town fire illuminating in the distance, I began to scour the edge of the darkness. Everything was quiet; not even the barking of a stray dog could be heard. I called for radio silence as we closed in on the target building. The guards standing outside were taken down in one quick motion, dark blood spilling from their throats, death found them quick and painlessly. Once inside, I gave the word to secure the building. Signaling to Ghost I would take the left, I headed into the dark corners of the house. Room after room was cleared, but we kept our guard up until the signal was given the girl was safe, and we could head to the rendezvous point. I caught sight of Ghost and gave him the signal my side was clear, and he returned it letting me know the same.

I had just stepped out of the house and onto the desert floor when it happened. From out of nowhere, a local woman came running at me, brandishing what looked like a hunting knife. She was quick as she swung the knife at me like a baseball bat, connecting with the lower half of my left arm. I could feel the warmth of my own blood run down my arm, but my adrenaline acted as an instant painkiller. I didn't hear Ghost run over, but he was quick to silence the screaming woman. He helped me sit down before taking off my belt and applying pressure to the gash in my arm.

"Can you make it, Viper?" I nodded and he helped me stand up again. With the girl in tow, we headed to our rendezvous point. I'd been shot at more times than I could count, had a big motherfucker try to drown me in Belize once, but this was the first time I'd ever been attacked by a female.

The trip back to the hooch felt like forever, I was a sweaty mess as I entered the infirmary. Corpsman came rushing to me; one with a stretcher helping me lay down as they began removing my pack and Kevlar. The second they removed the belt from my arm, pain shot up from my fingers.

"Motherfucker!" I spat between clenched teeth. Taking a look at my arm, I got to see what the crazy bitch did to me. The cut was deep, I could see muscle and, dare I say, bone. The blade must have been jagged, as the skin and surrounding tissue was mutilated. One guy on my right had my arm in a blood pressure cuff; while another told me he needed to give me a tetanus shot.

"I don't have to tell you it's a deep one, but it's fixable. We'll have you back out there in no time." Captain Taylor had arrived on the same flight as me. I had shaken his hand, telling him no offense, but I hope I would never need his help. He agreed, but wished me the same.

Another corpsman came in with a syringe full of clear liquid injecting it randomly into the torn flesh, causing the sting of the wound to become less and less. I watched Captain Taylor closely as he maneuvered the curved needle, suture, and forceps like he was sewing a pair of socks. Almost an hour later, I had a bandaged arm and thirty stitches with orders to take at least forty-eight hours off.

Back at my cot, I lie down with my left arm resting across my chest. The medication they injected me with kept the pain at bay, although I knew it would hurt tomorrow. I didn't want to dwell on it, so I went over the events that left me in this predicament. I had secured my side of the perimeter, but lost my edge, letting my guard down just enough it almost got me killed. Leaning my head back and closing my eyes, I thought of all the things I still wanted out of life.

A steady job and a house to call my own. Someplace to have cookouts on the weekends, and super bowl parties during the season. I wanted to wave at my neighbors and bitch when I had to mow the lawn. But most of all, I wanted a girl by my side to enjoy it all with me. I meant what I said to Savannah, I do believe there is someone out there for everyone. I could sense my someone was only a plane ride away.

* * *

Sleep could not find me, my overactive thoughts refusing to let my dreams take over. Pulling myself out of bed, I moved to the trunk that held my material possessions. Unlocking the metal flap, the lid opened with a haggard creek from months of not being used. I sifted through the various award letters and souvenirs I stored in there until I reached the bottom and the contraband I'd hidden there months ago.

Closing the lid, shoving the glass bottle into one of my pants pockets, "Freedom Rock, 0530." I ordered as my fist pounded on each door, continuing down the hall, not waiting for any of them to protest the early hour. Ignoring the smell of coffee and cooking meat coming from the mess hall, I flexed my stiff fingers of my injured arm as the meds they used last night had long since worn off. I didn't need to turn around to know three of my five men had already fallen in step behind me, silently following me into the shadows of the unknown.

Freedom Rock, its name coming from a gun battle between the first battalion of Marines who arrived here and Aarash's men. Two days of exchanging bullets, ten Marines dead, but the line they needed to push back had been established, which included the rock in the side of the hill, with the American flag still waving in the wind from the top.

The snapping sound of the flag whipping in the wind above my head was all I heard as I crouched down, my legs bent at the knees providing a place to rest my aching arm. Warm oranges, gold, and hues of pink announced the arrival of a new day, giving clarity to the decision I had made. Pulling the jar from my pocket, hoping it would give me the courage to deliver the news to my team. I set the clear liquid on the rock of the hill between my legs, waiting until everyone arrived.

"Well, y'all know this ain't a mission brief, but some heavy shit if Viper is violating military code with a jar of moonshine." Doc was right on all counts. This conversation was going to be one of the heaviest we've ever had, and the moonshine at my feet, could get me sent to a review board and a possible dishonorable discharge.

Doc being the last to arrive, his right boot was untied, the strings flapping around with each step. He dropped his tired body down on the rock to join the rest of us. With five sets of eyes looking back at me, I take in what I hope is enough air to get the words out.

"Ain't no easy way to say what I'm about to say." I began, refusing to look away from the five sets of eyes who watched me, my need to pay tribute to all of the times they covered my back. "Last night I let my mind wander and it nearly cost me my life. I've lost my edge." Swallowing thickly, my next words were almost a whisper. "I'm getting out." A collective silence remains across the group, not a single muscle flinching as my confession is reviewed.

Ghost is first to acknowledge my words, his head bobbing as he chucks a hand full of pebbles to the dirt below. "Me too," brushing the dirt and sand from his palms, "I wasn't certain until now, but this," he motions to the tent city below, "isn't how I want to live anymore."

"Ghost, while I appreciate—"

"What? You think you're the only one of us who has seen enough?"

"He's right, Viper." Havoc reaches over, taking the jar into his hand, unscrewing the lid, and taking a whiff. "Hell, I'm waiting for the Navy to kick my ass out any day now." He moves the jar in a toasting motion before tipping it back to his lips. His face squints as the burn of the alcohol goes down his throat.

"Might as well sign my package while you're at it." Reaper takes the jar from Havoc, repeating his toasting motion, as he enjoys his own drink, minus the admission of how strong the moonshine is.

"I'm the oldest some-bitch in this group, and I ain't got it in me to train another set of motherfuckers." Chief takes his turn at the community drink. "Hell, I've been ready to go stateside and get a real job for a while. "Chief motions for me to take the jar from his hand,

"Hurry up, Viper. Ramsey noticed you leaving in a huff. He's been sneaking up the side of the ridge for the past few minutes, looking over here with a set of binoculars." Nothing Ramsey did would ever surprise me, he wanted to be on my team more than he wanted his next breath.

"This goes without saying," the emotion of the situation hitting me like a brick. Taking a long pull from the jar, I ignore the protest my throat is giving me about the burn. "Y'all are my family. Anyone of you fuckers needs me—" Doc takes the jar from my hand, rescuing me from dealing with the emotions surrounding me.

"Hey, man, it ain't like you're getting out tomorrow." Kicking my boot, he flashes me a watery smile. "It could be worse, you could have the kinda time I have left." Doc had signed up so the military would pay for med school; he still owed them a considerable amount of time. "Hopefully, they'll stick me in some cushy stateside job until my time is served." Doc had a way of looking at things, always trying to get our minds off the madness around us, making light of the intense situation.

"With your luck, Doc," Reaper pulls the jar toward him, rising to his feet. "You'll spend the next fifteen months on bedpan duty." As the rest of us join Reaper, our bodies in a tight circle.

"Hey, you know me, I'll do anything to see a little ass."

We walked as a unit down the ridge, each of us calling out a hello to the hiding Ramsey as we passed the shadow he retreated into. Captain saw us walking across the camp, his gaze remaining on us as he stopped his forward progression.

"Lieutenant," shifting his stance, he was a smart enough guy to know when something was up. "Something I need to know about?" Eyes flicking back and forth between the six of us, his brow furrowing with concern. "Yes, Sir. You got a minute?"

Havoc had been right; his days in the military were numbered. Apparently, his last physical showed an area on his lung the military didn't particularly like. Captain gave him his word he would make sure his final duty station would be close to home. Chief hinted around he would consider a civilian job with the medical unit, but with no real training his odds were slim to none. Reaper was offered an extension with a considerable bonus, but he turned it down, saying he could make more money brewing moonshine. When Doc asked to return to Bethesda, Captain gave him a worried look, and then reminded him this mission was far from over and his skills as a surgeon were still needed here.

Ghost didn't say much of anything, thanking Captain as he signed his paperwork and left. We all knew he didn't want to return to Montana, fixing fences and herding cattle. He was a smart man and an incredible SEAL. Whatever he chose, he would do well.

To: CupCakeCutie
From: Michaels. Zach, L.T.
CC:
Subject: Need your help

*Savannah,*

*Remember when I was home last time and we talked about you renting a building for your store? Well, I want you to call the same lady who helped you and see if there are any openings for my tattoo shop. I made the decision tonight; I'm done with this part of my life. It's time to open a new door and live my dream. I need somewhere with a good storefront location. I'm open to buying or leasing, just check it out and if you wouldn't run a shop from it, then I wouldn't either. I need to have everything up and running so use that power of attorney I gave you to make this happen. I'm counting on you. Oh, and tell Zane to save me a ticket for his home opener.*
*Love,*
*Zach*
*P.S. We can talk on the phone if you can arrange it, just add in the time difference.*

Kennedy had been on my mind more than I was really comfortable with. It was unnerving for me, in nearly every one of my thoughts the faceless girl was there. Her last email had got me to seriously start thinking.

To: HorseWhisperer
From: Michaels. Zach, L.T.
CC:
Subject: anywhere in the world.

*Kennedy,*
*I must admit I am in agreement with you when it comes to staying in Georgia. I have traveled both with the Navy and on vacation with my parents to various countries. I've seen castles in Scotland, the Great Wall of China, and I floated in a gondola along the canals in Venice. The world is a beautiful place with mysteries yet to be solved and*

75

*lessons to be learned. However, nothing beats the view from the top of the Stone Mountain, standing in line at the original Coke plant, watching the first pitch on opening day of Braves baseball, or the leaves change with the season. You asked me where I would open my shop, without a doubt it would be in Atlanta.*

*You might be interested to know I've contacted my sister and she's going to start looking for a place to open my shop very soon.*

*When I enlisted, I knew my duty and I've done it to the best of my ability. Recently, I went on a mission and came back with a pretty, sizeable gash on my arm. I have a good amount of stitches, but more than that, I have a new perspective on things. I want different goals and new adventures. I believe my new way of thinking really started when I began this friendship with you. I hope you don't find it forward of me, but once I get settled in Atlanta, I would really like to take you to a game or stand in line at the Coke plant. I understand if you are too busy or not comfortable, but maybe if you give it some consideration your brother can come with you? Give it some thought; I look forward to your next email.*

*So tell me, if you could design anything for anyone, what would it be? Tell me about your horse. How would you handle having the freedom to work with them instead of what your mother dictates you to?*

*Yours,*

*Zach*

The pain medicine had begun to wear off by the time I shutdown my laptop. I had some oral meds the Captain prescribed for me, so I popped two in my mouth and closed my eyes drifting off to sleep.

\* \* \*

My arm was on fire when I woke the next day, forcing me to stop by medical, they gave me more painkillers and even added an antibiotic to the mix. I hated taking pills, but you never know what kind of shit was growing on the blade of a knife. My appetite was barely there but I knew I had to eat in order to take the pain meds and antibiotic. Once I forced some food down, I headed back to my cot to check my email.

To: Michaels. Zach, L.T.
From: CupCakeCutie
CC:
Subject: I'm brilliant!

*Zach,*

*I did get in contact with my realtor friend, Diane. She just got a listing for an existing tattoo shop. She faxed me the details and it sounded really good on paper. She did tell me she had a guy coming to look at it, so since she was going to be there anyway I made an appointment.*

*When I got there, the guy was just pulling up. He was so handsome, I nearly fell out of my car, except a really pretty girl got out of the passenger seat. He walked over to where Diane and I were standing and introduced himself. I was so enamored with him I couldn't look away. He introduced himself and the girl. I wanted to hate her, but when she shook my hand, she was so nice and polite. Thank God the girl turned out to be his sister, not his wife or girlfriend. Diane let us both have a look at the building and I have to tell you it's perfect. It has everything you need. The guy is selling everything—equipment, chairs, ink, you name it. I told Diane we were definitely interested, but she had to see if the other guy wanted it since he responded first. Diane gave him twenty-four hours to decide what he wants.*

*But the best part is, I got his number and we're having dinner tomorrow night. Now, before you wig out about me falling in love with him and getting hurt, Zane already had him checked out and Jason Forrester is an honorable man. Mom says she knows his mother from one of her charities, and dad has met his father for a business matter. So you can breathe and just worry about getting this building.*

*Love you!*
*Savannah*

The similarities were too great to ignore. The burning in my gut was much more than the side effect of my recent dose of medication. Could our lives be that intertwined? Could Savannah's Jason and Kennedy's brother be the same person?

"Lieutenant!" My rank being shouted caused me to automatically look away from my email to Savannah.

"Don't waste your time trying to send out an email, we're now in River City."

My answer was automatic and edged, "Who died?" With modern technology comes great benefits, and even greater challenges. A few years ago, a fallen soldier's family discovered his death by a message found on his Facebook page. Since then, an automatic shutdown of all communication happened until the family was notified.

"A new boot, Correra." Sadly I knew the name, the young man Reaper had messed with as we waited for the medical convoy to arrive. He had been cocky, stomping off when Reaper tried to help him grow thicker skin.

You never had to question when communication was restored, the common areas emptied out and the noise levels were near zero. I knew if I tried to log onto my computer, it would take forever to get enough bandwidth to open my email. Talking to my sister was worth the amount of money it would cost for me to call her. Doing a quick calculation of the time back home, I pulled out my cell and dialed the number that could set my mind at ease.

"Hello?" Her voice was slightly broken up by laughter, but the delight in her voice caused me to smile along with her.

"Savannah? It's your brother."

"Oh, my God, Zach!" Her excitement increased tenfold, the octave in her voice rose to painful levels in typical Savannah fashion, and she began to babble about what was going on around her.

"Do you know what happened? Of course you don't know, you're in another country. Well, let me tell you!" She emphasized each word as her jubilance grew. "I tried to send you an email, but it came back with that crazy message. You know, the one when they turn off your Internet? Anyway, I went ahead and had a meeting with Diane, who told me *Jason...*" It didn't go unnoticed the way she said his name. Something was going on there. "...Wanted the shop, but was only interested in renting because his father found out he doesn't want to be an attorney and has cut him off. Thank God for his little sister. Oh, you would just love his sister, Kennedy, she's so pretty and she just graduated, but her mother is being so silly by not letting her ride her horse. Can you believe that, Zach? Not letting her ride her own horse!"

Savannah was the type of person to get excited over a dental exam. When she was little, mom was concerned she had some sort of mental condition, so she insisted my father take her to a neurologist. My father tried explaining nothing was wrong with her mentally, she was thinking so quickly her mouth couldn't keep up. The pediatric neurologist confirmed what my father had said, and emphasized to my mother to let Savannah get her words out and not to encourage her to slow down. Over the years I have gotten used to the speed in which she does everything, I sit back and absorb.

"You got me that scarf, the one Lauren spilled her drink on. Oh, wasn't that a day! I had to leave the party and have daddy drive me because the stupid cow got her drink on my key fob and it wouldn't start my car." Her ability to branch off her main subject was rather annoying, but completely a part of who she is.

"But the guy at the dealership got me a new one and then Zane got my car. Oh, I'm sorry Zach; we were talking about Ms. Diane and my Jason. Well, aren't you in luck as we're having lunch at my shop, which is a half a block from your new shop. I went ahead and bought it using the paper thingy like you said to do and in three weeks, you'll have the keys to the shop. Jason's sister, Kennedy, gave him her savings to help him out, isn't that so sweet? Not that I wouldn't give you my money if you needed it, but she is just so nice and I am hoping to introduce her to someone. She's too pretty to be without a boyfriend, and I have decided to help her get one."

I couldn't explain the feeling I got when I heard my sister's admission. I should have been worried she had just bought a shop with my name and money attached to it, but the real reason for my discomfort was the likelihood Savannah would indeed find a guy for Kennedy. Granted this may not be the same Kennedy as the one I have been introduced to recently, but the fear is there.

"Savannah, did you say you're having lunch with someone?" If Savannah's Jason was Kennedy's brother, then I might have more success talking with him than Savannah. Besides, it would seem I have a business partner I needed to get acquainted with.

"I'm having a celebratory lunch with Jason. I invited Kennedy to join us, since his mother and father are being so difficult, but she's at a job interview. Oh, Zach, she wants to work with horses, just like Aunt Ella. You remember when Daddy got me the red pony when I was five and he tried to jump over the fence and hurt his leg. Aunt Ella called the doctor to fix him. " Now I was almost certain the Kennedy who had been writing me and the Kennedy who was now my sister's project, were one in the same.

"Savannah, hand the phone to Jason, please."

There had been few moments when my sister has been rendered silent. On her sixteenth birthday, when my father pulled some strings and had her favorite boy band play at her party. When she was awarded the National Merit Scholarship after she just knew she blew her interview and now, when I asked to talk to the man who she is apparently much interested in.

"Uh...um." I could hear the sounds of the street around her. A car that needed replacement brakes, the high pitched sound of metal on metal, a woman who was trying to hail a taxi, all the while cursing at the apparent moron had pulled directly in front of a large water puddle.

"Yes, sir, this is Jason Forrester. What can I help you with?" I could mentally picture my sister sitting across from this man with her fingernail held captive by her surgically enhanced perfect teeth, not caring she is completely distorting her expensive manicure.

"Well, first, hello, it's a pleasure to meet you. Second, since we're apparently business partners, it's Zach, and not sir." Jason had a good sense of humor, a quality I found vital in people. Not many wanted to be tied to someone who took life too seriously. Let's face it, if he had any intention of hanging around my sister, then he will need all the humor he can get.

"Good to meet you, Zach. Savannah was insistent you would be fine with having a partner you'd never met. She showed me your picture, so I do feel as if I have a slight advantage over you."

Savannah is one of those people who have never met a stranger; she sees the good in everyone, even slime ball men who try to take advantage of her. "Yes, well, it won't be too long before I'm back in Atlanta and helping with the shop. I want to know everything you know about this guy we're buying the business from, but first, I need to ask you a rather peculiar question."

I waited a beat, making certain I had the right words. The last thing I wanted was a pissed off sibling gunning for my balls the second I stepped off the airplane. "Your sister, is her first name Kennedy and did she just get her master's degree from University of Colorado?"

His response is understandably cautioned, "Yes?"

"Was she recently involved in an Internet scam for a dating website?" Part of me felt really angry about what had happened, but another part was thankful a door had been opened, giving me an opportunity to get to know Kennedy.

"She was, actually she is, as it isn't over yet. Listen, to be honest, you're really starting to freak me out with your questions, mind telling me what this is about?"

I had to laugh; if the roles were reversed I would want to know about Jason's interest in my sister. So, I told him everything: the letter, the emails and how I had grown to love hearing from her. He confessed he had noticed a big change in his sister in the last few weeks.

"She's at an interview now."

"Where?" I would have to send an email to my Aunt Ella, maybe she knew someone who was hiring or even had an opening herself. "Hart Stables. It's over on County Road seven. She's going to meet us when she's finished."

I smiled when he confirmed it was indeed my aunt's therapy center, I'd give her a call the second this conversation was over. Jason started telling me about how his sister emptied out her savings to get his half of the money to buy the shop. He explained Kennedy wouldn't get her trust fund for a few more months, and he worried if his parents found out she had helped him that they would cut her off as well. He explained he had a friend of his draw up some partnership agreements he was giving to Savannah for our attorney to go over. He told me in great detail the specs of the building and what he felt needed to be changed. I asked if he could send me some examples of his work, telling him I would do the same. He told me Savannah and Kennedy had taken tons of pictures of the inside and he had even asked Kennedy to come up with some ideas on how to make the most of the space. He said her eyes lit up like a Christmas tree when he asked her.

"Speak of the devil and she will appear. Hey, Sis, guess who I'm talking to?

# CHAPTER EIGHT

*Kennedy*

THIS INTERVIEW WAS THE SINGLE MOST important of my career. Hart Stables and Therapy Center was the only center of its caliber for miles. The center run by Ella Hart, a published author and world-renowned expert in the field of Equestrian Therapy. The pictures that greeted me as I opened the ornate wooden door were proof positive the articles on the web were true.

A small boy smiling, his arms wrapped tight around the brown haired beauty I knew to be Ella. A young girl in leg braces standing beside a gelding, her smile lighting up the photo. Seeing that smile, watching it form as my patients took steps doctors said would never come, that was the best feeling.

A horse neighing pulled my smile from the nerves, which had held it captive since I woke this morning. I couldn't resist the temptation, as I made my way around the entry and into the stables.

My heels clicked against the solid wood of the floor, the restriction of my skirt keeping my steps short and wobbly. I would have dressed in boots and a pair of jeans, but my mother had tossed the pair she found into the trash. The joke was on her as I have thirty-three pairs in a storage facility I rented with my brother. If by a stroke of luck, and maybe a little skill, I am chosen for this position, I plan to move into my own apartment and wear boots everyday for the rest of my life.

I love being around horses, the smell of the hay, and the sounds of them moving around in their stalls. Even the smell of manure isn't too unpleasant for me.

A stall at the far end catches my attention, its inhabitants actually. Above the stall, was the long proud head of a beautiful horse, chewing lazily on his breakfast. His black coat shines in the overhead lights. Every stall has a single horse, each giving me a look as I pass them by. The tall guy on the end though, has my attention for the moment.

Approaching cautiously, the black beauty is eyeing me with the same amount of apprehension. Horses are majestic creatures, powerful and yet, in my opinion, one of the gentlest creatures alive.

"Hey, boy." I said softly as I got closer, giving him time to investigate and decide if I pose a threat to him. "I'm not gonna hurt you." Letting him huff against my fist, the moisture his nostrils leave behind is a comfort for me. The nameplate beside his door reads, Hercules, and I wonder if he is here as part of the program or as a border.

"That's right, I'm not gonna hurt ya." Laying my palm flat against the plane of his nose, I slowly move my fingers up and down. Dark eyes never leave mine as he looks down at me. Hercules isn't quite as big as a Clydesdale, but he is pretty darn close.

"You make it a habit of touching what doesn't belong to you?" I would have jerked my hand back, but after years of dealing with horses and knowing the importance of never spooking one, I chose instead to drop my hand after patting him twice.

"Only handsome boys like this big guy." I know the lady standing against the stall three doors over is Ella Hart. I saw her picture on the webpage and in a few articles I found on *Wikipedia*.

"You're lucky you still have a hand, Hercules isn't known to be much of a gentleman." Pushing herself away from the wall, the knowing sounds of boots to wood is a major comfort in opposition to the clicking sound my overpriced toe pinchers made.

As far as first impressions go, I had effectively blown any chance of working here. "Most men aren't, you have to learn to work around their rough edges, until they turn on their backs so you can scratch their bellies." I began backing away from the edge of the stall, but Hercules was having none of it and nudges me in the shoulder.

"Looks to me like he has rolled over for you." I don't know Ella well enough to know if the humor in her voice is genuine or just to keep me smiling as she tosses me out on my ass. "You must be Kennedy," she places her own hand where mine had just vacated.

"Yes, ma'am. Kennedy Forrester, and I will be leaving now."

Cinnamon brown eyes drift to mine; her hand stills and then pats the horse twice just as I had. "Hercules, I need to borrow your new girlfriend for a few minutes." Wordlessly she turns away, heading back toward the front of the stables, carrying her slender frame with authority. According to various sources, she is in her early forties, single, and a force to be reckoned with.

Stopping just before the hall to the reception office, Ella opens a door on the left, sending me a smile over her shoulder. Standing in the frame of the door, she waves me into the small office, as the phone begins ringing from the desk.

"I'm sorry, Kennedy, this is my personal line and I have to take it." I wave her off as she answers the line and exits the office. Stopping to take a deep breath, I began to have a good look around the room. Her shelves were filled with pictures of her and who I assumed were her family. A handsome man was wrapped around her from behind, sitting on what looks to be a boat. Little girls in ballet attire, hair pulled tightly atop their heads. Boys playing soccer, hair wet from sweat covering their heads. Men dressed formally as if attending a wedding. My eyes continue to scan and imagine the story behind each image, I smiled until I come to the photo of the man dressed in a military uniform, and my thoughts fall to Zach.

I wish he would have given me an opportunity to apologize for any offense I had given him. He had tried to be a gentleman, getting my letter to the rightful owner. Perhaps I spoke too much, told him too many of my problems. He was fighting a battle and didn't need to hear about my issues. Still, as I look into the brown eyes of the soldier in the picture, I wonder what Zach looks like? Is he tall or short, dark haired like the man in the picture or is his hair light from the sun? Does he have facial hair or is he clean-shaven?

"Sorry about that," Ella apologized for the interruption as she reclaimed her seat, donned her glasses, and then took my resume in hand. "Kennedy, I see here that you graduated just a few years ago."

"Yes, ma'am. Top five in my class." Ella dropped my resume back to her desk, slowly and methodically removing her reading glasses, and then placing them on the desk. She folded her hands in grace and elegance. She was quiet for several seconds, although it seems so much longer.

"Kennedy, I'm going to be blunt. I have a stack of applicants for this particular position. I've sat through more interviews in the past week than I ever want to remember. Each of them swearing to work hard for me, telling me how good they are with people and of value to me and this company. So tell me, Kennedy, what can you do for me that all the others can't?"

When I was in high school, I had a teacher who was the most amazing person. He wasn't like the other staff who stood in front of the class and taught behind the desk. He walked around the room or sat in chairs that were vacant due to illness and what not. He would give us real life examples instead of textbook doctrine. He was exciting and fun and made learning his subject easy. I can remember one time; a classmate of mine was having an issue understanding something. She was giving an oral presentation in the class and lost her place. He told her, people will tell you to baffle with bullshit if you can't impress them with knowledge. He disagreed with that saying, instead he said be honest, own your mistakes and everyone will follow you. I'm choosing to take his advice.

"Well, Ms. Hart, if you hire me, I will most definitely keep you entertained. I tend to ramble when I'm nervous, as you can clearly see, and I'll tell you more about completely useless things than you ever wanted to hear. I tend to go overboard with the information I pass along. In all honesty, Ms. Hart, I want to work for this company because I live to see the face of a patient as they take that first step. I treasure each and every moment I can spend with the horses and people who care as much as I do about them" There, I had been honest, now let's see if she found

86

me to be of her liking. By acting on impulse in touching her property, I was using all of my luck with her not calling the authorities.

"Well, Kennedy, besides your inability to filter and condense what you have to say, is there anything else you would like me to know? Boyfriend, children, husband?"

"No, I'm single, I know there's someone out there for me, I just have to be patient and not get in a hurry. I know when the time is right, he'll be there waiting for me, as well." Silently, I hoped he would be as handsome as the soldier in the photo behind her. As strong and kind as the man I had most likely scared away. Ella assured me she would contact me either way regarding the position. I thanked her and quietly exited the building.

I made it to the parking space where I had left my Porsche. I hated this car, so much money spent on a name instead of something practical. Claudia Forrester didn't need a large event to spend astonishing amounts of money on things she wanted, this car was a prime example. With all of my money tied up in Jason's half of the shop, I would be selling this car and using the money left over to supplement my income. I wouldn't rely on the maturity of my trust fund to support me. I had a suspicion once my father got wind of my involvement with Jason's venture; my assets would be frozen as well.

Once inside the confines of the car, surrounded by almost complete silence and the smell of fine leather, I took the steering wheel in my hands and lowered my forehead to it. "Please, God, make my other half with a good heart like Zach's. I don't care if he is short and has bad breath, just make him a good man." With a kiss to my fingertip to send the prayer to God's ears, I pressed the button to start the car.

Pulling out of the parking space, I waved to Hercules who had ventured out into the paddock, silently hoping to see him again. Driving into traffic, I chose to keep the radio off, needing the silence to reflect on my interview. I had plans to meet Jason and Savannah for lunch, and was behind schedule, but Jason would understand. Traffic was heavy, as the rain had just finished, however as I grew closer to my destination, someone was pulling out of a parking space directly in front of me. Giving the customary 'thank you' wave, I pulled into the space.

Savannah was a breath of fresh air for Jason, different from Hannah in so many ways. He smiled more and laughed all the time. It was good to see him like this and I prayed it would continue. As I approached the table, I could see Jason talking on the phone. I also knew it wasn't his phone since it was covered in crystals and a bright pink bow. His eyes were camouflaged behind sunglasses, but his face was happy. Savannah was dancing in her chair to music only she could hear, swirling inside her head. I approached and was about to pull out my chair when Jason announced my arrival to whomever he was speaking to. I smiled as I turned my attention to Savannah, allowing him to conclude his conversation in peace.

"Oh, hey, how was the interview? I just know you got the job. Oh, and you look really nice. I told you that skirt would fit you and still look professional. Don't you just love garlic fries? I am so glad Jason ordered them also, that way we'll both have garlic breath."

As much as I enjoyed Savannah's company, she was quite excitable and quick to talk. Jason was trying to get my attention when my cell phone began to ring.

"Hello?"

"Kennedy? It's Ella Hart, I'm calling to officially offer you the position. I was serious when I said Hercules isn't normally as welcoming as he was today. I need someone who the horse's trust and he showed me today you're his choice. Your honesty today was refreshing and frankly, I could use some entertainment on a daily basis. Come in on Monday and let's get you started."

I thanked her several times and then hung up the phone. The feeling of being employed by the one place I wanted to work was the cream of my day. Jason finished his call and he and Savannah looked at me with anticipation.

"I got the job." I blurted out, not wanting to wait a single second to share my joy. Savannah jumped out of her seat and for the first time in my life I let all of my emotions emote from me. I hugged her back with the same exuberance. I didn't care if one of mother's friends happened by; my plans of being my own person were about to come to fruition. Jason shared joy along with me. It seems Savannah was correct in assuming her brother would be fine going into a blind partnership. Savannah began to rattle on about curtains and pillows.

"Wait a minute, Sweetheart. I know you're excited and all, but this is your brother's shop as much as it is mine." Savannah waved him off as she proceeded to eat her fries. "Zach is so easy going and has such a good heart. Don't get me wrong, since he joined the military and has done all the things he has, he is a tough guy as well. He just doesn't get upset about things like decorations." Jason placed his hand over hers, as she raised it to place another handful of fries into her mouth.

"No, babe, I was referring to having my sister decorate it."

I was happy for him and excited he wanted my input on the decor of his business, but I was stuck on the part where Savannah said her brother's name was Zach and was in the military. How many men named Zach were from Georgia? Atlanta to be exact and in the military. It's safe to assume more than one exists; however I wondered if Savannah's Zach was *my* Zach.

"Savannah, do you by chance have a picture of your brother?" Savannah was still so excited she scanned her phone and pulled up a photo. Handing it to me, I took a long look at the brown eyes that looked back at me. It was the same man I saw in the photos in Ella's office. I took a chance and moved to the next photo and found the same photo, which was framed on her shelf.

"Savannah, how do you know Ella Hart?"

# CHAPTER NINE

*Zach*

I HADN'T EVEN PRESSED THE END BUTTON on my phone when the alarms started to wail. Ignoring the pain in my arm, I grabbed my boots and stormed to my post. Even in the bright daylight, you could see the trail the missile left behind. All the training we did, training which most of my men complained was useless as the enemy never fired at us, took over and we returned fire. Our training and Reaper being a good ol' boy from the Appalachian Mountains who grew up, "shooting for his dinner," giving him a perfect kill record.

The colors, which lit up the already bright sky, would rival any Fourth of July fireworks display back home. Reaper said he joined the Navy to get out of the Mountains, to see the world on someone else's dime. He told me one night, while we were on patrol; he also left when he saw his best friend kiss the girl he'd thought was his. I wish I could say that was the first time I had heard that kind of story. If it wasn't a reason for leaving, it was the reason they wouldn't return home to the girl. Far too many women vowed to be patient and wait, but the true test of time proved to be too much and heart after heart was broken in the name of war.

After making certain we could offer no help to the victims of the attack, we silently made our way back to our base. Each of us mulling over the fact an organization could do something so evil to its own people. With my gear secured, I plopped down on my bed and opened my mail. I needed to escape the images that have permanently scarred my memories. Kennedy's email was dated nearly a week ago, causing my breath to hitch and my heart to speed up just a little.

To: Michaels. Zach, L.T.
From: HorseWhisper
CC:
Subject: How are you?

*Dear Zach,*

*I have such exciting news! Jason was able to secure the shop for his tattoo business. He had me go with him after signing the contracts. He wanted me to look at the set up and help him get a feel for where to go with what is there. I was overwhelmed with ideas. I can picture the different rooms and how to make the business appealing for both male and female clients. He has met the most wonderful, yet excitable, young woman. He is completely taken with her, however he is worried what will happen when she realizes who our mother is. I won't leave you hanging on my last statement; my mother is what one would term a social climber. She spends every waking moment trying to find a new edge in the hunt for her next "new best friend." I also won't admit who the ultimate prize in this quest of hers is, on the off chance you know her.*

*In more pleasant news, I have an interview with the one place I want to work for. Not to say I haven't had many, many interviews, trust me when I say I have sat through so many meetings, completely set up by my mother's "friends," to keep her network functioning.*

*However, seeing Jason tossing caution, and his trust fund, to the wind has inspired me to cut ties with my parents. My mother purchased this ridiculous convertible for me, but I need something much more practical. I've done a search with the DMV and have happily found the car is indeed registered to me. Once I have secured gainful employment, I plan to march over to a dealership and trade the overpriced convertible for a more sensible mode of transportation.*

*I've been scouring the newspapers for an apartment to rent and although the money my parents have placed in a trust for me would offer me a lifestyle, which would be ideal, it would also be dull. I want to work for the food I place on my table and complain when my alarm goes off before the sun comes up, but rejoice when a client is brought to tears after they take those first steps. I don't want social status or society chairs for organizations that are more about who the president is rather than the people they help. I want to live and be a productive member of the community. I want to walk down the street, instead of riding in the back of a limo. To shop in second hand stores instead of media enhanced mall fronts. I want to know who my neighbors are instead of reading about them in the society pages. To have cookouts and dinner parties with my friends and coworkers. To marry for love and not because he works for my father.*

*I'm sorry...I know this sounds like the ramblings of a twelve year old, but this is how I feel. I know I shouldn't bring you into my American tragedy, but I feel as if I could tell you anything and you would cheer for me, encouraging me instead of laughing at me and telling me to go shopping with daddy's black card. I can't imagine what a day is like for you. I do pray for your safe return.*

> *Your friend,*
> *Kennedy*

I wished I could have read this prior to talking with Jason, however I was in the mindset to get the shop up and running. I was just like Kennedy in her desire to be a productive member of society. I wanted many of the same things she did, it made me wonder. What if fate had a way of steering you in the direction you needed to go? What if two people, born into the same world, never knew the other due to circumstances beyond their control? What if I was destined to meet this amazing creature named Kennedy Forrester? Saving her email to the folder I had created in her name, I found another from her written the same day I had made a call to Savannah.

To: Michaels. Zach, L.T.

From: HorseWhisper
CC:
Subject: I'm sorry

*Dear Zach,*

*I feel this will be my last letter to you. I want to apologize if I offended you in any way. I have a feeling; even with my attempts to keep my mother's name in the shadows, you, being an intelligent man, figured it out. I understand your desire to stay as far away from me as possible. Please, don't hold your distaste for her against Jason. He is working so hard to make the business a success. He offered me the apartment that sits above the building you guys own. I have declined and will keep my distance.*

*Thank you so much for your service and for being such a kind man in trying to help me. May you return safe and secure, and be prosperous in your new business.*

*Regards,*
*Kennedy Forrester*

I was confused as I re-read the last letter over again. She certainly hadn't offended me and I had no clue what she was talking about in regards to her mother. I didn't really keep up with my mother's charities and organizations. I knew she was cautious with whom she associated with, as she and my father had talked about some pretty aggressive women who behaved as Kennedy described. Closing out my email, I checked the time and then opened my *Skype* program. My mother may have the ability to raise millions and millions of dollars, but she was clueless when it came to modern technology. My aunt Ella, however, was a master. I knew she would be in her office or at least near her cell phone at this time of the day. I clicked on her name and waited as the line tried to connect.

"Well, good evening my favorite SEAL." My aunt's voice carried over the speakers; I had forgotten to place my earphones on so as not to disturb the rest of the guys around me.

"Aunt Ella, how are you?" I spoke softly, again being considerate of those around me.

93

"I couldn't be better, Zach. I just got a call from a client who has been approved to come to the center. He's a motorcycle accident victim and hasn't walked in nearly a year. Based on his medical records, he is the perfect candidate for our services. I also hired a new tech. She comes from Colorado Springs with a glowing review from Sabrina Moore, a colleague I went to school with. She has such a way with the horses, almost like she can communicate with them."

I couldn't help but smile, I had my suspicions about who her new girl was. My aunt's voice was full of joy. Aunt Ella had been in my corner more times than I could count. I knew she was excited for the girl more than what it would mean for her in the end.

"So, you're impressed with your new hire?" Finally, the picture went from black to reveal the beautiful woman that was my mother's sister. My mother, Emma, was four years older than aunt Ella, but you would swear they were much closer. Ella chose to go to school and never marry, while my mother chose to be a wife and mother, yet both were really great at what they did.

"Kennedy is a breath of fresh air. She's here before the sun gets up in the morning and is always going nonstop with her ideas. Hell, she even has Hercules following her around like a lost puppy." This surprised me, Hercules was a rescue horse. It had taken Ella and her staff months to get him to settle down enough to put a saddle on. He had even bitten his handlers, and I knew several grown men who wouldn't go anywhere near him.

"Kennedy, you say?"

"Oh, Zach...she is just the prettiest thing and so sweet and caring. Your sister likes her, which, as you know, is a big thing. Not only that, but her brother Jason...wait, why am I telling you this? You already know. Savannah said you and Jason are partners. Savannah said she was helping put your shop together."

"Ms. Hart, I can't find the—Oh, I'm sorry, you're on a call."

I heard the feminine voice of whom, I was confident, was the woman I had called my aunt about. Her voice dropped to nearly a whisper as she discovered the situation my aunt was in.

"Oh, Sweetheart, please come in. I have someone I want you to meet." I could see the caring expression on my aunt's face, her heart full and it radiated to her beautiful features. Her smile could warm the coldest heart and make the devil himself feel bad about the evil he did. Many men have tried to get her attention, however my aunt has remained single. I watched her face while she motioned for Kennedy to come around her desk. I waited with anticipation for my first glimpse of the girl who had changed my world. Ella's smile grew and, as the seconds passed, mine did too.

"Kennedy, this is my nephew, Zach Michaels. He's calling me from somewhere in the God-forsaken desert." There was no mistaking the gasp, it was quick and quiet, but I heard it loud and clear. Slowly and carefully, I could see the shadow on the wall shift and change to indicate her enclosing presence. I held my breath as her face came into view. Her eyes looked sad and the memory of her letter was fresh in my mind. Ella didn't know about our history, unless Kennedy had confessed it, however I was certain she wasn't the gossipy type.

"Zach, this is my new horse whisperer, Kennedy Forrester." Kennedy's face took on a smile as fake as the people she had described in her letters. I didn't like it, just like the wrong in what Virginia Greyson had done; I was about to correct it.

"Actually, Aunt Ella, I do know Kennedy. Although this is the first time I'm laying eyes on her beautiful face. She has been faithfully writing to me and until about a week ago, I was responding to them. However, due to recent enemy activity, my lines of communication were severed. I just got communication back and was about to respond to her email, although given the situation I like this much better." I gave Kennedy the smile and wink combo my mother has made me swear to use sparingly.

"Kennedy, you deserve an apology as I neglected to inform you of situations that happen all too frequently here in the— as my aunt so poetically puts it— God-forsaken desert. There are times, and sadly there are many, where we have no way of contacting the outside world."

Color started to spread across the beautiful face of the woman who is decorating the screen. She isn't a runway model, as she admitted in her letters, but she isn't the monster she painted herself to be either. She's what writers describe as the girl next door. The one you take home to your mother and pray she says yes to your proposal. She is the girl my father told me to look and search for. The one I will find my sanctuary in.

"How about I let the two of you catch up?" My aunt winked as she pushed her chair back, closing the door to give us privacy. Kennedy moved to her left, taking the vacant seat, scooting closer to the screen.

"Kennedy, you lied to me."

"How?" Her eyes growing large in disbelief, shock in her reply.

"You said you weren't beautiful. Which, from where I'm setting, is a boldface lie." I watched as a myriad of emotions crossed her face, sadness the one remaining. "Hey, I'm teasing you. It was meant to be a compliment, not make you sad."

Kennedy shook her head as she looked down, "No, you're fine, I'm distracted today." she filled her cheeks with air, and then released it in a rush.

"With?" I prodded, feeling the need to know everything about her. Crossing her arms on the desk, she takes a few deep breaths as she begins. "When I lived back in Colorado, we had a reporter who wanted to do a piece on the horses and how the program worked. When he arrived, he brought with him a freelance photographer, Ethan Porter. After the article was finished, Ethan asked me out on a date. I didn't really have a reason not to, so I went out with him. One date was all it took for me to realize there was no spark, not even a blip between us. He continued to pursue me, by sending flowers and calling. I finally had to invite him over and remind him I was moving back home."

Patiently, I watched and waited, knowing there had to be more to this story. Keeping my face neutral, even as the jealousy crept up my spine. "I take it by the look on your face, he didn't take the news well."

"He said I couldn't get rid of him that easily." I didn't like the way her voice sounded as if she had given up. She had no idea what I was capable of, what lengths I would go to in order to keep her safe.

"I'd forgotten about him since leaving Colorado, until today, when I got a bouquet of flowers." Her eyes locked with mine on the screen, a new emotion I couldn't label colored her face. "I sent them back, but I have a feeling this won't be the end of him."

"Good, I hope he calls you." I leaned forward, not giving her time enough to question me. "When he does, tell him to move along, before your SEAL boyfriend has a conversation with him."

# CHAPTER TEN

## *Kennedy*

"KENNEDY, YOU DON'T WANT TO LIVE LIKE ME." Jason and I had been up late trying to get the shop in some state of order. The dust was thick and the old owner had left behind some questionable items. Nothing sexual or anything, just nothing you could identify.

"I have no money, Kennedy. I can't even take Savannah out on a proper date. Hell, I would completely starve if it wasn't for you."

Since the afternoon in Ella's office, Zach and I had been *Skyping* nearly every day. He was always so excited with what I would tell him about the shop and working for Ella. We had arranged for him to be able to see the inside of the shop. I had taken my computer down there one evening and let him look around. He and Jason began to solidify plans for what they wanted. Which included the naming of the place, *Second Skin*. I then took Zach upstairs and showed him the apartment located there. It was decided Jason and I would occupy it, making sure someone was around to discourage looters and such.

"I happen to like living here where no one is telling me to sit up straight or that my skirt isn't short enough."

It was a silent agreement life for both of us had gotten so much better. I went to a local dealership where the salesman asked me several times if I was certain I wanted to trade in my Porsche. I walked away with a used full size truck, something my mother would gasp and clutch her chest about, and a little change in my pocket.

Savannah had been another change for us as she stayed over most nights with Jason. If she was bothered by his lack of fortune, you would never know it. When Jason and Zach asked for my design ideas, so much came to mind. I got lost in my own world when I walked around and told the two of them what I thought.

So for the past two months, we have cleaned, painted, and gone to meeting after meeting to obtain a business license. They had to deal with tax ID-numbers, credit card machines and permits. Opening a business is quite the undertaking. Zach also announced his time in Afghanistan was nearly up and he would be heading home at the end of this week. The grand opening was scheduled for the next Monday.

My friendship with Zach had blossomed; he was a funny guy who could turn any situation into a joke. We avoided talking about what he does when he has to go out in the field. He had gone out on, what he said, was his final mission three days ago. Savannah and Emma, their mother, had begun planning a huge welcome home party. I got the impression it would be a family event, so I never assumed I was included.

* * *

"My sister tells me my mother has this huge party planned for me the Saturday after I return." His eyes were devilish, with an air of charm about him, making it hard to concentrate when he spoke. I wouldn't delude myself into thinking his feelings for me went anything beyond friendship. However, sometimes the things he said confused me and made me think things I shouldn't.

"You know if the other Zack would have been real, I don't think he could have tried to scam you when he saw how pretty you are." I was stunned by his words. "Come on, Kennedy, you have to know how pretty you are." His voice and face implied he was speaking from his heart.

"Well, Mr. Michaels, if that were true, I wouldn't have been on that website looking for a date now would I?"

Zach shook his head looking at me straight in the eyes. "Guys are just as intimidated as girls when it comes to approaching the opposite sex. Trust me, if I were sitting there with you, I probably wouldn't have the courage to say anything to you." His admission caught me off guard, he seemed so sure of himself, not shy and reserved like he was admitting to.

"Well, I should have known Zack was full of it, he put those electronic roses across the top of his email."

"What, no real flowers showing up at your door? Total cheap skate. So, are you coming to my party?" His quick subject change was a relief for me. I wasn't comfortable with the path we were headed down.

"I was under the impression it was for family only, and I wasn't actually invited." His grin, which had made me melt from the beginning, was there as he spoke the words that would change everything.

"Well, it's my party and I'm inviting you."

"Zach," I started, my eyes drifting down briefly. "I don't know if attending a family function is such a good idea, considering who my mother is. Wouldn't you agree?"

"Sorry, Kennedy, but I beg to differ. You are more than welcome, your mother, not so much. Please say you'll come. I know my mom will be fine with you there." With a ton of reluctance, I agreed to attend his welcome home party. Zach had to cut our session short as his CO needed to speak with him.

Just after lunch, Ella came into the stables holding a massive bouquet of yellow roses. I felt the need to hit Ethan with the pitchfork I had in my hand. Ella, noticing my frustration, halted my nefarious thoughts. "Hold on. Before you plot his murder, read the card."

Trading the wooden handle for the attached card, I slid the flap open and pulled out the thick card.

*Kennedy,*

*I may not be able to scribe roses across the top of an email. But I can put a dozen in your hand, where you can enjoy the beauty and fragrance as you think of me.*

*Yours, Zach*

I didn't want to read anything into Zach's flowers or the words he said, especially as I had no one to talk to about this. My mother was out, as she only wanted one thing, Zach's mother. Emma Michaels was the queen bee of charity work and to be in her inner circle was a huge honor. No one dared say no to one of the chosen. If my mother knew who Jason was seeing or that I had been talking to Zach, she would try to weasel her way into having Emma over to her home. My sister would run to my mother and Savannah would head straight to Zach and tell him anything I confessed to her.

Jason, while on my side, remained a guy and therefore clueless. His head floated high above the clouds around Savannah. Which brings me back to my confusion. I knew Zach could be a huge flirt, I'd witnessed it too many times. He called every woman he knew beautiful, something more than likely his parents taught him.

Isolation from social life is bound to cause some backup. What if his invitation and flower delivery, were more of his natural flirtatious personality and not from any deep seated feelings he harbored for me? This explanation made the most sense, and therefore was the most logical. Zach Michaels was being a nice guy.

* * *

It was the Thursday before Zach was due back in the states. Every detail about his party had been carefully planned and his entire family would be waiting for him at the airport. They wanted to welcome him home with a hero's reception. The shop, however, was a mess with open boxes and half full shelves. Jason had finished the private room and it now looked more like the waiting area of a spa than a place to put on a tattoo.

The guy who was putting the lettering on the front glass had just arrived and was setting up. Jason had painted the ceiling black, which caused the bucket lights to be more pronounced. He even found a company who specialized in neon signs and they had just finished a sign for another company. Although the color had come out all wrong for what they were going for, it worked well with the theme Jason was going for, so he bought it.

Framed samples lined both walls of the entry. Zach had emailed all of his designs and I had to admit he was quite talented. I personally had never wanted a tattoo, but Zach had insisted Jason was going to give him one once he got home. Savannah already had him do something on her lower hip, it was hidden beneath her clothes and I didn't want to know what he had created. Zach offered to do one for me, a thank you for all of my help, but I declined, as a tattoo wasn't on my radar. I also never questioned if Zach already had a tattoo or if he had something pierced.

Appointments began pouring in the minute word hit the streets a SEAL co-owned the place. Military men seemed to line up to have one of their own do something for them. Although, a fair share of women were also booked for a chance, I was certain, to see the artist.

Second Skin was beginning to take shape along the top half of the entry door. The old English script would match the logo, which had been placed on the front of the reception desk yesterday. It took what seemed like forever to get it centered perfectly, the poor guy had to start over four times as Jason wasn't happy.

I was on my hands and knees, sorting and organizing the piercing jewelry to be sold. They had everything from skulls to initials. I had also arranged the supplies for the aftercare behind the counter. I took in the scene around me; Jason was filling the toolboxes that would house the supplies he and Zach would work from. Savannah was setting up the credit card reader in a system she herself used in her own shop. She had also contacted every newspaper and radio station in the city, announcing the grand opening. A friend of hers was a host for one of the popular morning shows here in Atlanta, and he would be doing a live broadcast while Jason did his tattoo.

Music played overhead, something from the fifties, with a catchy beat, making you want to dance. This was how living simple was supposed to be. Putting yourself into what you loved and believed in, and feeling good about it at the end of the day.

I looked around at the patterns and colors Jason had placed together. I had no doubt patrons would walk through the door and be amazed at how it all turned out. Even though I had no desire for a tattoo of my own, I appreciated the art.

My knees were protesting from the abuse I had inflicted on them by kneeling for so long, but the display was perfect. The lighting caused the brilliance in the diamonds and metal to stand out. I could literally look at it all day.

The guy applying the lettering to the door, glanced at me so I smiled a friendly smile in return, but paused when I noticed the figure directly behind him. A man, tall and well-built, complete with brown camouflage and a hat atop his head. His pants were tucked inside his brown boots and a bag slung over his right shoulder, its top edge sticking out over his head. If I hadn't seen his face nearly every day for the past few months, I probably wouldn't have reacted the way I did.

His eyes landed on mine as I pushed the door open with more force than I intended, causing the poor sign guy to curse under his breath. I can't explain why I ran to him the way I did or why I had tears in my eyes. But as I stood in the center of the sidewalk, with the late afternoon sun beaming down on me and the breeze from the passing cars pushing my hair into my face, I couldn't help the way my hand covered my mouth as I took him all in. Zach was here, a day early, and looking so much better than he did on my computer screen. His smile widened, as he dropped his bag to the sidewalk, and took his hat in his hands.

"Kennedy?" His voice was so much richer, his smile somehow bigger. I could only nod my head as the sting of tears began.

"Oh, God, I was so wrong." His voice sounded pained as he closed the distance between us.

"About what?" I asked, confused. His eyes were so bright, his body solid as his arms encircled me, picking me up from the sidewalk. His warm lips crashed to mine as strong fingers buried themselves in the hair at the back of my head. The kiss lasted until breathing became necessary, each of us pulling back, sucking in the same breath. Eager and happy eyes locked as the sounds of the city filled the air around us.

Zach and Jason walked around the shop talking about items in the drawers, using terms, if I had been a fan of tattooing or interested in having one myself, I would most likely understand. My heart was in my throat as Zach took me by the hand, allowing me to lead him to the room Jason took such pride in pulling together. The pounding of my heart kept time with the sounds of his boots, as we got closer to it. At first, I thought he was trying to find the words to tell me he hated it, but when he turned from the plush sofa, he had the widest, brightest smile on his handsome face, flooring me even further than the kiss on the sidewalk; if that was even possible.

"Babe, it's more beautiful than I imagined." He punctuated his words with a kiss to my temple.

* * *

Zach commented several times on the changes in the city he noticed as I drove everyone to the Michaels's estate. It's sad how you could become immune to your surroundings. New buildings and businesses became the norm and were no longer appreciated once the shiny exteriors faded away.

Watching a trembling Emma run down the steps and practically leap into her son's arms made me smile a teary smile, and also burn with jealousy. My mother would have scoffed at such a display of emotion. I waited, with my car door open and my leg still inside, as they hugged for what seemed like an eternity. Zach and his mother exchanged several words before she insisted we all come inside. I stopped Zach and tried to get him to understand he needed time with his parents. Emma encouraged Jason and I to at least come in and have some iced tea. Knowing if I refused and word ever got back to my mother I would never hear the end of it, I accepted her invitation and joined them on her deck.

As I sat and listened to Zach and his father talk about the shop and what he had planned for the grand opening, I wondered what my mother would say if I were to snap a picture of where I was and send it to her. No doubt she would make an excuse to come and join me.

After finishing my tea and reassuring Zach I would return the following day to attend his party, I spent the remainder of the night over analyzing everything that happened. When I couldn't stand laying wide awake any longer, I slipped down to the shop and resumed my task of arranging jewelry and doing the final clean ups. With the silence in the room, it allowed my mind to roam free and explore every angle of the situation with Zach. I came to the conclusion that I had nothing to lose by exploring a relationship with him.

# CHAPTER ELEVEN

## *Zach*

THE PLANE RIDE FROM LONDON TO ATLANTA was full of turbulence; halfway through, the Captain made the flight attendants get in their seats and buckle up. Passengers around me were silently praying, I, however, snuggled in and fell asleep. When I finally got my luggage and a cab, I was still trying to get my bearings. The cabbie refused to take my money, telling me his brother had died in Vietnam and he'd made it his life's mission to never charge a returning soldier for a ride home. I tried to argue with him, but he refused, so I decided I would figure out how to give back in the same way.

Standing outside the building I had seen only by way of a Skype session, I took just a moment to live in the moment; my reality now. An older man was applying vinyl to the glass doors that housed my dream and future. A bright red potted plant sitting in the middle window of the second floor, caught my attention. It was evident Kennedy must have placed it there. I could almost imagine her humming as she filled the pot with dirt, taking careful precaution not to disturb the delicate roots of the tiny plant. How she would lovingly water it and gently stroke its petals. I wondered if she ever thought of me as she looked down on the streets below. Oh, how I had thought of her. Too many thoughts, which would remain hidden in my mind. Thoughts of a life of laughter and adventure with her. Of holding her as she cooked dinner or folded laundry. Sunday mornings wrapped around each other in fluffy white sheets. Standing at the end of an aisle, watching her face as she slowly walked my way. Again, thoughts that would, for the near future, remain in my head.

All the times I had laid eyes on Kennedy had done nothing to prepare me for this moment. Watching her move across the sidewalk was like watching a figure skater doing a perfect maneuver, minus the roar of the crowd. I watched the flow of her hair as it whipped around her face, and saw the smattering of freckles across her nose and cheeks. Her eyes were as bright as mine when I searched her face; longing to know what secrets they held.

"Only you could pull a stunt like you did and have mom too happy to see you to be pissed." Zane stood beside me, but his attention was focused on his children playing a game with our father.

I smiled quietly to myself since he was correct; I had ruined her plans of a large welcome in the middle of the airport. "Don't get too upset, everyone knows I'm her favorite."

He glances in my direction with a look of surprise on his face and a grunt rising from his massive chest, but didn't answer, instead nudging me with his free arm. "So, she must be someone pretty special to bring home to the 'rents so soon. Although she is giving you the stink eye right now."

I hadn't noticed it before, but Zane was right. Kennedy was talking with Meghan, and a friend of hers, beside one of the food tables. I wouldn't categorize her look as angry, but more...perplexed? Going for broke, I flashed her a smile and added in a wink. Her eyes moved to Meghan's face before touching her forearm. Maybe Zane was right, had I upset her? I was just about to walk over and ask her when Zane halted my momentum.

"Wouldn't do that if I were you? I have a feeling Meghan just told her how she and I met. Good thing my Meghan loves you, as by the looks of things this could get ugly."

"Zane, when will you get it through that thick skull of yours, I—unlike you— keep the women in my life happy. Kennedy knows how I

107

feel about her and she is well aware there are no other ladies sniffing around after me. When I finally laid eyes on her, I made sure she knew I had been wrong about my feelings for her."

"Explains the stink eye you're getting." Zane's words are followed by his body convulsing in laughter. "Come on you douche! You spend months sending emails back and forth and the first thing you say to her is you were wrong about her?"

"No, you idiot." I smacked his chest with my fist and told him what happened. Kennedy was a genuinely good person, a beautiful and gifted girl. So much so, when I saw the excitement leave her face for one tenth of a second, I ignored the risk of being slapped or, worse, having an angry brother come storming out and punching me. Everything about her called to me; her enduring rambling, her generous nature, her endeavor to hide her personal life from her mother's watchful eye, but most of all, her drive to be her own person. She was so excited to tell me about opening her first checking account and applying for a credit card in her name. I wanted to see that joy every day; I wanted to *be* the reason for that joy.

Abandoning all of the warning bells in my mind, I tossed caution to the wind and chose to see for myself if her lips were as soft as they looked. I closed the distance, lacing my hand in the hair at the back of her head and pulled her soft body against mine. The electricity that flowed around us was like an invisible bubble protecting us from the reality that begged to interrupt. The moment our lips connected, all my doubts were erased. The way she molded her body to mine, fusing us together in more than just flesh, connecting us on a level few had experienced. It was in that moment I knew those thoughts I had carefully tucked away, were a glimpse of what we could be.

"Wow." With the raw talent we both possessed and years of education between us, something better than 'wow' should have come out. When Zane was actively pursuing Meghan all those years ago, his teammates gave him shit for picking such an ordinary girl. Yet, he never let anything they said change his mind. I knew Kennedy thought of herself as simple and plain, but to me, she was perfect.

"Let me tell you this, little brother, if what I suspect about Kennedy is true, you're going to have to drill into her head this isn't just a dry spell hook up." My confused look gave him the opening he needed to finish his thought. With a wave of his hand that still housed his beer, he looked over my shoulder and continued.

"Meghan was, and still is, the most beautiful woman I have ever met. However, she fought me so hard because she believed all I really wanted was to get into her pants, some type of varsity challenge or some shit."

He didn't have to remind me of this, I was the one who kept encouraging him to be patient with her. "You forget, Zane, I was there when you had your balls in your hand, panting over her."

"I am aware, smartass. What I'm trying to tell you is, you're going to have to be direct and quite frankly blunt when it comes to Kennedy. If you want to hold her hand, you need to make it clear it isn't to help her cross the street or keep her balance. If you want to touch her, you'll need to set her straight as to why you want to do that. Don't give her any reason to justify your actions with innocent excuses.

His eyes never wavered, looking at Meghan with fondness in his eyes. "I'm telling you this and I know it sounds harsh, but I wish someone would have given me the handbook when it came to girls like ours."

"It would have been no good, they would have changed the rules on us."

* * *

My parents refused to sell the house we had grown up in, even after all of us had moved out and started lives of our own. My mother spent endless hours in the back yard, planting and tending to the flowers and shrubs she loved so much. She was angry with my father for days once when he offered to hire her a gardener. She preferred to be up to her elbows in rich soil and covered in grass clippings, than be dressed in the expensive clothing she had collecting dust in her closet upstairs. My mother was a simple girl at heart, a heart my father worked hard to cherish and keep.

"Can I get you something to eat?" My loving, but overly emotional, mother was driving me crazy. I knew she meant well, but I had been able to make my own plate for most of my life. I knew it was just her joy in my being home, but it was also tiring and I had to be very careful to keep my tongue reined in.

"You spoil me, but I'm fine." I chose to answer, avoiding hurting her feelings and causing my father's brow to rise.

"You're my son, it comes with the job." Her warm hands were on either side of my face as her brown eyes shifted between the matching pair I inherited.

"This was a great party, thank you for this, and for not saying anything to Kennedy."

Her hands dropped to her sides and the smile vanished. She leaned further into me as she spoke in a hushed tone, giving a quick look to any possible eavesdroppers. "I will say this one time, Zach." Her finger was sharp as it met the soft skin of my chest. "Kennedy is every mother's dream for their son, but if you have less than honorable intentions for her, I will call a car service right this second."

Taking a small step back and pulling my mother off to the side of the house, the tone of this conversation was unfamiliar to me. She had always defended our family, not one of Savannah's many boyfriends or any of the girls that sniffed around Zane or myself. "What's going on, Mom? You never do this, defending someone outside of the family."

She inhaled deeply and then pulled me in for a hug, the gesture making a large lump form in my throat. "When I was making the rounds of our guests, I overheard Kennedy and Meghan talking."

I pulled away, taking her hands in mine. This wasn't a conversation I wanted to risk being overheard and spreading like cheap gossip. I nodded in the direction of the house and she followed me. Closing the door to her sitting room, I looked at her to continue.

"As I was saying, I overheard Meghan and Kennedy talking. Sharing the story of a kiss, in the center of a busy Atlanta sidewalk, the gentleman dressed in a military uniform and the girl wearing a shocked expression." I waited for the punch line, a clue as to where this was going.

"Kennedy confided in Meghan she had never been kissed in such a fashion. It seems certain emotions were stirred up by your kiss."

I remained stoic, still unsure of where this was going. I took a seat on the sofa with a clear view of the backyard. Upon examination, Meghan

110

and Kennedy were still standing in the same spot, the smile still had not returned to her face.

"Okay, so I kissed her, big deal." I shrugged.

"Perhaps it's not to a mature man who is well trained and worldly. But to a shy young lady whose upbringing dictated a certain level of morals..." Silence fell jagged between us, her eyes pleading with me to understand.

"Kennedy is confused." My mother held her hand up when I tried to question her statement. "She was under the impression you had been a gentleman in helping get a certain letter to its owner and then continuing to be gracious by corresponding through emails and other forms of communication. She doesn't understand the feelings the kiss brought forward and is convinced you have one thing on your mind. Meghan explained to her the similar situation she found herself in and gave her what I would agree was solid advice." This couldn't be good, I knew what Meghan had put Zane through and the heartache he had experienced.

"She told her to avoid having sex with you. If sex was your true intention, then you'll tire easily and move on to the next girl."

The sun had gone down and the sky was now a dark purple with oranges and dim yellows. I had watched the sun set in the desert many nights and wondered what Kennedy was doing at that moment. With determined steps, I flew out the back door, directly to where Kennedy was still standing. I passed many of my guests and even bid some of them goodnight. Meghan was wrapped in Zane's arms, the children in the house I'm sure. Kennedy's eyes met mine and I could swear she gasped as I reached out for her.

"I'm sorry to interrupt, but I've waited for quite a while to sit with Kennedy and have a discussion." I didn't let go of her hand until I had insured she was comfortable. I made certain we were face to face as I wanted her to have no doubt about my desire for her. Not to one day warm my bed, but to own my soul.

"I know I should apologize for kissing you yesterday, but that would indicate I had remorse for it happening, which would be a lie."

Kennedy tried to look down at her lap, but I refused to let her run from me or change the subject. Zane was right, women like Kennedy are so closed off to themselves they miss out on what is right in front of them.

"I've wanted to kiss you since the first email I got back from you. I didn't care what you looked like or if you had three heads, I wanted to be near you and get to know the amazing creature half a world away." The smile I longed for so much returned to her face and it gave me the encouragement I needed to continue. Squeezing her hands in mine, our eyes reflecting what our hearts surely already knew.

"I want to make myself perfectly clear. I want to have a relationship with you, one in which kisses like the one we shared yesterday are expected and wanted. I want to be able to give you cute pet names and call you those names when we are alone or surrounded by our friends and family. To see the look of hope and contentment on my mother's face when I kiss you again as she watches from the kitchen window." Kennedys eyes and attention stayed with me, never turned her head to see if I was correct, seeing for herself my mother was indeed biting her nails as she watched this play out.

"When you told me about Ethan bothering you, my comment about being your boyfriend was real, not empty words to scare some creep away. I'm asking you to trust me, a man you barely know, a man who wants nothing more than to make you so happy you want to share it with the entire world. A man who would do anything, give anything, to be by your side."

With my words hanging in the air, I searched her face for any sign she was about to bolt. When I couldn't take it anymore, slowly and cautiously, I lowered my head to hers waiting until the last second to close my eyes before placing my lips to hers. There was no deepening of the kiss, or groping of body parts, just two sets of lips joined in agreement.

Kennedy was the first to pull away and for a second I thought this was it, this is the moment she gives me the 'just friends speech'. As the smile formed on her face, the light from the fire dancing in her eyes, I knew this was the beginning of the best thing to happen to me.

Only family remained as we sat around a now dying fire. Mom and dad had excused themselves an hour ago, insisting on giving the children baths, and then putting them to bed. Meghan rolled her eyes as Zane made a sexual gesture in response. I was content to have my arm behind Kennedy's head, my thumb rubbing up and down her shoulder. The first time I did it, she shivered and I knew it wasn't from any chill in the air as there wasn't any. Kennedy was talking softly with Meghan about Hercules and a big biker guy she was working with. Aunt Ella had already informed me of their new patient, so I was content to listen and continue touching her shoulder.

"Hey, Zach, before we head out, I got you those tickets for the home opener." I remove my arm from around Kennedy and stand up to say goodnight to my brother and sister- in-law, but capture Kennedy's hand, pulling her up with me. Now that she knew how I felt about her, I would definitely be reassuring her this was for real.

"It's Sunday, right?"

Zane confirmed the date and time and assured me he would be at the grand opening on Monday. Once I saw the taillights of Zane's car, I turned to Kennedy and offered to drive her home.

"It's all right, Jason said he would come by after he drops Savannah at her apartment." I shook my head and pulled her close, whispering softly in her ear. "Now what kind of boyfriend would I be if I let your brother come all the way back here to get you? Besides, it will give me more time with my girlfriend."

"You're serious about this?" Her nervousness was adorable.

"Well, if you would rather just be friends, I'll take what I can get. I mean, I know I'm not the most handsome guy on the block." Her eyes became huge as she immediately threw her hands up, tossing them from side to side in rapid movements.

"No, Zach, that's not what I meant! It's just that...well...it's just—"

She was so damn cute and I wanted to take her back in the house and lock her away forever.

"I just don't understand why you want me?"

"Well, I could stand here for the next week and give you reason after reason, or I can take my time and show you."

* * *

My mother was still awake when I returned from taking Kennedy home. I knew I wouldn't be able to just slip into bed without having a conversation with her. As I rounded the kitchen counter, she slid a glass of whisky in my direction. My mother was old school and believed in keeping things in the family. She was a great listener, but an even better disciplinarian.

"So, I take it by the way you glued yourself to Kennedy's side the talk went well?" Her eyes weren't meeting mine, instead watching her fingers as they circled the rim of her glass. I knew from experience she was collecting her thoughts, searching for the right words.

"We had a good talk, so yes, things are going well."

"I'm happy to hear it. You deserve to be with someone like Kennedy. "Her eyes met mine with a happiness that shown on her face.

"One thing concerns me." She looked down as she pulled the bottle of Jameson's toward her, refilling both of our glasses.

"Oh, what would that be?"

She tossed her drink back before she answered me. "Her mother." I let the statement hang in the air for a few moments. I already knew Kennedy's concerns with how her mother felt about her new life. She had confided to me about Jason being cut off due to the disrespect he had shown their parents.

"Kennedy was worried you held an opposition to her coming here today, I assured her this wasn't the case. I don't think she knows about my return, and I know for fact, she has no clue about Savannah and Jason." Mom nodded still watching me.

"I had a long talk with Jason when I visited him at the shop the other day. Savannah is head over heels for him and I think this might just be the one that sticks for her. However, I also know the second Claudia figures out who the new people in her children's lives are, she'll most likely use this as an avenue to weasel her way to you." I knew the way Kennedy had spoken of her mother wasn't in the positive. Growing up as my mother's son, I knew how to deal with people and their ulterior motives.

"Don't worry mom, Kennedy's parents will know that she's dating an ex-military, tattoo artist. I'll make sure the first time I meet them I dress the part. I'll even arrive on a motorcycle to give it the full effect." I kissed her goodnight, after placing the whiskey back in the cabinet. I love my mother dearly, but sometimes when she had a lot on her mind, she could drink herself silly. I would be the good son and save her from a nasty headache.

# CHAPTER TWELVE

*Kennedy*

CLARITY IS A FUNNY THING. When you feel as if you have all of the facts in a situation, only to be given a different perspective, everything, which was murky, becomes clear.

Keeping my word to Zach, I arrived to his party on time. Emma informed me he was upstairs taking a much-deserved shower after working out with his brother's football team. She introduced me to several of the ladies in attendance, everyone was friendly and I knew my mother would never fit into the inner circle Emma had created. Each person she introduced me to was interested in what I had to say, answered every question I asked and laughed when it was appropriate. They were all genuinely good people. There weren't any hidden agendas, ulterior motives, or anything to gain by speaking to me.

Meghan was the last lady I was introduced to. She was bent over, speaking softly with a little boy who I would guess to be about two or three. He had tears on his face, but after a few words from Meghan, a smile lit up his features and he was off and running with the rest of the children.

"Wouldn't it be nice if everything in life was as simple as a hug from your mother?" Her eyes remained on the now happy child.

"That would be an ideal world wouldn't it?" I voiced, and then really thought about what I said.

Meghan moved closer to me extending her hand for me to shake, the smile caressing her gentle face was real and not forced. I hated when people had to force a smile, it made you wonder what was really going on inside their heads.

"My mother-in-law tells me Zach brought you over yesterday." Eyes drifting behind me and without seeming rude, I turned to see a large guy standing just outside the patio doors, a beer in his hand, and Jonathan, Zach's father, standing beside him. He was incredibly good looking and I scanned the lawn trying to see who the lucky girl was wearing the matching wedding ring that decorated the third finger of his left hand.

"Yes, he and my brother own a shop downtown." It was the simplest answer I could give. Disclosing what had transpired between Zach and I would serve no purpose, therefore I kept it to myself.

"He is persistent. Hell, all of them are."

I looked at her with a questioning expression, but before she could elaborate or I could ask her the question that was on the tip of my tongue, we heard a conversation that was currently transpiring between several of the younger girls who were enjoying the music playing overhead.

"Can you imagine not having the opportunity to date for as long as he's been away?"

"Forget about dating! Imagine how long it's been since he's had sex. I mean hasn't he been surrounded by men for the past few years?"

"He's still single, which can only mean one thing."

"Well, if it's dry spell relief that he needs, he can certainly have his pick."

Meghan grabbed me by the arm, pulling us away from the rest of the conversation. Her movement allowed me to see a sight that would cause even the most seasoned girl to swoon. Zach stood, beer in hand, with a red ball cap on backward and a sleeveless shirt giving me a glimpse of the tattoos decorating his arms. Muscular tan legs, perfected from hours of training and hard work, peaked out from the bottom of his tan shorts. Raising the bottle to his mouth, I couldn't help but watch the dip of his Adam's apple, as he took in the cold liquid, all while looking in my direction. In all of my thoughts last night, I never considered Zach would be in the need of sex. It wasn't unreasonable to think he would feel comfortable approaching me with his need.

"I swear, if gossip was an art form, those two would be a couple of Picasso's. They don't care whose bed they fall into as long as it's lined with money. Listen, Kennedy, I don't know anything about you except what Emma has told me, but what I do know is how these Michaels boys work." For the next few minutes she told me of her introduction to one of the Michaels men. She indicated the man who was the subject of the conversation was the handsome man who stood beside Zach. Meghan wasn't a drop dead gorgeous woman, looking at her was like looking at a version of myself. She lived to be comfortable, not fashionable. Given the appearance of her husband, it was not the social norm.

"Maybe those ladies are right, maybe that is what he's after, but nothing says you have to sleep with him. If he is only after what you can give him, it's simple, don't give it. But if he's anything like Zane, and I don't have to even guess, then you're about to be swept off your feet and taken for an amazing ride."

Her rationale seems so plausible, and maybe it was. After listening to her share the details of her courtship with Zane, I found myself stuck on a loop of sorts. By definition, not everyone is attracted to the same type of people, much like ice-cream flavors and brands of cars. We all have different tastes; it makes the world less dull. With the understanding of Meghan and Zane's relationship and the way Zach was currently expressing his interest in me, it allowed me just a glimmer of hope he wanted more from me than simply a tour of my panties.

"Well, something is definitely up." Meghan's sweet voice called my attention back to our conversation. I looked over to see what she was referring to before following her eyes and the nod of her head as a very determined, and dare I say fixated, Zach was currently headed in our direction.

\* \* \*

Zane shared a story of one of his players who was having trouble keeping his focus on the game. They had sent him to see the team physician, but the visit revealed nothing.

"If his arm wasn't as good as it is, his ass would have been traded."

"Sounds like he's more interested in the cheerleaders instead of his teammates." Meghan voiced the thoughts I was thinking. Men lose the ability to function normally when a pretty face and a short skirt are involved."You're probably right, babe. Now, tell me how to center his attention on the ball and you just might be able to rule the world."

Zane pulled his wife in closer to his chest. A move, even with the talk Meghan and I had, still baffled me. Meghan was not a stunning beauty, her hair could use a trim and her nails were chipped and broken, but that didn't seem to matter.

Zane asked if Zach would be willing to come and help out with the game as his assistant was out with a broken foot. They lost me with talk of yardage and tight ends.

"You'll be there as well, right, Kennedy?" Meghan nudged me as she and Zane stood to leave.

"Um...well, I need to take care of some things at work."

Meghan passed off my comment with a wave of her hand. "Oh, your work will still be there after the game. At least come and keep me company."

\* \* \*

The white ceiling above my bed a backdrop for the shadows reflected by the headlights from the street below. The leaves and flowers from my potted plants on the ledge allowed distorted shadows to dance around the room, much like my thoughts.

Zach's kiss had left me to re-evaluate every conversation and email we had exchanged. He was a handsome man, with a strong work ethic, and endless doors of opportunity, which were open because of his family name.

I have never deluded myself into thinking an attractive man would flirt or be the slightest bit interested in me, I found it was easier that way. Knowing your limitations went beyond cutting yourself off before you

119

drank too much wine. Embarrassing yourself by creating a scene in front of a man of interest never seemed like a good idea to me. So, when Zach held my face in his hands, placing those lips I had watched so many times during our *Skype* sessions against mine, my common sense left me and I allowed myself to fall into his embrace. Letting the hope and desire I had denied myself spring to life.

When Zach brought up Ethan, I held back the chill, which begged to travel up and down my spine. I found the remnants of the bouquet smashed against the back of the shop. Crushed petals littered the pavement beside my car and down the sidewalk.

Last night after Zach dropped me off, I found another leaning against the door to the apartment. No card attached, but I know who they were from, and I know this wasn't the last I would hear from him.

My inability to find a reason that would negate my attendance was the reason for my scanning the stands looking for Meghan. Zach picked me up from the shop, with a quick kiss and the capture of my hand in his. We arrived to find the stadium filled to the rafters, a sea of red and black. When Zach led me to the field instead of a seat in the stands, I didn't question it, allowing him to guide me onto the field. With his Falcons ball cap and team polo, he could easily be mistaken for a player.

"Michaels!" Came a shout sounded from behind me. Zach pulled me to stop as he turned in the direction of the voice. Standing with a beer in one hand, the other waving overhead as he tried to get Zach's attention, was a tattoo-covered man.

"Hey, man, long time no see." Zach released my hand, reaching out to greet the man in a sporting hug.

"I didn't think you were due home till next year." The tattooed man remarked, his smile sparkling as the two pulled back.

"I took an extra assignment so I could get out early." This was news to me, although I guess it wasn't really my concern. Tattoo man shot a glance in my direction, Zach noticed and brought me into the conversation. With both men now facing me, Zach's hand extended in my direction,

"Viper, how the hell do you know this knock out?" I didn't want to know the answer Zach was about to give. After everything that had

120

occurred last night, he could respond we were good friends, or he could use the word so many women like myself seek to have as a title.

"Hey, Babe, come here I want you to meet a friend of mine." Although Zach's smile was bright and the term 'babe' was a step in the direction of a title, it was also a common word used in everyday conversations among men. Disguising my nervousness with a tight smile, I stepped in his direction as his arm went around my shoulders, not a gesture I would associate with friendship.

"Tombstone, this is Kennedy. Kennedy, this is Tombstone, we went to SEAL training together." My smile still gleaming, yet my spirit dropping at the words he chose. My need to avoid bad manners, enabling me to extend a free hand, and move slightly away from Zach side. This was not an avenue I was comfortable traveling down.

"Kennedy, the pleasure is all mine, but I have to ask again, what is a beauty such as yourself doing with this ugly fuck?"

"Well, Mr. Tombstone, Zach was kind enough to help me when I found myself in a situation without my consent. He has been wonderful in making the tragedy a little less...bleak."

"Sounds like Viper, all right. Always did have a soft spot for a damsel in distress." I held my breath and squared my reserve; refusing to let my smile drop or tears fall. I tried to listen as Tombstone told the story of his injury, which put him in the hospital for a while. Since returning to the states, he'd come home to find his wife and children gone, with a note and divorce papers left in the middle of the floor.

I thanked Tombstone for his service and followed Zach, since I had no real idea where I was to keep myself as Meghan was nowhere in sight. I was doing my best to stay out of the way of the players and coaches, yet not appearing to be snobbish or rude.

Zach was talking with Zane about the strengths and weakness of each player as they walked across the field. My attention was drawn away by the sounds of the cheerleaders standing directly behind me. Taught bodies with pristine smiles, all dressed up in a little as possible. Caroline had been active in cheer and dance, using her pom poms to grab the attention of her husband, Richard.

Shouts of "watch out" cried out behind me, before a loud slapping sound resonated behind my head, causing me to snap back around to face the playing field. Mere centimeters away from my nose, Zach's hand was clenched tightly around a football. Zane shouted for someone to get off the field and get over to him. My eyes left the white stitching across the side of the ball, looking up into Zach's face, glancing back and forth with the realization of what almost happened.

Had Zach not caught the speeding ball, I would have been hit and injured severely. I changed of my line of sight back to Zach's face, waiting as his eyes locked with mine. His brown eyes bore into mine as he tossed the ball back to the players. The gravity of the situation finally registered and I could do nothing to stop my body from its intended actions. My hands and lips acted of their own accord as they came in contact with Zach. Hands needing to feel him, knocking his ball cap off in the process. My legs stretched to the limit as I pushed myself up on my tiptoes. Zach pulls me close as my feet leave the ground, ignoring the cheering and catcalls raining around us.

Never in my life had I ever initiated the physical side of a relationship. However, as my fingers found their target at the back of Zach's neck, his hair stubble from his required military haircut, my tongue demanded to explore his. The kiss may have lasted for centuries or more realistically a few seconds, but we were both breathless when it ended.

"I'm sorry about your hat." My voice raspy with my need for him. "I don't give a shit about my hat, not when my entire world is right here in my arms."

\* \* \*

The grand opening for the shop had people lined up around the corner for a chance to look inside. Savannah, true to her word, had every newspaper and radio station who would broadcast, standing outside and asking questions. I watched Zach give two men free tattoos once he found out they had recently returned from the Middle East. After the excitement of the day had passed, we were laying on my couch when I commented about him being a good guy. He told me about the taxi driver who wouldn't let him pay for his cab ride from the airport and how he wanted to pay it forward.

Jason had never looked happier than after the initial success of the shop. He even refused to question the amount of bookings it would take to get them in the black at the end of the month. However, the silence from our parents hadn't gone unnoticed by either of us, we just chose to ignore the sleeping giant, as I had labeled it.

The next day at lunch, Ella said something about Zach buying a house, she suggested I take the guys something to eat and see if Zach had any potential properties in mind. Walking in with an arm full of deli goodies, caused Jason to jump from behind the counter and help with the heavy entry door. Zach was bent over a large bald guy, working on what looked to be a naked girl on his chest. I didn't want to interrupt, so I told Jason I would place the food in the break room and talk to them later.

"Sure, let's see if that really happens." The teasing way Jason spoke, placed a smile on my face. I followed him down the hallway, passing a group of young girls who were pointing at different tattoo examples displayed on the walls. Several middle age men were also looking at the same wall, however I'm certain their interests were on the assets of the ladies, not of the art. Placing the perishable items in the refrigerator, I made my way back to the front of the shop. I would speak with Zach later about his house hunting.

By the time I entered the main room, the bald guy was finished and one of the young ladies stood with her stomach bare and the button of her jeans unhooked, her hands shimmying her jeans and panties lower on her body. In my opinion, these were women who were direct and to the point. Tossing aside the need to be pursued and fully prepared to make their intentions with members of the opposite sex perfectly clear. You could accept they sometimes tired easily when the object of their affections didn't respond or you could get mad and get in their face. I was never one who enjoyed causing a scene and chose to let the pretty blonde fall on her face. While I observed her unbridled flirting, I also noticed Zach's eye roll and hand gesture for her to just hurry up.

"While I'm still young, girly."

123

When his eyes recovered from their three sixty, they came to rest in direct alignment with my own. I smiled brightly and blew him a quick kiss, giving a slight wave as I headed in the direction of the front door.

"Ah, hell no. You better deliver that kiss." Zach possessed a commanding voice; one I imagine rang proud and true for his men during their missions. Now, it filled the room and silenced any conversations. With just a hint of embarrassment and more joy than sorrow, I fulfilled his request. I crossed the floor and kissed him soundly on his lips.

Being with Zach had brought out a boldness I never knew I possessed. After his bare handed catch of the football, any childhood instruction on public displays of affection went right out the door. I had since become quite brazen in initiating contact between us. This was new territory for me, a frontier I couldn't wait to explore and conquer.

"Is this your sister?" My head turned on its own toward the voice belonging to lady who was now not only half naked, but by the hands resting on her bare hips, irritated. Add in the harsh tone of her words and her irritation was clear. I was ready to simply bid Zach a quick goodbye and be on my way. However, Zach being Zach, he wasn't going to settle for what I had planned

"Fuck no, she ain't my sister!" Closing the distance between us with purpose, he pulled me flush against him. "She's the goddamn mother of my unborn children." His voice was elevated and brash, his grip on my hips tightening to a slightly painful level and yet it was, shockingly, erotic. He never let go of my body as he began to usher her out of his chair. "Now take your skinny ass out of here."

The poor blonde was more shocked than anything and I wanted to feel bad for her, but again he was bringing out a new person in me. One who didn't have to smooth out everything or worry about what would get back to my mother's judgmental ears.

The blonde and her friends scurried out the door, gone long before the seat they occupied was cold from lack of body heat. Zach pulled me closer to his body, his hand keeping my hip captive, now rested securely along my right ass cheek. It was bold and brazen, and I couldn't get enough.

124

"Any of you other motherfucker's got a problem with me kissing my girl?" The remaining men shook their heads, no one daring to disagree with him. I felt his body vibrate with a satisfied chuckle, then he buried his face in my neck and hair. Closing my eyes, I enjoyed the feel of this man who was wrapped around me; the smell of his clean shirt, his deodorant, and the salve he used on the new tattoo Jason had given him.

When the shop first opened and the media came inside, they found a calm Zach sitting in Jason's chair. Zach wanted a symbol of the new chapter in his life, a representation of everything new in his world. So he had Jason place a Phoenix on his right shoulder, its significance evident to everyone—a new beginning.

The vibrating of my phone was like an alarm on reality. I pulled away from Zach, knowing it was still working hours for me. Zach knew how seriously I took my job and didn't stop me. One glance at the screen however, told me the giant Jason and I had tried to ignore was now awake. Placing my hand on Zach's chest, I closed my eyes and braced myself for the wrath I was certain would come. Zach sat in his chair, pulling me into his lap.

"Hello, Mother. I wasn't expecting your call." When I was a little girl, my mother hired a lady to come instruct me on how to properly address someone. We spent several sessions on how to answer a telephone. I gripped Zach's shirt tighter the second the words left my lips, knowing they were all wrong and improper.

"Kennedy, it seems you have been slacking on your social skills. Perhaps we should rethink this new venture you have set upon." Even if I thought long and hard for several days, I don't think I could remember the last time my mother said a kind word about anything I did or said, unless it was to place her in a better light.

"I'm sorry, Mother, but I am trying to conduct a business meeting and have a client. Can I phone you back later?" My voice was fake and I hated the sound of it. I got the feeling it bothered Zach as well, as his hands left my body and found their way to the back of his neck.

"Really, Kennedy? Is this the same client from the deplorable display your father showed me on one of his sports channels? Or could this be the client whom Buffy Thompson saw you kissing in the middle of a public street where everyone could see?"

Had this conversation occurred a month ago, I would have been so embarrassed. I would have excused myself from Zach's presence, caught the first cab I could find, and then cried all the way to my parents estate. That wasn't the case today. No, today I was a different person, one who now craved life. One who wanted everything to change, experience all the adventure and danger it had to offer. To be like the people I had read about, tossing pride and expectations aside and just living in the moment. Moving out of Zach's lap, I turned to face him, raising my left leg and gliding my foot over his jean clad legs, I came to rest with my cotton-covered core over the leather of his belt. His smirk came to life, the one I loved so much and truly believed he saved only for me.

"Yes, Mother, the very same client. However, today, I'm not only kissing him in public, but I'm straddling his lap, leaving only a thin layer of clothing between us." My eyes were lost in his, my own smirk, which I did save just for him, was on display for his enjoyment. My fingers traced the edge of his collar, watching this Adam's apple bob with the shifting of his hips. "I'm also enjoying the sight of his ink covered arms and the vibrations of his motorcycle as we fly down the street at dangerous speeds."

I knew my mother said something in anger and distaste back to me, but I was too lost in Zach to care what it was. So lost, I didn't protest as he took my phone and tossed it behind him. I knew there would be a fall out from that phone call, yet being here in this moment, with all of my walls lying in ruin around us, I felt like I was living for the very first time.

The bell announced the opening of the front door, reminding us we really did have to leave the world we had created and go back to being responsible adults. With a final kiss, I rose from his lap. As if the phone call wasn't enough, the tiny girl who had caused so much heartache stood inside the door providing the perfect cap to the day. I looked to Jason who was now headed in her direction.

"What do you want?"

Living with my brother, I've had the opportunity to see him in many different situations. I've watched as he took on a bully who tried to shove him in gym class. Cheered for him as he broke the school running record for most yardage during the homecoming football game. Defied my father in denying his place at his firm. Now, I will witness him confront the woman who toyed with him, broke him down, and then had him believing her lies.

Hannah was a beautiful woman. Her family's money and regular appointments with the country's top plastic surgeons had insured that. Her cold and evil heart was the only original part on her and she perfected it well. Her walk was rehearsed, calculated, and purposeful. She used whatever measures available to her to get where and what she wanted. For the longest time, she wanted my brother. Everything changed when he chose to open this shop, instead of the door to the corner office in our father's firm.

Zach moved from his chair as if he was going to intercede, but I knew Jason needed closure. He needed to show Hannah he had moved on and the hold she once held over him was broken, replaced with the love of a girl who deserved him. One who would make him happy no matter what his occupation. I placed my hand in the center of Zach's chest, instructing him to let it be, sit back and be a spectator this time.

"Is this anyway to address the woman you love?"

Etiquette ruled me to remain silent, "*let the adults have a conversation, Kennedy.*" Living in the moment, however, allowed me to snort, causing Zach to pull me into his chest, a protective cage he created with his arms wrapped around my middle.

Hannah had no inkling of the man who stood before her. A man who rose from disappointment and heartbreak, earning new battle scars and life lessons. The man Hannah had left cold and bleeding died, leaving a new and improved version that now stood proudly in his place. He was loved and respected by those he chose to surround himself with.

"The woman I love isn't in this room, unless you're referring to the love between a brother and sister. Although, everyone knows that isn't what you're referring to." Jason's voice was calm as he turned his attention away from the she-devil standing before him, cleaning his station with pride and determination.

"Jassie, I was wrong."

127

Clearly she was wrong, in more ways than just creating a situation that caused Jason to break things off with her. My brother was never one quick to anger, a quality I wanted to find in the man I gave my heart to. But as the expression goes, everyone has their breaking point and by the look of Jason, she had pushed him to his.

"My name is Jason, not Jase or Jassie or any of the other ridiculous names you degraded me with while we were together." All those years of resentment came bubbling to the surface. Resentment for sitting back and letting her be cruel, for doing what our father asked of him, and dating her only to please our parents. He needed this, a cleansing of sorts. I prayed he and Zach kept something stiff to drink hidden around here somewhere as I suspected he would need it soon.

"Actually, your name is daddy."

The woman had no boundaries, no level she wouldn't stoop to. Our mother would have been proud at her antics. It wouldn't surprise me if she had paid a visit to the queen bitch first and got some pointers.

Jason's movements stopped, and I watched sadly as he eyes closed tightly. The feelings changed as I witnessed the smile that slowly took form on his hidden face. With grace and determination he shifted his body, closing the drawer he had been working from, purging himself of the negativity he had been forced to carry for so long.

"You expect me to believe you're pregnant?" There was no mistaking the amusement in his tone, or the anger in his stance. Even knowing I was in no danger from him, I pushed back into Zach's body, seeking protection that was not warranted.

"The chances of that actually happening are a bigger miracle than Jesus himself walking in here and asking for a piercing. Especially since you haven't let me get my fucking dick near you in over a year." My eyes were wide with shock, my hand covering my mouth to keep me silent. "Only allowing me to pleasure you on occasion, and only when you felt that pussy of yours was, as you proclaimed, perfectly groomed." His anger was evident in not only his tone of voice, but by the redness covering his face. She had hurt him, made him to feel belittled and humiliated when he should have been loved and cherished.

128

"So you can take your snake oil and peddle it somewhere else, cause I'm not buying." Jason tossed the rag he had used to clean his area onto his empty chair. As he was walking away I noticed Savannah stood at the end of the hallway, her arms open wide and her face covered with a warm smile. I swear I saw him run to her, pick her up and disappear into the back alley. Hannah didn't linger in the shop or even acknowledge my presence. However, it didn't escape me the second she left the shop, her cell phone was pressed to her ear. There was no doubt in my mind who she was calling.

* * *

Caroline called me out of the blue one afternoon, feeding me some line about how important it was to spend time together as sisters. Zach was assisting his brother with a Monday night game, so I agreed to have dinner with her. She made reservations at one of the city's most exclusive restaurants. You had to be someone, or know someone, to even get a reservation. The interior was designed around old style dining. Plush benches lined the walls, with small tables situated against them and linen tablecloths created the illusion of elegance, yet the room was comfortable. So much so, I failed to look around taking in the design of it, but more importantly the fellow patrons. It was during my initial perusal, I noticed them. Sitting in a corner booth, their hands clasped tightly together, and looking as if they were the only two people in the room. My breath caught, alerting Caroline something wasn't right.

"Kennedy?" Her questioning, concerned tone did nothing to avert my attention.

"Is that...?" I didn't have to finish my question, we both knew who the couple was.

Seeing my father sitting at a table less than thirty feet from us, holding hands with a woman I recognized as Leeann Charles. I had been introduced to her during a charity event my mother chaired. Leeann didn't really fit the image my mother imagined for her worker bees. She had a brain and, much like myself, would, and could, think for herself. Leeann's first husband, Thurston, died in a plane crash leaving her a substantial amount of money. She continued to support various events, so I had seen her several times. Just never with my father.

My mind started conjuring up different reasons for her to be in this restaurant with my father. Perhaps he was representing her as legal counsel or maybe my mother had sent him to get a donation for whatever event she was currently working on. All that flew out the window when I watched, in shock, as he leaned over the table, kissing her on the lips.

While my mother wasn't the most pleasant person in the world, she didn't deserve to be cheated on. They had been married for over twenty years, I just couldn't understand.

"Kennedy, you cannot be surprised." Caroline reached for her wine glass, peering over the top at my shocked face.

"Forgive me for assuming our parents would stay within the confines of their marriage." Tossing my napkin over my empty plate, I could feel the anger raising my blood pressure.

"Women of our social status understand the needs of men as powerful as ours will never be satisfied by a single woman. It is understood we are to turn our heads when we see something unpleasant."

"Turn a blind eye, you mean? Give him permission to have a girl on the side, so long as the money keeps rolling in."

"Yes, and if something catches your eye that is pleasing to you, all the better." Her coy smile gave me all I needed to understand she had cheated on Richard.

"So let me get this straight, you pretend to have a headache so Richard can go off and shove his dick in one of your friends. Or perhaps you invite all of them over and crawl under the table to suck each other's husbands off. Taking turns as if it is a goddamn carpool." I want her to be as angry as I am, to see for herself how ridiculous she sounds by her admission.

"Don't you judge me, Kennedy. You have no idea what it is like to marry a man because of where he can take you. You can't imagine sleeping beside a man who has no clue how to please you sexually. Look around this room, Kennedy. Half the women here find letting their husbands do as they please a small price to pay for living as we do."

"Then buy a fucking porno and a vibrator. Or better yet, show him how to make you scream his name, not hand him off to your girlfriend so she can babysit him while you diddle the pool boy. You will have to forgive me, my small minded need to have my husband love me, taking joy in fucking me until I lose consciousness."

"Then you had better get comfortable being alone. There isn't a man out there who can be everything you need." Having heard enough of her justifying her actions, I tossed some money on the table, pushed away and left. Outside, I waved down the first cab to come in my direction. It was late, nearly midnight, as I stood on the wooden front porch of the home Zach had purchased. I knew Zach would be asleep, but I didn't care.

I could hear the sounds of the doorbell chiming inside the house. With my fist pounding on the wooden door, I begged him to come and open the door, to rescue me from the nightmare that had unfolded inside the restaurant. I could hear the sounds of his feet descend the stairs, getting closer to the place where I needed him. The light above the door illuminated as the locks on the door clicked open. The opening door gave my body permission to break down. Zach stood in the dark house, shirtless, with only a pair of gray basketball shorts on. His sexiness was lost on me as the tears started to fall, making my body rock with emotion.

"Baby?" Zach pulled me to his chest, slamming the door behind us. He didn't ask me any questions as he picked me up and carried me into his kitchen, the hum of the refrigerator's motor the only noise in the room. He placed me on the counter wrapping me tightly in his arms without a millimeter of space between our bodies. Clasping my arms around his midsection, my hands came in contact with the gun he had tucked in his waistband. He had never hid the fact he owns a gun. Given his former job, it is to be expected

"Are these tears a result of something I did?" His usual commanding voice was raspy, no doubt from his disturbed sleep. I shake my head against his chest as he rubs my back gently. As cliché as it sounds, he allows me to cry myself out. He never moved or tried to get me to talk, held me as my body shook with my sadness. When the last hiccup escaped me, he let go long enough to pull a glass from his cabinet, fill it with an amber liquid and instruct me to sip it.

Zach continued to touch me in a way letting me know he was waiting until I was ready to speak. With the glass half empty, I looked up at him and told him what I had witnessed. Taking the glass from my hands, Zach leaned back against the counter on the opposite side of the room. His right hand scratching at his chin.

"Kennedy, I can see how that would upset you. I can't imagine my father stepping outside of his marriage. Zane either, for that matter." I could tell by the way his words came out, a but was about to be delivered. "Please understand, I'm one hundred percent on your side in this, but—" I took a deep breath and wondered if he knew something I didn't? Maybe he had heard something from his parents about mine and hadn't had an opportunity to tell me.

"Your parents' marriage really isn't your business. Don't get me wrong, I know this hurts like hell, but your father is a grown man. If he wants to have an affair, it's between him and your mother."

As much as I wanted to argue, he was right. The relationship my dad had with my mother wasn't really my business. "You're right, I just don't understand. I mean, my mother is no saint, but no one deserves to be cheated on. Caroline said this was something I would have to do. I would have to turn a blind eye to my husband's infidelities." Zach shifted his position resting both elbows behind him on the countertop.

"I agree with you, Sweetheart. I can assure you I would never be able to do that to you, nor will I ever expect you to act like your sister. But do you know for certain they are having an affair? I mean, there could be a valid reason for his actions." I loved this about Zach. He was rational and able to look at this from a multitude of angles.

"Somehow, I don't think so. The way he touched her was too—"

"Intimate?" He finished for me. I nodded in agreement.

"Well, there is nothing you can do about this tonight. It's late and maybe, just maybe, things will look better in the light of day."

Zach suggested I stay with him. Agreeing, I sent a text message to Jason letting him know I wouldn't be home. There was nothing sexual about lying beside Zach. I didn't even bother asking to borrow clothes as I kicked my shoes off and crawled under the covers. Zach asked me in a whisper if I wanted to be left alone or if he could hold me. Holding out my hand to him, he took my fingers and laced his through mine. It was enough for me to lay beside him, knowing he was available to me if I needed him, but far enough away I could be alone with my thoughts.

As the sun began to illuminate the sky the next morning, I walked downstairs grabbing my phone and sent my father a text informing him I would be at his office first thing this morning.

* * *

When I was a little girl, dad would bring me to his office on the days mom would go have her hair done. I would crawl into his chair, pretending to be just like him. Somehow the more successful my father became, the less like him I wanted to be. John Forrester dealt with personal property law, wills, estate planning and the like. He once told me he loved working for the District Attorney's office after graduating law school. Telling me how he worked with people who depended on him, saw people at their lowest and gave his all to help them.

I pushed open the door and came face to face with the man who gave me guidelines on what kind of man I should allow in my life. However, with recent events, those guidelines needed to be re-evaluated.

Ignoring my deep-set manners, I walked around the room before taking a seat on the couch without waiting for an invitation. Dad's face told me he was surprised to see me and my boldness made him uneasy.

"I didn't expect to see you this early."

Leaning forward in my seat, I felt the need to purge myself of these feelings of hurt and betrayal. I needed to tell him what a jerk I thought he was being.

"I saw you last night," I began. "With Leeann."

Brown eyes that matched mine stared at me from across the desk. There was silver decorating the hair near his ears, and his face, always freshly shaven even on the weekends, suddenly looked older to me. I believed, my entire life, my father had the answer to every question. Now, as we sit staring at each other with the minutes ticking by, there are no answers, no pearls of advice, not even a go ask your mother.

He removed his glasses, tossing them to the center of his desk, his paperwork long forgotten. "Kennedy, do you have any idea what it's like to live with someone who hates you?"

I'd always assumed my parents were on the same team, both having the same agenda and goals in life.

"Being tied to a woman who married you because your name was the same as her obsession? Being compared everyday of your life to a man who has been dead and buried longer than she has been alive? Someone who fashions her world around a woman she never met, even naming her children after this obsession?" It was true; Claudia Forrester possessed an unhealthy obsession with Jackie Kennedy Onassis. When Caroline was born, she had slapped the name on the birth certificate before my father could hold his daughter. When I came along, she told him from the second the pink line appeared, my name, regardless of gender, would be Kennedy.

"Then why do you stay, Dad?" I could have answered him with a simple yes or no, but I honestly didn't want to admit I knew my mother didn't care for me, as a mother should.

"Leeann asks me the same thing, telling me I should put my happiness first. "This was the father I remembered from my childhood, the one who laughs, smiles, and tells the occasional joke.

"She doesn't push me to do anything I don't want to do, to be something I'm not. She also doesn't give a shit about how much money I have or how many properties I own. Just being in her company is enough." His eyes were downcast, his fingers busy with the edge of his desk.

"Again, Dad, why do you stay?"

His eyes flashed to mine, the truth shining brightly. Good or bad, it's there and I want to hear what he has to say, what he has been hiding from us. "Honestly, I didn't want to see the disappointment in your eyes when your mother made our business your business. I guess my carousing did just that, making you see me in a negative light."

I nodded, understanding where he was coming from. I worked my whole life to keep my parents from ever being disappointed in me. "Daddy, I'm not here to judge you. Hell, I know firsthand how hard it can be to live with mom, but no one deserves this." My eyes were pleading with him and praying he didn't shut me down. "If being with Leeann is making you as happy as you claim, then why not just be honest with her and, more importantly, yourself. Be the man I know you can be. Be the man I have compared other men to my entire life."

I watched as his face went from pale and pained to content and resolved. Having a conversation with my father was always easy, always level and calm. My mother on the other hand, not so much.

"Tell me, Kennedy, when did you get so smart?" His joking voice made the moment lighter.

"I've always been smart, I just got some really great advice lately."

Leaning back in his chair his smile returned, the one I have always loved. "Really? I heard your mother talking about a young man you've been seeing. Is he the one giving this good advice?"

I thought about Zach. About kissing him on the sidewalk, straddling him in his chair, falling asleep holding his hand, but more importantly, being able to run to him when I needed a friend without having to separate the friend side from the sexual side.

"He is an amazing man who was a friend when I needed one."

"Just a friend?"

I shake my head, not bothering to hide the smile thoughts of Zach created. "No, he is so much more than a friend."

"So, how serious are we talking? Are you being careful?"

I thought about laughing. My father was attempting to have the talk with me, the one my mother hired a nurse to have with me. "We're getting to know one another better. He's open with his feelings for me, but to answer your question, no we haven't—" I motioned with my hand, avoiding the word.

"Well, that's something, I guess. Do I get to meet this young man?" Knowing my father wasn't on my mother's side anymore, I felt as if I could tell him about Zach. I don't have to worry about him running back and telling her everything I was about to say.

"Daddy, I'm dating Zach Michaels." I waited for him to show some form of emotion, but he never moved. "Dad?"

"I'm sorry, I didn't expect to hear...well this. Wait a second, I just want to enjoy this for a moment, knowing something your mother doesn't, something that would cause her to have a heart attack."

This was the side of my dad I had forgotten existed. Now that it has resurfaced, I wanted to hold on to it, keep it in a secret place I can visit as often as I needed. I missed being able to confide in him and have the relationship I always wanted. For the next hour we talked about Leeann and Zach. He shared how they had been spending time together for nearly two years, yet swore they hadn't had sex.

"Listen, I need a favor from you. I need you to not say anything to your mother or to Leeann if you happen to see either of them."

Not that I saw Leeann that much. However fate has a way of making life interesting, so I knew she would cross paths with me in the not so distant future because of this conversation alone. Although, his request gave me an idea.

"Dad, I'll make you a deal." He leaned forward, ready and waiting. I knew this would intrigue him, especially with his skills of being a lawyer. "I'll keep my mouth shut to mom about Leeann if you'll do something for me."

I waited until I knew his curiosity was greater than his need for my silence, fully intending to get what was best for everyone.

* * *

Getting ready for work was an exercise in patience when you have one tiny bath and an open floor plan. Jason would let me shower first as I had more hair to wash. In turn, I would let him dress in the closed bathroom. Today, we were both running behind, creating something resembling a three-ring circus. I was in the kitchen, making us each a piece of toast when the doorbell rang. Jason came out of the bathroom to see who was there.

As I spread a healthy portion of peanut butter on the browned bread, I glanced up to see Jason enter the room holding what looked to be a large manila envelope, a shocked expression covering his face. I moved cautiously across the tiny room until I was standing directly beside him. I suspected what was inside the envelope, hoping it would be a fresh start for all parties involved. Jason slowly opened it up, pulled out a sheet of paper and started to read out loud.

"Dear Jason, as an attorney, it is my job to counsel those who seek my advice. I've always prided myself on giving fair and accurate information. Recently, I found cause to receive advice from an unlikely source. I send this to you as an olive branch, if you will. You may choose not to accept, for which you will have just cause, or you can accept the apology of a foolish old man who let the unimportant things in life cloud his judgment. Enclosed you will find the bulk of your trust fund; it was promised to you before you could even understand what money really was. It has been yours and I had no right taking it from you. Son, if I can leave you with one pearl of advice, one quality of being a man that is important: always be a man of your word, the rest will follow easily."

Jason was speechless. I knew he would take that money and use it to build the business further. Dad was wrong for keeping it from him, just as he is wrong for stepping out on mom, no matter how wretched she may be. I was proud of my father, the way he showed me he was indeed the man I should judge other men by.

My brother's eyes brimmed with tears as he looked at me. Joy was masked by the lump in my throat, excited over what this meant for my brother. "Kennedy, can you tell Zach I'll be late this morning? I'm going to the bank before dad changes his mind again." He wasn't looking at me as he scurried to put his shoes on, grabbed his jacket and was out the door. He didn't even take time to see if I was listening.

As I resumed getting ready for work, a knock at the door once again pulled me away. "Did you forget your ID?" I called as I twisted the knob open. Standing on the landing, a bouquet of daisies in hand was Ethan. With his hair damp from the rain, and a smile on his face, he pushed past me into the apartment.

"You've been avoiding me, Kennedy."

"Ethan? Why are you here? You need to leave." I kept the door wide open, knowing there was a chance Zach was downstairs and would hear me if I had to scream.

"I've sent you several gifts, but they have all been returned. And here I thought you southern women were full of sweetness, without a mean or rude bone in your body." Setting the flowers on the kitchen counter, crossing his arms over his chest, staring at me.

"Ethan, I told you before I have a boyfriend, one who would not like it if he found you here." Ethan shook his head, with a forced smile on his face, glancing to his feet as he pushed away from the counter. "Your new boyfriend, the guy who owns the tattoo shop down stairs? The one who was kicked out of the military because he couldn't keep his nose clean? You think he works with half naked women and doesn't take a sample every once in awhile. Don't be naive, Kennedy, tattoo dude keeps you around as a back up."

* * *

Zach was pulling equipment out of a machine he told me was used to heat his instruments so hot it killed any germs left behind. His black long sleeve t-shirt with the company logo sprayed across his back fit him tightly, hugging his muscles. I couldn't help myself as I crossed the room, carefully wrapping my arms around his middle. I felt him jerk in surprise, but ended up wrapping his around mine.

"Hey, everything ok?"

"Everything is great." I am trying my best to tap down the doubt Ethan planted in my heart. Zach turned around, wrapping his arms around me, capturing my lips with his.

"You know, that front door is gonna be locked for at least another half hour." His lips moved to my neck and collarbone, causing my eyes to close and my breath to hitch. Zach never pushed when it came to intimacy. "I also received a text message from a certain brother of yours about ten minutes ago, letting me know he wouldn't be in until his first client at eleven."

"Umm, but I have to be at work in fifteen minutes." My voice was laden with nervousness. I prayed he wouldn't pick up on my hesitation.

"I can be quick." He teased.

"I do have a reason for coming here this morning." I kissed him quickly, pulling away so I could get my thoughts together.

"I know and I like it." He pulled me back and continued to kiss me, causing laughter to rise from my chest.

"No, really, I have something to ask you."

"Yes, I'll make sure you finish first." His teeth nibbling at my neck. I pushed him away, giggling as I managed to free up some space between us. Knowing if he would just give me a second, I would cure the issue he had brewing inside his Levis.

"Zach, I'm serious, I need to ask you a couple of things." I tried to sound annoyed, but I loved it when he teased me like this.

"All right, all right," he held his hands up in surrender. "What's so important?"

"Well, I need to ask you about when you got out of the military." Zach gave me a strange look. "Did it involve drugs?" Suddenly my shoes looked interesting and I questioned why I thought this was a good idea. Why I had allowed Ethan to get to me. Zach stepped away, leaning against the edge of the counter.

"It did, but not in the way your face is telling me you're thinking." His voice formed an edge to it, his body stiff. "I spent the last five years of my military career chasing after this smug son-of-a- bitch, Aarash Konar, a modern day heroin dealer. I got sick of capturing him, only for some government loophole let him go back to the caves he hid in. Now tell me who made you question me, cause I know this was never an issue before." In embarrassment, I told him of Ethan's visit, how I knew this wasn't the last I would see of him. He stood statue still for a few minutes, "You said two questions, what's the second?" His voice still held an angry prickle, but I knew better than to tell him to forget it "What would you say to meeting my parents?"

# CHAPTER THIRTEEN

## Zach

MY NINE THIRTY WAS LATE, which was pissing me the fuck off as I had squeezed him into my schedule. At this point, he would be lucky if I didn't toss him out on his ass. When Kennedy came in earlier this morning, I thought for a second I would get a few minutes alone to satisfy some fantasies I had involving her and my chair. She doused any thoughts of us getting naked by telling me about Ethan.

From the first mention of his name, I've had an ear to the ground where he is concerned. She doesn't know I have cleaned up several crushed flowers outside of the shop out back. I have Ethan on surveillance, pacing back and forth mumbling before tossing the flowers to the ground. There is no point in calling the cops, pacing and throwing flowers isn't a crime.

I kick my feet up on the edge of the counter and cross at my ankles as the shop phone rings. Reaching over to grab the handset, I take just a moment to think this had better not be my nine thirty.

"Second Skin?"

"Viper?"

"Hey, Diesel." Some habits die-hard as the name gets my attention quicker than the one my parents put on my birth certificate.

"I tried your cell, but it went to voicemail." Checking my pockets, but coming up empty. I remember getting Jason's text as I made coffee, but I must have left it on the counter.

"It's cool, must be important if you've gone to the trouble of tracking me down."

"Well, I think it is. You recall the files we found with your information on them?" How could I forget? It gave me the bright smile and soft skin of the girl driving me crazy at the moment.

"Yeah, what about it?"

"Well, the bitch who orchestrated it, got herself in deep with a man not to be messed with."

"Who?"

"Andrey Korin, a Russian mobster."

"Can't say as I've ever heard of him." Scanning my memory, I came up empty, which bothered me for some reason. "But you did say Russian, so not much has surfaced in the last few years."

"You would know him as Drew Korin, he took over after his father was killed in an accident. Rumors flew around somehow Aarash was involved."

Like a snap of my finger, the name finally registered. "Wait, wasn't this the family whose mother and daughter died in a car crash?"

"One in the same. Victor Utkin was driving, killed the wife and daughter of Korin, and the wife and daughter of his right hand man, Petrov."

"Any mumbling in the trenches?"

"Not really."

"What do you mean, not really? It's either yes or no." Diesel knew the first thing I would want to know is if there was anyone bragging about pulling some shit.

"Wow, if I didn't know better, I'd say a pretty hand has you by the short hairs."

There was no point in denying it, given the uncertainty of this Ethan fuck; I may need some recon done. "She is gorgeous, and I plan to keep her away from the prying eyes of Aarash."

"Wait, what?"

"Right after you called me about the file you found, I got a letter from a girl here in Atlanta. She had been scammed by this Virginia, posing as this douche bag with a name similar to mine. We traded emails back and forth, and now she owns my fucking ass. She's cooperating with the feds on this case, just waiting for word on a court date."

"Which brings me to the reason for my call." I sit up in my chair, placing my feet on the floor, as if what he is about to share would need me to be more alert.

"There isn't going to be any trial."

"What the fuck?"

"Calm down, Viper. It isn't what you think, no loopholes were involved." Diesel knew my hatred for fast talking lawyers, and slick politicians. I've stared down the barrel of too many guns where the man on the other side laughed as those loopholes set him free.

"Virginia Greyson is dead."

"No shit?"

"Like I said, she got in bed with someone she shouldn't have. One of Korin's men took her out during a prison transfer."

I had to see this for myself and have something to show Kennedy, to put a smile back on her face. Logging into Google, I find an article on a major news page.

*What started off as a security breach within the OPM, Office of Personnel Management, has turned into a Federal nightmare involving the armed forces. In a report released today, the Department of Justice admits a security breach, which occurred previously, is at the center of an Internet scam. MilitaryConnections.com, was an online dating website geared toward matching civilian men and women with active duty military personnel who were looking for a connection. The free service collected information, fed it into a database, and then matched you with the perfect person. Seemed simple enough, no money to participate and no face to face searching required. All moves along while you correspond with the guy, or gal, you've been assigned. Too bad the person isn't real. Two names were created, Harmony Wells and Zackery Michels, each given to the seventy thousand subscribers.*

*Investigators say during the OPM breach, a little known hacker named Virginia Greyson, developed a software program where the information the user gave was given back to them in a series of emails. The victims were convinced the relationships were real and blossoming. In documents filed with the department, an email was sent detailing a mission the active duty was given, detailing he or she would hope they would wait for them to return. Days later another email was sent, depicting an emergency at home, with the soldier unable to help a sick relative. Once the money changed hands, the service member became lost in action. Records show, one million dollars was stolen from victims spanning the globe.*

"Viper, I can hear the keys clicking, you forget my brother is a computer geek. So tell me about this girl, the one who owns your balls."

I can't contain the smile as I think about her. "Her name is Kennedy. She's beautiful and smart as fuck. She works with veterans and others with spinal cord injuries. Her brother co-owns the shop with me."

"I'm happy for you man, a good girl will do wonders for you. Wait until you have little ones running around."

I won't lie, I've thought of what our children would look like, with Kennedy's bright smile and my hair and eyes. "Maybe someday. Until then, I need you to keep an ear open for any movement from this Russian fuck or Aarash. I have a bad feeling he's planning something."

\* \* \*

"Tell me you're not fucking with my sister." Jason walked into the shop just as I said goodbye to Diesel, slamming limp and damaged flower stems on the desk. "Cause I swear to God, I will beat your ass."

Anger radiated from Jason's body, his shaking hands evidence of the adrenalin running through his bloodstream. I've dealt with my fair share of pissed off big brothers, angry with what myself, or Zane, had allegedly done.

"Where did you find those?" Keeping my tone level, as I had no real gauge for how quick Jason was with his fists. I kept a handgun in the drawer to my left and one in my station, but didn't feel we had reached that level.

"Outside my front door. There's glass on the step and a bunch of these things down the stairs." Reaching inside the drawer, I pulled out my gun and slid it into the small of my back. "Where are you going?" Jason shouted from behind me, the anger he had moments ago changing to confusion.

"Come on, I'll show you." Retrieving my phone from the counter, I pulled up the app that held my security footage. "I'm not fucking with your sister, but this motherfucker is. Some douche bag named Ethan. He followed her from Colorado, even after she told him she had a boyfriend. When she came down this morning, she asked me if I'd left the military because of drugs. That bastard planted a seed in her mind, making her question who I really am."

"So why is he hanging around, breaking flowers outside of my door?" Jason's hands were on his hips, his defense of Kennedy switching from me to Ethan.

"Either he's a desperate son-of-a-bitch, or he's someone I need to call my team in to help deal with." My phone began to vibrate in my pocket; silently hoping it was Kennedy calling to say she missed me. The name on the screen put my defenses on high, "Aunt Ella?"

"Zach, I need you to get out here. Some man showed up demanding to talk with Kennedy. She asked him to leave, but he refuses. I've called the sheriff, but you know how long it will take them to get here."

Jason locked the front door as I ended the call with my aunt. Trying not to think of what Ethan could do to Kennedy before I got there. There were so many things I still wanted to do with her, places I wanted to share with her, tell her I love her.

"Hey, man, sorry about earlier." Jason apologized as he climbed into my truck. When I saw my girl jump down from the cab of her truck, a yearning filled my chest. The next day, I went to the dealership and grabbed one for myself.

"No need to apologize. It's your job as her brother to protect her, just as I'll do for Savannah." As soon as his door closed, my foot found the floor, the gas pedal smashed in between.

Jason flings out his arms to steady himself, smacking his hand against the glass, and then reaching for the 'oh shit' handle, as I jump into traffic. "Dude, you're gonna get us killed."

Shooting him a slide glance, a wisp of a smile creeps onto my face. "Clearly you've never had to out run an RPG."

I thought Jason's neck would snap from the force of him looking in my direction. Under any other circumstances, I would have found this situation amusing, giving him a reason to shit his pants. While breaking a number of traffic laws and nearly hitting a few cars, growing up in this area, I knew of a few short cuts to avoid traffic. The last two miles separating me from Kennedy housed a field partially owned by my Aunt. I ignored the dirt road since it would have taken us a few more minutes to get to the entrance of the stables. Choosing instead to cut through the field and across the dried up creek bed. I slam my truck in park as the white fence of the stables came into view.

Jumping over the fence, I didn't care if Jason was on my heels or tossing his cookies in the loose gravel of the drive. Raised voices combined with the high-pitched sound of an upset horse guided me to the stall where Aunt Ella housed one of her more difficult horses. The sound of a scream and loud crash of wood made my world stand still as thoughts of an injured Kennedy filled my mind.

# CHAPTER FOURTEEN

*Kennedy*

**B**RUSHING THE COAT OF A HORSE was a mindless task, one I've always enjoyed. My new friend, Hercules, loved to stand and let me brush him for as long as I needed, never giving a care which side I chose first. My favorite gentle giant gave me much more than what he got.

Mr. Hawthorne had phoned just as I got into my truck this morning, letting me know my testimony would not be needed due to Miss Greyson's untimely death. As crazy as it sounds, I felt a hint of sadness for her family. Mr. Hawthorne didn't supply many details surrounding what happened, but it didn't take much to imagine someone being killed while in jail.

A clicking sound from behind interrupts the marinating of my thoughts. Standing with his camera to his eye is Ethan. "You know, I fell in love with you the first time I took a picture of you grooming a horse." Ethan lowers his camera, the worn strap around his neck, its logo lettering faded from years of use. A sly smile paints his lips as a gleam of something evil coats his eyes.

"Love is a four letter word." I comment, pretending to be uninterested. I hope he will act like a professional and not the lunatic I'm afraid he is becoming. Hercules takes a step back, irritated by the interruption as my hand stopped moving along his back. "A word men like you toss around when you want to separate girls like me from our panties."

Hercules begins to whinny from the stranger invading our space. Horses are known to have sensitivity when it comes to fear, and I am trying to keep my nervousness to a minimum.

"Had you given us a chance, you would know I am a man who gives my all to the woman I confess my feelings to."

Looking over my shoulder, I grasped Hercules's reins tightly in my fist, steadying my reserve, worried about what he was going to do. "Ethan, we've had this conversation, a few times. I don't have feelings for you."

His head shakes from side to side as he pushes on the bottom half of the door; the latch catches, keeping him out, as he mutters an oath of his frustration. "You didn't give us a chance, Kennedy." Reaching inside the stall, he pulls up on the latch until it gives and walks into the stall as if he owns the place, giving little concern for his safety or mine.

Hercules eyes grow large, his feet stomping hard against the floor of the stall. Ethan's eagerness to get inside the room causes the door to slam against the side of the stall. Ethan's momentum causes him to tumble in, tripping over his feet; increasing his aggravation and extracting more swear words.

I hear Ella call my name down the hall. If I don't answer, she will be here in less than fifteen seconds and I'm counting every single one of them. "Ethan, you can't be in here, it isn't safe." I warn him. Hercules is now raising his front legs in his own form of alarm. Pulling at his reins, I try to calm him down.

"I suggest you listen to Kennedy, I've already called the sheriff and my nephew." I wish her voice brought with it a level of comfort, but Hercules is now completely agitated.

"Whoa, boy." My soothing is useless, as he has already made up his mind about the stranger bothering him. In a quick motion, Hercules pulls his front legs into the air, his eyes wide with fright as he comes down a few inches from where Ethan has stumbled. "Get out of here!" I shout,

147

anger and worry filling my chest. I'm no match for the strength of this horse, but I refuse to let him hurt himself. Hercules once again rears up, this time kicking at Ethan, knocking the camera from its strap. A cracking noise sounds, followed by a cry of pain from Ethan.

"Kennedy, get out of there." Ella orders, but I ignore her, trying again to calm the horse.

"Hey, boy, it's okay. Ethan is leaving." I look over my shoulder in what I hope is an authoritative glare. "Get out of here! The next time he will aim for your head and, trust me, he won't care if he kills you." I can see a cloud of dust coming down the road; it's either Zach or the sheriff. I'm hoping it's Zach as the sheriff is more figurative than enforcive. "Go on, that's the sheriff pulling up now."

Hercules rears up once again, his hooves spinning wildly in a circle and I know he is going to do some major damage when he comes down. Ethan watches as the motion of the hooves change, deciding I'm serious about his intentions and jumps over the side of the door, running off into the pasture.

"Kennedy?" I hear Zach call my name, but I'm too concerned with a still angry horse. He knows Ethan is gone, but his adrenaline is still pumping and he wants to fight.

"It's okay, big guy." With the brush still in my hand, I try and see of he will calm down for another massage. The sound of heavy boots running down the wood floor of the hall tells me there is more than just Zach coming toward us.

"Babe, you okay?"

Hercules is breathing heavy and his muscles are tense, but he doesn't seem to want to rear up anymore. Brushing his back, I lower my voice as I talk to him, reassuring him he is safe and no one is going to hurt him.

"I'm good, Zach. Just give us a few minutes." I don't dare look away from Hercules, not until I can assure him I'm okay. "He's gone, no need to worry, big guy." I can feel Zach's eyes on my back, feel the apprehension from what he has witnessed.

"Kennedy," Zach's voice cautions, but I can't turn around to look at him. "I don't like you so close to a pissed off horse."

His concern is refreshing, something I've not experienced in a long time. Ella has rejoined the party, telling Zach how Ethan showed up and most likely broke something when Hercules kicked at him.

I hear the latch engage as Zach enters the stall, Hercules is still jumpy, but not as much as when Ethan was in here. "Hey, boy. Thanks for helping my girl." Zach places his left hand on my shoulder, the warmth spreading across my shoulders and wrapping around my heart, while the right brushes the side of Hercules, assuring him he means no harm. "Remind me to get you a girl of your own, as a thank you for protecting mine." Hearing Zach take possession of me, knowing he has such deep-rooted feelings for me, does something wild and primal inside of my soul.

"You okay?"

"Me or Hercules?" I tease, trying to rid the room of the tension.

"Hercules of course, why would I be worried about you?" For a tenth of a second, I consider he isn't teasing, using humor as his own form of releasing the tension. Shifting my face over my shoulder, his worried eyes finding mine, cancels out every ounce doubt I created. His thumb caresses my cheek, soulful eyes searching mine. Hercules has become bored with us, as he knows the danger has passed, the oats in his pail gaining his attention once again.

"In all seriousness, are you okay?" His concern is real, his feelings for me valid and I want to take away the worry discoloring the handsome face he is blessed with.

"I swear," placing my hand to his face. "I'm fine, Ethan left before Hercules could do any damage."

Pulling me closer, his hands on my shoulders. "You scared the shit out of me. Not many people can lay claim to scaring me, but when aunt Ella called me, all I could think about was getting to you, making sure you were safe." His lips descended on mine before I can assure him I really am fine. We both need this. Personally, I crave this, the closeness, the intimacy of his touch. "Don't do that again, scared isn't something I want to feel for you ever again."

Tires on gravel remind me of the real world around us, "That's the sheriff." I sigh against his chest, the feel of his lips against my forehead provide more comfort than the arrival of the police. "I'll be right here beside you as you tell him what happened."

Nodding my head against his chest, knowing the character of Sheriff Barnes and the way he handles most things around this county. He wears the uniform because it is what his family has done for generations. Each one exceeding the worthlessness of the one prior. "Not like it will help much."

Zach holds my hand in his as Ella shows the deputy to where we are. Wesley Proctor and his five foot nothing stature, walk into the stall. Poised with his hands on the edge of his gun belt, his cowboy hat on his head and his mustache moving to the rhythm of his gum chewing. "Evening, y'all." Flows from his lips, hidden behind the mammoth cluster of facial hair he calls a mustache. "Heard you had some trouble."

Ella suggests we go to her office where we can all have a seat, so I tuck myself under Zach's arm as we walk as a unit down the hall. Twenty minutes, three pages of Deputy Proctor's notebook and several repeats of the same story later, Zach is on his feet as Wesley tells me not much can be done. "Explain to me, how you can stand there and tell us there is little your department can do about this?" I've seen Zach lose his cool on a customer, heard a few stories of how he handled things in the Marines. But to see him tower over Wesley, rage and disbelief in his voice, makes me jump with intimidation.

"Sir, as I explained to you and Ms. Kennedy, the man who you accuse of coming into the barn didn't harm anyone, didn't hit her or threaten her. The premises is considered public, so he wasn't trespassing."

Zach stand with his hands on his hips looks to Ella and then back at me. "So what your sayin' is he can come in here, walk into a stall where he doesn't belong, nearly injuring a horse and there is nothing you and your office can do about it?"

"No, Sir. I can't even open a case number on this."

The deputy begins to shove his notebook into his back pocket, reaching for the handset attached to his collar board. "So if I tell you her father is John Forrester and she is dating the son of Dr. Jonathan Michaels, your answer will remain the same." I hated name-dropping, something my mother and sister had mastered. I knew Zach felt the same way, so for him to stand before me, utter those words and not choke spoke volumes.

But not as loud as the way Deputy Proctor handed him his card, complete with a case number and his personal cell number. "Make sure you have your daddy file the paperwork, let him know I'd be honored to serve the order myself."

* * *

Three days ago I called my mother, confirming she didn't have any plans for this afternoon. Her response would be considered brash, but given the source, she was pleased. Dad and I had agreed not to tell her about the incident at the stables. Ethan had been served with the paperwork the next morning at a hotel near my work. Sheriff Barnes called my father personally; apologized for any misunderstanding his deputy may have caused, came by his office and took the papers to serve Ethan himself.

"I have someone I would like you to meet." It was the only detail I would give her. She badgered me for nearly half an hour as to the identity of the person, but I stood firm. I wanted to set the stage for what I had in mind. Zach offered to drive in one of his family's more expensive modes of transportation, but I declined, opting for something a lot more risqué, more suited to the image I wanted my mother to witness.

"Kennedy, are you sure you don't want me to dress up? It's your family after all. I have a closet full of clothes, with names that would impress your mother and her friends."

Again, he was so wonderful. He cared enough to put himself into a situation, which would have made any gladiator turn and run. He was doing this for me, and my happiness. "Zach, I have never once seen you wear anything other than t-shirts and jeans, well, except for the occasional workout shorts. As much as I appreciate your willingness to dress to impress, I want her to meet *my* Zach."

I remember the day we moved into the estate where my mother lives. Once my father's practice took off, the success brought with it a few benefits. I never understood why he kept the downtown apartment we moved from after he built this for her. He would spend several nights back at the apartment, giving the excuse his meeting ran late and he didn't want to disturb us. Thinking back, it was his solitude. He placed my mother in a home where she could be queen to impress her transparent friends so they would like her, tolerate her would be more accurate.

Like a fortress, the heavily decorative iron gates came into view long before the house did. Mother insisted on the illusion, she wanted her visitors to anticipate their first glimpse of her castle. For me, it was more like a prison than a fairytale story.

Zach shut off the engine, allowing me to press the security call button without needing to shout. You could hear the humming of the camera as it focused in on the image of us waiting to pass through the gates. There was no mystery as to who was adjusting it for a better look. In a measure that would cause a huff to escape her lips, I removed the helmet Zach had secured before we left his house, smiling like a twelve-year-old fan girl at a meet and greet. With a thud, the gates slowly began to open, but the moaning of the metal was soon drowned out by the roar of Zach's engine.

How many hundreds of times have I traveled this very road, journeying to a place I once considered home? Now it was simply a visit, wrapped around the man who is now my solitude, just as the apartment is for my father.

As Zach rounded the final curve, a break in the trees revealed the stone facade of the house and with a pair of shadows stood under the awning. Mother never greeted any guests from the front entry, always wanting to make a grand entrance, complete with music if it wouldn't have been considered in poor taste. There she stood, in her white linen suit shipped from London or Paris, my sister Caroline beside her in nearly matching attire. Zach pulled to a stop shutting off the engine once again, but stayed seated atop the monster he called a bike.

Standing with pride and assurance, I tapped his shoulder letting him know I would be dismounting this beast. His arm extended in assistance to help me climb off. Once my boot-clad feet touched the cobblestone drive, a quick snap of the chinstrap and my brown hair was released in a title wave of curls. I placed the helmet on the seat pad, unzipping the leather jacket Zach had given me after dinner last night. He had me try it on, commenting on how sexy he found me, and increasing the need for the self-love session I participated in.

Her face reminded me of the time I forgot to put sugar in the lemonade I'd made for my dad. His poor face had contorted so badly when he took a large sip from the glass I gave him. "Kennedy, what is the meaning of this?" She pointed first at the motorcycle, and then at the handsome man who commanded it, while she spoke.

I turned in the direction of said man smiling as he had already taken off his own helmet, his hands smoothing over his hair that had grown in nicely since his discharge from the military. "I told you over the phone I wanted you to meet someone." My voice too jubilant, she was making this too easy, allowing me to enjoy this far too much.

"Honey, come meet my Mommy." Claudia Dwyer Forrester had many titles, but mommy was not one she allowed. It was mother or ma'am, but never mommy. Her disdain for the word made me want to say it over and over.

"That's far enough, Kennedy." Her arms now crossed under her surgically enhanced chest. She offered to have mine done when I turned sixteen, but thankfully the surgeon deferred until I became of legal age.

I ignored her instruction, adding fuel to the fire, as I took Zach's hand in mine climbing the stone steps toward the dais she had created. "Young man." I inwardly snickered at the words she chose. "You need to take that...that...death machine and leave the premises." Snapping her fingers in my direction, "Kennedy, you will wait for me in your room." Once upon a time I would have lowered my head, shot her a quick, "yes ma'am", and followed her orders. Those days were over. Standing on the same steps where I took those orders, swallowing everything down to avoid her wrath, was a new woman. One who was in charge of her own destiny and in love with a man who treated her like she was the most valuable thing he owned.

"Are you asking him to leave?" I expected this, prayed she wouldn't disappoint me with her reaction.

"Yes, security will be called if he isn't back on that bike in ten seconds. Kennedy, really what has happened to you? You're a mess! You're...you're wearing jeans and leather!"

153

Her face is contorted in disgust despite the gallons of Botox she has injected; her nose was practically sticking straight in the air while motioning toward my clothing.

"You're certain he needs to leave? You don't want to offer him a cup of tea? Or a place at the dinner table?" She ignores my question, turns to Caroline and tells her to call security. With all of the crime that occurred in the area, security was more of a selling point than actual protection. The sight of the custom golf cart, complete with flashing blue lights, which whirled along with the electric motor and rain guard, made my smile brighten just a little.

Mr. Preston is on duty today, a retired police chief from a small town not too far from here. His wife works as a cook in the home of the Spencer's, a bigger gossip than my mother. What was about to happen here today would be all over the community before we made it to the gate. Officer Preston pulled the cart so it blocked Zach from immediately leaving. Ridiculous if you ask me, he could just back up and be gone in a flash.

"Mrs. Forrester, what seems to be the problem?" He questioned as he adjusted his ball cap. His pepper spray and radio were housed in the black utility belt that sagged around his hips.

"Officer Preston, I need you to remove this hooligan from my property. He is trespassing and unwelcome." This was easier than I thought, words meant to embarrass Zach would ignite the spread of the gossip. Officer Preston turned his attention to a slightly smiling Zach, leaning against the seat of the bike. Looking sexy as hell with his amused expression and lickable lips.

"Sir, can I see some identification?" I didn't expect that, but it was going to make what was about to happen that much sweeter.

"I don't want to know his name. I want him escorted off my property, immediately."

Officer Preston ignores my mother, signaling to Zach he did indeed need to see his identification. "Ma'am, I have to know who we are escorting off the property so we can place him on an alert list. If he returns after I escort him off, he can be arrested." The pleased smirk, which appeared on my mother's face, would be short lived. Preston took

Zach's driver's license, adjusted his eyeglasses and addressed him with respect. "Zachary Michaels, you are hereby asked to remove yourself from—"

I've never seen my mother do anything quickly, with the exception of handing her credit card over to a sales lady. However, the moment the officer spoke Zach's last name she shouted a firm, "Stop!"

All eyes turned in her direction. "Wha...what did you say?" This was my moment. I wouldn't get the opportunity to watch my father ask her for a divorce. To witness him separating her from the life she craved and the reality her reign was about to end, but I could see the beginning of her dethronement.

"Oh...did I forget to mention I was dating a Michaels?" I placed my hand over my mouth and widened my eyes in mock surprise. "Well, it must have completely slipped my mind." I turned to see Zach placing his driver's license back into his pocket; a smile forming, as he knew this was pure enjoyment for me. "Doesn't really matter now though, because you've asked him to leave."

"Wait!" The desperation was vibrating in her voice, a nightmare being created right before her very eyes. "For what, Mommy? You've asked Zach to leave, which is what we're doing. I wouldn't want to get him arrested knowing his mother would be upset. Although, I'm not certain she won't be, once she learns how you asked him to leave when he was invited by your daughter." Not wanting any real response from her, I turned my attention to Officer Preston. "Thank you so much for your quick response, we'll be on our way. Please give your beautiful wife, Carol, a hug from me. I do hope she is doing well."

Turning away, I ignored my mother calling my name, pleading for me to stop and listen. I straddled the bike wrapping my body around Zach. He gave her a two-finger salute and tore out of there as if we had just stolen the bike from her. I reveled in the feeling of freedom. Not only from riding on the back of this monster of a bike, but freedom from the chains my mother had shackled me with, dominating my every move, thought, and controlling every action and reaction. I can finally place that part of my life behind me, like the distance we were traveling, the memories faded with each passing mile.

Squeezing Zach's midsection tighter, I place all my trust in his skills. I enjoyed the rush each twist and turn along the back roads gave me. With a final switch of gears, he pulled the bike over onto a secluded dirt road, adjacent to a small pond. Not a word was said as we held each other, and gazed out over the still water, enjoying the moment. The hard ground caused my butt to become numb and I finally relented, needing to get up and move around. Attempting to free myself from Zach's caged arms was a struggle as he wasn't ready to let go.

"Just a second more," he whispered against my temple. His fingers found my cheek turning my face toward his. "I was proud of you today. I know it took a lot of courage to stand up to your mother." His eyes flicked back and forth between mine, searching for something; reassurance, courage, I didn't know. What I did know, was the man who sat silently and gave me the stage to handle the situation as I chose, was my entire world. In a perfect move that completed a perfect day, his lips touched mine, reverent and respectful.

"You are an amazing woman, Kennedy. You always try and see the positive, even when nothing but negativity is looking back at you." He pauses, but the way he looks at me, tells me everything I need to hear. "I love you. It was easy as breathing to fall for you." His touch tells me this is for real, that it's okay for me to admit what I kept hidden for so long. Too worried he wouldn't return my feelings.

"I love you, too."

As the sun took its final dance against the peaks of the water, I embraced the man who had, not only rescued me from my dreary life, but also gave me hope something much better was on the horizon.

\* \* \*

"Surely you can understand my concern, Claudia."

Emma Michaels had the voice of an angel, even when she was telling someone something they didn't want to hear. Just as I suspected, the ladies in my mother's neighborhood had spread the news of Zach being asked to leave the property.

"I have spoken in great length with my son, and your daughter, for that matter. Everyone's story is exactly the same, except for yours."

156

Zach had driven me over to his parent's house after our confession, Emma was in the developmental stages of getting a group of ladies together for a new campaign she wanted to start. Just like at my mother's home, Emma was waiting on her front steps, only she was smiling and welcoming me with hugs and praises.

"Honestly, Claudia, I had you on my short list as chairperson for the committee. You can certainly understand why I will need to remove your name, as this incident shows me exactly the type of person you are."

Last night, we sat around Emma's kitchen table where I spoke in great detail about why I did what I did. I shared with the both of them how good it felt to speak my mind and not what was expected of me.

"Claudia, he was wearing a five thousand dollar leather jacket! It was not something I bought on the clearance rack at one of your resale shops." It was a jab, and a good one. Mother's biggest charity was her thrift store on the lower east side. She had never stepped a foot inside it, but boasted about how it helped the neighborhood.

"I fail to believe you would not recognize the maker of the jacket since I know for a fact you were in a bidding war for a handbag with Lauren Wilkins last fall." I remember the event fondly. The same company who made Zach's jacket released a line of handbags, only five of which were sold in the US. Mother was determined to have one in her collection. When she learned Lauren was bidding against her, the gloves came off. I don't know the particulars, but Lauren owns the bag in question.

"Furthermore, the death machine you are referring to, is a custom made motorcycle and we won't even speak of the costs. Claudia, we can have this conversation for as long as you wish. I can appreciate your explanation of the events, which occurred; however I cannot be swayed to change my mind as to your place on my team. I refuse to have a member who shows such distaste for a human being, only to flip on a dime when it's discovered who he is or, more importantly, who his family is. Do not think for one moment I have not heard how you abandoned your own son due to his choice in occupation. And ordering your grown daughter to the confines of her room because she showed up on the back of an expensive motorcycle, instead of the back seat of a Rolls-Royce."

157

My eyes bugged out my head and my hand covered my mouth. Emma's voice was slightly elevated and I detected a slight attitude in her tone. It was joyous, yet frightening at the same time.

"My daughter!" Emma shouted into the phone, her hand coming to rest on her chest. "If you would have kept the lines of communication open with your children, not shutting them out because they've chosen to avoid the mold you crafted for them, you would know that my daughter is practically living with your son—the tattoo artist. And while we are on the subject, you might want to remind your oldest daughter to use an alias when checking into an Atlanta hotel with a man other than her husband."

After Emma's declaration, the room fell silent and I could tell by the look on her face the conversation was at a standstill. I could mentally see my mother, standing in her ten thousand dollar shoes, gasping for air. This was so much better than anything I could have planned myself. Jason would only be upset he didn't get to watch our mother fall apart with his own eyes.

"You need to take a minute and do some serious soul searching, Claudia. Get a handle on the things in your life before it's too late, if it's not already."

\* \* \*

The hearing to decide if my petition for a restraining order would be granted was this afternoon. Dad and Zach showed up as a unified front, dressed in tailored suits with shaved faces. We climbed into my father's town car, his normal driver holding the door open wide for us. Zach wrapped his arm around me, tucking me into the protection of his body. As we made our way into the city, the car swayed with the irregularities in the road as we approached the Court House. Dad assured me I had nothing to worry about, and the way Zach held me confirmed his words to be true. Today must have been a busy day for hearings; the hallway outside the courtroom was filled with men in orange waiting to have their time before the judge. I was about to tell Zach we could go sit down, when a deep voice to my left spoke my name.

"Kennedy?" Jerking my attention in the direction of the voice, I came face to face with Ethan. Dressed in jeans, a button up shirt and boots,

158

with his left arm in a sling, and a bandage over his right eye. I would have thought the horse defending me would have been a deterrent; apparently this was not the case.

"Ethan." Fear tickled at the edge of my resolve, causing me to pull at Zach's arm involuntarily.

"I've told you we're meant to be together, why you fight it I cannot understand. If I were you, I would find something else to do besides testify at this trial." The threat coming from his menacing voice hung in the air. I was frozen, until I heard the response from behind me, a response that was equally as menacing.

Zach's fingers dug into my shoulder, pushing me toward my father. "You're really gonna do that here? Threaten her like that?"

Ethan never responded with words. With a sneer growing on his face, he looked to Zach, and then to my father before walking into the courtroom. Zach pulled out his phone as the door closed behind Ethan.

"He can't hurt you, Darlin'." My father assured me as he kissed my temple.

The door opened again and a man in uniform stepped out. "Forrester?" he called in a raised voice, the sound echoing in the massive hall.

"That's us, Darlin'. Remember what I said, he can't hurt you."

Zach is still on his phone when I turn around to look for him, his eyes full of anger and determination as they lock with mine. I watch as he tells whomever he is talking to he will see them later, ending his call.

I'm not sure what I expected out of the hearing, but in less than seven minutes, after my father stood before the judge presenting the facts, I was granted an order of protection. As the gavel came down on the wooden desk of the judge, Ethan laughed, shook his head and muttered something under his breath as he left the room. Having this order of protection gave me permission to let out the breath I had been holding since he walked into the stables.

* * *

Since the beginning, Zach and I have spent every possible hour together. He usually tried to bribe me to spend the night with him, kissing

159

my neck or using his wandering hands. Tonight as I washed the final plate and he dried, placing it back in the cabinet, I waited for the groping to begin. When he grabbed his car keys and explained he had an early appointment in the morning, I nodded, trying to cover my disappointment. The ride back to my apartment was quiet and I wasn't certain if it was due to my repeated decline of his advances or something, *someone*, else.

I tried not to read anything into his mood, after all we are all entitled to be 'off' every once in awhile, but as I stared at the shadows on the ceiling, my mind refused to shut off. Finally, in exasperation, I tossed the covers back and grabbed my own set of keys.

It was well after one in the morning, so the streets between Zach's house and mine were empty. I tried to plan what I would do. Would I just crawl in bed with him and try to make up for all the refusals I have dished out over the past several months? He had given me a key months ago, encouraging me to come and go as I pleased.

Pulling around the house, I locked my car and slid my key into the lock of his back patio door. Oddly, his alarm wasn't engaged; perhaps he was too tired and simply forgot. Stepping into the kitchen, I notice movement to my right. Shifting my eyes, I expected to find Zach standing with a bottle of water or a late night snack. Instead, I found a dark haired, wide-eyed girl, dressed in a t-shirt and nothing else.

"Hello?"

"I'm sorry, who are you?"

"Oh, um. Zach is—"

"No," I interrupt, my hand extended in her direction. "No need to explain." Turning as quick as I possibly could, I ignored whatever the girl is calling after me. Climbing into my truck, the engine roars to life as I turn the ignition, slam it into gear, and pull out of the driveway.

When did I become so desperate for love and affection that I tossed away my sense of self-preservation? How blind had I become to let a man pull the wool over my eyes? Zach came in like a superhero, dressed in camouflage and a bright smile, swearing to me he was, "just trying to do the right thing." The irony of the situation, I'd assumed because Zach had a good story to tell and didn't ask for money, he was one of the good guys.

I watched the sun filter through the clouds as I waited to see Zach pull up to the shop for his early morning appointment, but it never happened. Jason came strutting up the sidewalk with a smile glossing his face, looking happy and content. I wouldn't rob him of that just because I had the ability to attract the worst people in the world. Taking my keys in hand once again, I powered off my phone and made the six-mile journey to my father's house.

I have always loved the condo my father kept downtown. It's quaint and has comfortable furnishings, not to mention, my mother absolutely hated how simple it was. I was taking a huge chance my father was home this morning or if he would be alone. To my knowledge, my father had still not presented my mother with divorce papers, or stopped seeing Leeann. My hand reached up, grasped the ring that ran through the nose of the metal horse, and tapped it against the door three times. I was about to turn around and leave when the door opened, revealing my father in his suit and tie, a steaming cup of coffee in his hand.

"Sweetheart?" My father's voice laced with concern, giving me the needed courage to throw on the fake smile I wanted to hide behind. If only for today, I will  pretend my life was anything but what the evidence was telling me.

"Dad, I apologize for showing up unannounced."

He held out his hand inviting mine to join his. "This is your home, too. You never need a reason to come over."

I remember when I was six, sitting at the bar in this kitchen, swinging my socked feet back and forth as I watched my mother cook eggs. Once dad started making money, those duties fell to the staff she insisted on hiring. Now, I sit in the same chair, albeit a little more worn than before, drinking the coffee my father proudly made for me.

"I know you're a very busy man and have more clients to see than hours in the day, but—"

Taking my shoulders in his hands and looking directly in my eyes, he responded with some of the sweetest words any man has ever uttered to me. "My day can wait. I would be honored to spend time with my little girl."

After a quick call to his secretary to clear his schedule, we settled onto the sofa beneath the bay window in his study. I loved this room, with its abundant light and soft colors. We laughed and spoke of events going on in the city. Eventually, we decided to attend a street festival happening around the corner. Never once did he question me about where Zach was or what he would think. It was just my dad and myself, enjoying the different merchants and the arts and crafts they sold. As we visited the last booth, the rich smell of cooking food caught our attention. Dad said there was a little diner just up the block, so we began to make our way in that direction.

The diner was more of a sports bar, complete with pool tables and a plethora of television screens covering the walls. I found an empty booth and slid into the seat. The men sitting at the bar were laughing as they told tales of women and war, each trying desperately to out tell the guy next to him. I enjoyed people like this, they were real and genuine. The man behind the bar took our request for draft beers and delivered them with a smile. Dad ordered the largest hamburger they had on the menu and I followed with chicken wings.

"To more days with my beautiful girl." My father toasted, holding his glass high. I smiled as I accepted, clinking my glass and then nearly devouring the cold beverage. Dad leaned back, his face telling me the quiet and gentle part of our day was about to end. He wasn't a stupid man; he knew I would have a motive for showing up on his doorstep at the crack of dawn. However, a man yelling, "turn it up" from the back of the bar caused both of us to look at the massive television screen hanging behind the bar.

Breaking news flashed across the screen. A man in a suit with a microphone in hand filled the picture, while his lips moved as he motioned to the events happening behind him. The barman turned and pointed the remote to the screen and the indicator at the bottom showed the level of the volume increased. A hush came over the bar as the newscaster began his tale.

"*Police are reporting a man's naked body was found by hotel staff at approximately eight this morning. The coroner's office reports they have a positively identified the man as Ethan Porter, a Colorado Springs native. Investigators have not released any information on how Mr. Porter died, however foul play is not suspected.*"

My father picked up his phone and started making calls, talking about autopsies and the grand jury. Reaching into my back pocket, I retrieved my own phone and powered it up, the signals of awaiting messages sounded in repeat succession. All appeared to be from Zach, but the last one caught my attention and held it.

**Baby, please call me, we need to talk.**

# CHAPTER FIFTEEN

*Zach*

"HEY, MAN, YOU MADE GOOD TIME." I hollered as I closed my truck door after dropping off Kennedy. I hated the doubt in her eyes, especially since yours caused it truly, but Ethan needed to be dealt with. From what I knew about him, no piece of paper signed by a man in a robe is going to keep him away from her.

Reaper stood in my driveway, leaning against the hood of a massive truck, his arms wrapped around a beautiful, dark haired girl. I expected him to look different; several months out of the military will change a man. Even in the dark of the night, I could see something new in his eyes; something good had come into his world.

"How fucking far away do you think Charleston is, Viper?" His voice was different, or maybe it was the smile on his face, no doubt a result of the girl he still hasn't let go of.

"You kidnap this beautiful creature?" Extending my hand out to Reaper's girl. She is shy, which is evident in the way she ducks her head into Reaper's neck.

"This is Rayne Winters, the woman who single handedly saved me from myself." Reaper pulls her closer, reaching his hand up into the back of her neck as he leans over to place a kiss to the crown of her head.

"Well, Miss Rayne, it's a pleasure to meet you. My name is Zach Michaels and please, forget everything this guy here has told you about me." I teased in an attempt to coax a smile out of her.

"Pleased to meet you," she responds, her eyes on the cement of the driveway as her shaking hand extends in my direction. "Matt told me you saved his life, and I thank you for that." A chill crawled up my spine as the memory of the single incident where I questioned if I was going to make it home rushed to the forefront. Drifting my eyes from Rayne to Reaper, I wondered how much of the story he shared with her.

"No need to thank me, he saved me a few times since then."

We had been three miles on the wrong side of enemy lines when all hell broke loose. As I went to jump across two large boulders, my boot slipped on some loose gravel, causing me to smack the shit out of my knee and sending my gun to the ravine below. With the amount of bullets flying, we were trapped against the side of the hill. Reaper stayed at the top of the boulders while I crawled the forty feet to the bottom. With all of the commotion going on, neither one of us noticed the lone shooter to the left of us. Reaper had his attention focused around the edge of the bolder he was hiding behind, while the man with a gun took his time aiming at Reaper's back.

"He's right Rayne, we've saved each other plenty of times."

I took a single shot with the pistol I kept, ending the man's life before he could take Reaper's. We sat behind the boulder for nearly ten hours, under near constant barrage of bullets, waiting for the enemy to run out of ammunition.

"Let's go inside and talk about this problem you need my help with." Reaper nods toward the house. Agreeing, I move to help my friends get their things inside. Rayne stays close to Reaper and I wonder what her story is. Last time I spoke with the guys, Reaper had been adamant when it came to relationships. Unlocking the backdoor, and silencing the alarm, I hold the door open so Rayne and Reaper can enter.

"You live in this big ass house alone?" Setting the pink duffel bag on the kitchen island, Reaper turns around to face me. Rayne takes a long look around my kitchen, her fingers drifting to the hard surface of my granite countertop.

"Not by choice. I have a girlfriend, Kennedy, I'd like her to live with me, but she...it's complicated."

"The good ones usually are." Reaper pulls Rayne into his embrace, placing a kiss to her lips. She raises her hand to caress his clean shaved face, something I'm shocked by. I was assuming he would have continued to hide behind the mask of his beard.

"Which is why we're here." I begin, knowing what I'm about to ask could blow up in our face, and quite frankly land us in jail. "Earlier today, I went to court with Kennedy and her father in hopes of an order of protection being granted. Ethan, has been stalking her, coming by her work and generally harassing her. Today, he had the audacity to threaten her."

"Is this an ex-boyfriend or husband?"

"Neither, according to Kennedy. They had one date and she gave him the cold shoulder. She moved from Colorado Springs to Atlanta and the fucker followed her."

"Has he touched her?" Reaper leans against the counter, his grip on Rayne a little tighter, leaving no doubt in my mind he's battled something similar with her.

"No, but I'm not willing to let this shit go any further. You and I both know a piece of paper isn't going to keep him away from her. Hell, she told him about me and that did nothing to deter him."

"All right, but where is she?"

Taking in a deep breath, I know this has all the ingredients for being a disaster. "At home, most likely in bed, or contemplating driving by the house to see if I'm really at home."

"In other words, she doesn't know about this little plan of yours."

"No."

"And if she comes by and you're not home, she's gonna think the worst."

Taking a deep breath, I brace myself against the counter, "Then at least she'll be safe."

* * *

I'd given Rayne a tour of the house, welcoming her to anything she wanted. I also warned her Kennedy had a key to the house, and not to be surprised by a late night visitor. After securing my truck in the garage, I climbed into Reaper's and we headed off toward Ethan's hotel.

When I was standing with Kennedy in the hallway of the courthouse, the fear was rolling off her in waves. It had taken everything I had not to reach over and strangle him with my bare hands. Ignoring the possibility of her hating me for the rest of her life, or the threat of jail time, I had phoned Diesel for help. He had gotten his brother, Austin, and Reaper on the line. Austin was able to track Ethan down to a hotel not far from my aunt's stables, which is where we were headed.

Reaper pulls into the parking lot of the one story motel. The dilapidated building has seen better days. Its neon sign missing several letters and there is a group of questionable guys standing outside one of the doors.

"A few bucks and I bet we can seal their mouths." Reaper nodded to the guy with a beer in hand, laughing at something one of the others said.

"Austin said he was in number ten, the last one on the end." Scanning the windows, most were as dark as the surrounding buildings, including the room in question. Austin had given us the make and model of the car he drove, but so far there was no sign of the late model Jeep.

"There's supposed to be a window on the back of the building, we can do a scan and see if he is inside." Sliding my night vision goggles into place, and my earpiece with Austin and Diesel already tuned in.

"Diesel we have a visual on the premises, no vehicle in the vicinity."

"Roger that, Viper."

Reaper is out of the truck and around the building before I can get to the edge of the property. Both of us check several times to see if the partiers have noticed our presence. "Window in the back is too small for a fucking Elf to get through."

Redirecting my attention to the front door, I'm assuming with the age of the building, there won't be a computer reader to mess with. Falling to my knee, I use a tool Ghost gave me back when I locked myself out of my room back in Kabul.

Reaper is on my six as I push open the wooden door, careful not to draw attention from the guys out front. Removing my night vision, I pull my flashlight out of my pocket.

"Well, fuck me." Reaper steals the words from my mouth. Covering every inch of wall space, are different pictures of Kennedy. Some are close up, while others show her riding a horse in the mountains. A few show her dining with a woman I know to be Caroline, her sister. "Fucker doesn't seem to care about you does he?"

Reaper has his light centered on the wall to the left, walking closer, I find a photo of Kennedy and myself, from the first time we met face to face. I have my arms around her, but my face is cut out.

"She is beautiful, good job, man."

Chatter in my ear pulls me from the creepy photo. "I need visual, Viper." Flipping the switch on my night vision, I let Austin and Diesel see what is going on in the room.

"Zach, there's a computer to your left, open it and let me have a look." Austin hasn't been trained like the rest of us, something we will have to rectify, if Diesel has his way. On the way over, Reaper had hinted the guys wanted to get together, forming a Mercenary for hire company. Evidently they had already done a couple of jobs together.

"Open the cover and let me see the drives."

I do as he asks, disbelieving he will be able to do much more than order replacement parts. As the lid opens and the screen comes to life, the box in the center tells me we need a password. "Any other ideas?" I ask knowing he sees what I do.

"Type in exactly what I tell you to." I listen attentively as he rattles off ten thousand letter and number combinations, my level of confidence this is going to work decreasing with each keystroke. "And hit enter." Like something out of a movie, the computer screen flashes and changes to a wall of blue folder looking icons. "Thanks, Zach, you can move along now." The mouse on the screen moves on its own, clicking on the first few folders.

"Viper." I respond in a harsh tone.

"Excuse me?" The mouse hovers, but doesn't move.

"We don't use names, only call signs, mine is Viper."

"Hey, Viper," Reaper calls from behind me. "You might want to check the security of your house." Illuminated by the light from his flashlight, is a photo of Kennedy and myself in my kitchen, she is sitting on my island, legs spread and wrapped around me. There are boxes in the background, which makes me think this was the first night I moved in.

"Reaper? Viper? We've got bigger problems than a sideshow peeper." Diesel calls over my earpiece. "Get over here and see what Keys found." I would laugh at the call sign Diesel has just assigned his brother, but the photo on the screen nearly takes my breath away.

"I've run her face through a recognition program I acquired access to." The image is the body of a girl, lying on the floor, arms tied behind her back and throat slashed. "Layla Evans, nineteen, of Coopers Park, Montana. She was reported missing three years ago, on June sixth when she failed to show up for work." Layla's eyes are wide open and, even in death, filled with fear. The mouse moves again and the photo of another girl fills the screen. "Marian Hope, twenty-two, of Deer Park, Wyoming. Reported missing six months later, also by her employer." This girl resembled the first, dark hair and expressive eyes. "There are at least thirty pictures of girls in the same position, all dead and all with one thing in common." Sweat began to bead on the nape of my neck, somehow knowing what he was about to say next. "They each worked with horses."

During SEAL training, one of our instructors told us to always follow our gut. When I learned Ethan had moved across the country to see Kennedy, I knew this wasn't your standard crush. Ethan Porter was a serial killer and my Kennedy was slated to be his next victim.

"Your call, Viper. We can call the cops and have this guy arrested, or..."

"Oh, we'll call the cops, but not until there's a conversation between Ethan and my fucking fist."

169

"You could serve him a Havoc cocktail, but it's your girl, so it's your call."

I'd already considered the many ways I could put an end to this motherfucker. Using a chemical cocktail formulated by Havoc was an option, but would minimize any gratification I would feel.

Headlights flashed the room, making a path across my face and blinding me momentarily. A late model Jeep, the same Ethan is known to drive, pulled into the lot. "Get ready, Reaper. Time to make him feel their pain."

Sliding into the corner behind the door, I make ready to knock him to the ground the second he enters. With my back against the wall and my fist clenched and ready, I listen as a key slides into the lock. Waiting for him to turn the knob felt like an eternity, just like it had when I'd gone over to John Forrester's condo to explain what I knew.

I expected him to demand all the facts behind what I had planned. However, as he stood with his arms crossed, the soothing sounds of music rising from hidden speakers, I saw the face of a man who loved Kennedy as much as I did.

*"Sir, I know I'll be taking a huge risk in her finding out what I'm about to do, but I have to make this monster go away. I know if he's left on the streets, he'll be another number in the game. Kennedy will be looking over her shoulder nearly every second of every day and questioning every man who passes her on the street. I can't let that happen to her, she deserves more."*

John had looked at the floor; his hands resting on his dress pant covered hips. *"I don't want to know your plans, ignorance is bliss. I won't lie to my daughter, not anymore, but you're right, she deserves the best of things our money can't buy."* He moved to the business side of his desk and picked up his reading glasses. *"You make certain the son of a bitch doesn't see the light of another day."*

Shaking hands with John that night had done more than signal the meeting of the minds. It was the beginning of a new relationship, a turn in the road. My plan was set. I was risking everything, including the future I had planned with Kennedy. Her safety and reassurance were more important than anything to me. Even if she found doubt in me, time would restore her trust.

The door creaked open, groaning in protest of the movement, much like an aging man getting out of a chair. Reaper didn't give him time to reach the switch on the wall as he grabbed his arm and yanked him into the room, tossing him to the dirty floor.

"What the fuck?" Ethan tried to stand; long enough for me kick his knee, sending him crying to the floor once again.

"What do you want?" He cried as he held his leg. I ignored his question and the pain in his voice as I drew back and kicked him three more times. Reaching down, I grabbed him by the back of the neck, tossing him onto the bed not two feet away.

"You've got the wrong guy! I ain't done nothing to anyone."

Stepping over to the desk where his computer sat, I switched the lamp on, causing Ethan to squint from the light filling the dark room. "No motherfucker, we've got the right one." I pointed to the girls on his screen. The number of pictures multiplied, women all tied up and dead at the hands of this bastard.

Ethan tries to get out of the bed, scrambling to reach the computer and its contents. "You've got no right to look at them." Reaper shoves him back on the bed, his head hitting the headboard. "They're mine, you can't have them!"

Walking over in three heavy steps, I pull Ethan up by the hair at the top of his head. "And her?" I shake him, pointing to the wall covered in photos of Kennedy. "She isn't fucking yours, she's my girl." Tossing him back against the headboard, hoping to fuck I crack his skull.

Ethan is either on something or stupid as fuck, as he tries to scramble to his feet. "Sit down, motherfucker." Reaper plants his boot in his chest, preventing him from rising again.

Ethan's eyes are wide and he gasps for air, like a fish out of water. "You fucked with the wrong girl, my friend."

Ethan slumps back, a trickle of blood rolling down from his nose. This sliver of blood is only the beginning of what he is about to shed. "Tell me, Ethan. Did you move across the country after all of these girls or is Kennedy special?" He leans over, spitting a wad of red to the dingy carpet, ignoring my question, just as I had his. "Or did she not succumb to your charms, preferring a southern gentleman to a seasoned killer?"

171

"You can talk all you want, hit me as many times as you feel man enough, but at the end of the day we both know any decent attorney will get me off with a twenty minute psychological test. You and Scarface here can hold me until the cops arrive, they'll see the pictures and decide I have to be a sick individual. Without a body, there's no way a jury will ever convict me. And maybe I'll go to jail for a little while, show the powers that be I'm a changed man, and they let me out. Guess what I'll do then?" His body quakes with his silent laughter. "I'll find Kennedy, and this time, I won't wait to have a sample of her."

He expects me to hit him, his muscles tightening in anticipation, but I have other ideas. It's time to give him a taste of what those poor girls went through. "Cut his clothes off, Reaper. Time to teach this fucker a lesson."

I walk back to the computer, "He's right about not having any bodies to charge him with those murders." Perusing the many innocent faces of the women he has killed. Ethan Porter may be as American as I am, but it doesn't separate him in my mind from Aarash or any of his men who preyed on the innocence of his own people.

"What was it you said earlier about my lack of training in knowing your call sign?" Austin's voice interrupts my disappointment in giving the families of these ladies the closure they deserve. "With us working together in the future, try and remember there isn't much I *can't* pull from a computer." Maps and grid markers begin popping up on the screen. "Here's the location of every young lady who died at the hands of Ethan Porter."

Reaper has Ethan naked and in the bathtub, water covering three quarters of his body, a washcloth shoved in his mouth to silence his screams. At least thirty girls died at his hand, and he would feel a level of pain for each life he took. During SEAL training, I learned more than how to function as a team, and hold my breath for five minutes. I gained the skills to get information out of someone, especially when they weren't too keen on giving it to me.

"I'm assuming you raped each of those girls? Bastards like you think you can take what you want and not care what happens to your victim." I grabbed a wire hanger dangling on the back of the bathroom door, twisting off the top hook to deliver the first dose of pain. Reaching down into the water, I grabbed his dick in my gloved hand, shoving the metal into the slit of his flaccid cock. "How many of those girls were virgins, saving themselves for their wedding night?" Ethan thrashed about, spilling some of the water onto the floor. I made sure the hook disappeared into his flesh, rupturing his bladder in the process.

"Alice Bennett, eighteen, has a burn mark on her left shoulder. It looks to have been inflicted just prior to her death." Austin's voice holds an eerie calm, considering the line of work Diesel said he did.

Reaper picks up the discarded remnants of the hanger, bends it, and then places it under the flame of his lighter. Pressing Ethan's head against the tub, he jams the red hot metal into one of his nostrils. "How do you like that? Smells real good, huh?"

"Lori Stone disappeared on her twenty first birthday. She had gotten engaged the weekend before—to a Marine." Reaper and I shared a look. We would never know the name of this marine, but it didn't matter, Ethan would feel his grief. I pulled the two bottles from the pack on my back, being careful to mix them in the proper order. "Open his mouth and shove this in there." Handing the tube to Reaper.

"Did you follow her home from the bar, lie to her and say you wanted to help her?" Pouring the acid into the funnel, I watched Ethan's eyes as it entered his mouth and began to burn. Giving him the Havoc cocktail would limit the pain he would feel, given what he had inflicted on those girls. "Start reading off each of those names, Keys."

As he read each name, Reaper and I repeated them, and then slashed his skin with our knifes. When the last name was set free, the water in the tub is clouded red with his blood, our mission complete.

Reaper cleaned up all the evidence of our visit, turning up the volume of the television so security would be called to investigate. By the looks of the room, it had been a while since the cleaning crew had even stepped foot inside. I almost felt bad for the poor bastard who found him several hours from now, his death a guarantee. Reaper's final check was to Porter's carotid. "Welcome to Hell, Motherfucker."

* * *

I knew Kennedy had been to my house the second I walked in the darkened door. I could smell the faint scent of her perfume still lingering inside.

The sun would be up any minute and I hoped she was still fast asleep. Deep down, I knew she was as awake as I was, her imagination of why I hadn't been home running like wild fire. Wondering about the strange girl she had found in my kitchen, according to Rayne. I knew I stood a good chance of losing her. There was a real possibility she wouldn't accept my explanation, the only one I would give her.

The exhaustion of my night reared its ugly head, but I knew sleep would not be found until I was able to speak with Kennedy. Just as I was about to head over to her apartment, my cell phone chimed with a text message. I sent a silent prayer before looking at the screen; my heart sank as I read the message sent from John.

**Good luck, she just showed up. Taking my girl out for the day.**

# CHAPTER SIXTEEN

*Kennedy*

IN THE PAST YEAR A BOY HAS STALKED ME, while another didn't exist. Now, the one I gave my heart to, played with it until it broke. I wasn't naive enough to think the news report and my father's sudden urgency to return to his office were coincidental.

My father was a man of means. He was quite capable of hiring a man of certain characteristics to tidy up the situation with Ethan. The media can spin any explanation they want on how he died, but it doesn't take a genius to know a man on a mission isn't suicidal.

I pulled into the stables where we kept my horse, Chestnut, a racehorse who had outlived her usefulness to her previous owners. She was found by a couple of hunters when her foot got caught in a barbwire fence. They called a family member who happens to be a veterinarian, but Chestnut had been too weak to do any real damage to herself. My mother agreed to let me have her after I let it slip the media had done a story on her, in hopes of finding her a forever home.

I walked over to the stall where Chestnut has made her home since that fateful day. How many times have I come here to share the secrets I couldn't tell anyone else?

A perfect black nose greets me before I can get my hand out to stroke her face. "Well, hello to you too." Running both hands along her healthy features, she nudges around me; looking for the crunchy treat I usually bring her. "Sorry, Chestnut, I didn't have a chance to stop and get you an apple."

Unlatching the door, I keep one hand on her coat as I pass over the threshold. "Things have become complicated and I needed to see you." My voice cracks as the hurt I've been holding back rushes forward, demanding to be heard.

Chestnut allows me to lean against her, letting the tears roll off my face, sobs racking my body as the images of the girl from the night before haunt me. I'd never seen the shirt she had on, but I imagine Zach has a million stuffed in a drawer in his bedroom. I know I'm torturing myself as I ponder where he would have found her. Was she a client or someone from his past? Whatever the case, she had been beautiful.

"Come on, Chestnut. Let's go stretch those legs." The stables employed several handlers to prepare the owner's horse for riding, but I'd had my fill of men with fake smiles and ulterior motives. I've known how to saddle my own horse since I was ten. With the straps secure, I hoisted myself onto the back of Chestnut, kicking her into a walk, with no real destination in mind. Giving Chestnut the freedom to walk where she wanted, I lost myself in the trees and blue sky above, falling into my thoughts.

I had to place at least half the blame on my own shoulders for thinking a man— particularly a man in Zach's position—would hold out until the perfect moment. A man who had spent that much time away needed to relieve the tension built up by his months of celibacy. The remaining half of the blame needed to be placed on his broad shoulders. He could have, at any moment, ended things with me and went searching for someone to bed.

I refuse to accept any blame in the Ethan situation. I had done nothing to give him any hope I returned his feelings. Clearly, he had something twisted deep in his psyche.

With my head somewhat clear, I focused my eyes on my surroundings. The edges of Ella's fence stood out in the distance. Chestnut had walked the miles, which separated the two businesses. With her age in mind, I needed to let her rest and get something to eat and drink. I would call the stables in a little while and have them send over a trailer.

Letting Chestnut continue at her leisurely pace, I cringed as she rounded the main office. The parked truck of the one man I didn't want to see, was sitting in the spot I usually filled. Of course he would be here, telling his family how my working here would be a conflict of interest, as he no longer wanted to play the game with me.

Pulling back on the reins, I let Chestnut know her job is done and slide off the saddle, guiding her the rest of the way by hand. The stall beside Hercules is empty. I know I can keep her there long enough to cool her down and get a trailer over here. Swallowing the new set of emotions brewing in my chest, I walked past Ella's office and down the long hall.

"Hercules, this is my girl, Chestnut. You be nice to her, she's had a long day." Settling her into the stall, I remove the saddle and blanket. Hercules is acting like a busy body, staring at us through the bars separating the stalls. "Oh, don't be a creeper, she was my horse long before I met you."

I run my hand down the side of her neck, letting her know this is a safe place and the mammoth beast beside her would do her no harm. "I'm with you, Chestnut, boys make me jumpy too."

"Not every boy." My body flinches and I turn to look at the man I'd spent the day trying to forget, standing not three feet away. "At least *I* didn't used to."

Shaking my head, I let my breath out. Responding to him would mean I want to talk, which I certainly did not. "What are you doing here?" I avoid looking at him, giving my attention to Chestnut instead.

"I know you came by the house. We need to talk."

"Talk about what? How you lied to me about having a meeting and needing to get some rest."

"I didn't lie, Kennedy. I did have something to do."

"Oh, really? Don't you mean somebody? Since you know I came by your house, you also know I saw the half naked girl in your kitchen." Regret fills my mind, I didn't want to have a conversation that escalated like this. The last thing I want is to have someone in my life who is there for the wrong reason.

"Kennedy, I had to meet one of the guys from my SEAL team. We had a mission we had to carry out. The girl—"

"Stop! I don't want to hear anymore. If you think for one second, I believe you were on some secret mission for the military, you're crazy. Even with all the technology we have today, there is no way you traveled across the world and returned in less than twenty-four hours. Unless you want to try and convince me NASA has been hiding a time travel portal in *Area 51*. Or are you just that elite, where you can jump in and disarm the situation in seconds, hopping back in your *Doctor Who* telephone booth and arrive back home in a few hours."

"Kennedy, not all missions take place overseas. What I needed—"

"Stop, I don't want to hear about this secret mission you had to go on. I don't want to hear how the half naked girl appeared in your kitchen." I looked at my watch, sick to my stomach with the direction this conversation has headed. "Don't you have a shop to run?"

"I'm the boss, so it opens when I say."

"Well, I'm not the boss around here and I have things to do. If you will excuse me, I need to get Chestnut home." Stepping around him, I pull my cell from my back pocket, and charge down the hall, not really caring if he followed me or not. I had nearly made it to the front of the building when Ella blocked my path.

"Hey, did I hear my nephew's voice?" Her eyes say it all, as she reaches out for me. "Kennedy, are the two of you arguing?"

"No, we are in complete agreement. He wants to see other women and I won't stand in his way." I move again, sidestepping around her. "I'm sorry, Miss Ella, if you would excuse me." She could find her nephew and get all the juicy details from him.

Walking until I was a good distance from the barn, I chanced a look around, recalling the first time I set foot on this property. It was my dream to work here, to learn from the best of the best. Now, I wanted to rewind time and never send that letter, staying ignorant of the skills Ella has shown me. As I scrolled through my contacts, trying to find the number of the stables, I passed a number I hadn't had to call in ages.

Glancing over my shoulder, I made sure Zach hadn't followed me out. Leaning against the edge of the fence, I pressed the green circle beside her name.

"Hello, Kennedy. How are you?"

Hearing her voice brings the sting of tears to my eyes and I fight the sob bubbling in my chest. "Hey, Sabrina, I'm fine. Missing you, but fine." Glancing up, I notice Zach is standing at the edge of the yard, his eyes in my direction.

"You don't sound fine, my love. Want to tell me what's going on?" I don't. I don't want to admit to anyone I allowed yet another man to pull the wool over my eyes. "Sabrina, you were married to a military man for a number of years. Tell me, how did you handle him going off and not being able to tell you where he was?" Zach walked over to lean against the edge of his truck , even from this distance; I could see the exhaustion in his eyes.

"Honestly, it wasn't always easy. There were a few times he was called to work and I didn't see him for a few days. I'd question if he was out catting around. But when he walked through that door, looking tired and happy to be home, I tossed those thoughts away."

"So you chose to believe him?"

"No, I chose to love him. The rest seemed to fall into place."

I changed the subject to a technique I'd been working on with Ella. I watched as Zach waited for a few minutes, but seemed to surrender to his body's need for rest. As I was finishing up my call with Sabrina, he climbed into his car, not saying a word as he passed me on the road.

# CHAPTER SEVENTEEN

## *Zach*

"ZACH, I'M SO SORRY ABOUT KENNEDY." Rayne and Reaper had agreed to hang around for a few days until I could get Kennedy to listen to me. "It was so late, I never dreamed she would come over and find me in your kitchen."

I tossed my head against the back of the couch, feeling like a dumbass for not being able to figure this shit out. "Rayne, it's not your fault. The second she went upstairs and found my bed empty, she would have been just as pissed off." I reasoned.

"Would an Uncle Ray story cheer you up?"

I turn my head to Reaper, "Not unless it holds the secret to getting Kennedy back."

"Maybe I could talk to her? Let her know I'm with Matt, and not you." While I knew her intentions were good, I needed her to understand why this was such a bad idea.

"Rayne, let me ask you a question? Let's say the roles were reversed and it was Kennedy standing in Reaper's kitchen. The relationship is fairly new and you have just been through a terrible experience with another man. How about we add into the mix, you and Reaper haven't gone much past a heavy groping session. Would you really want to talk with the half naked girl, when she shows up at your front door?"

Rayne lowered her eyes to the rim of her coffee cup, "No, I wouldn't want to speak with her. Rip her eyes out maybe, but no way would I talk with her." It was oddly adorable how gentle and kind Rayne is, considering the gruff, mountain of man Reaper is.

"Wait, you went through all of that last night and today, but you haven't slept with her yet? Hell man, either she is more like a little sister or a good friend, or..."

"I bought the ring two weeks ago." My admission hung heavy in the room.

Rayne rose from her seat by the door, walking with a smile on her face as she sat on Reaper's lap. "You know, Zach, back before I met Matt, I was getting ready to marry a man I didn't love, or really even like. The people around me convinced me there was no one out there who would want to wake up to a woman who looks like me." Her pleading blue eyes, latched onto my soul, pulling me into the deep pools her heart swam in. Rayne, like Kennedy, was a classic beauty. Both were blessed with simple features and soft lines. They didn't need pounds of makeup to make them look natural.

"I worked for a funeral home, getting people who have passed ready for their loved ones to say goodbye to them. I felt safe doing it, avoiding the judgment I found in the eyes of those around me. My brother had asked his long time girlfriend to marry him and she made it clear there was room for only one female in the home she would share with him. So I started looking around for a place to stay, no small task considering the size of the town I lived in. Anyway, one afternoon I was leaving the post office and ran into Matt here."

Sliding her eyes to meet Reaper's, glowing smiles forming as they both relived the memory. "He seemed larger than life. When I looked into his eyes, what I saw looking back at me, made every bad name I had ever been called and every cruel joke seem to disappear. Mrs. Merkel, who ran the post office, tried to tell me he was some shifter blowing through town and to keep my distance. But when I needed his help, he was right there to save me." Rayne turned in my direction, immeasurable joy on her face.

"Matt told me why we needed to come here. I have to tell you, he made it clear if I chose to get in his truck, I was stuck with him forever. What Kennedy needs, is living proof of the kind of love you have for her."

Rayne didn't need to come out and say I had to be honest with Kennedy, but she was right, actions always speak louder than words.

"Zach?"

"Oh, God, that's creepy. You calling me by my first name." I shivered, unable to recall Reaper ever using my name.

"Tough shit. If I keep using your call sign for every day, when I need to use it in a mission, it won't protect you." Fucker had a point. "I spoke with Chase and his brothers today while you were over trying to salvage your relationship. They're offering to bring you in if you're still interested. According to Chase, they have more work than they know what to do with."

If I chose to join this group with my old teammates, it would mean admitting to Kennedy what I did when I was away. Hell, what I did for her last night. I can hire another artist to help Jason, only working there when we didn't have a mission.

"But you should know." His voice is serious, which causes me to sit up straight. "I have to leave in a few days to go help Tombstone."

"What the fuck happened?"

"You know he got shot and had to go to Germany to recover, right?" I nod my head, allowing him to continue. "Once he was well enough to fly back to the States, they tried to get in touch with his wife. When all attempts failed, his parents showed up and helped him home. He opened the front door to an empty house and divorce papers in the middle of the living room floor. His ex-wife had fallen in love with some guy she'd found in an Internet chat room and took off with him. While he wants nothing to do with her, he does want his kids back. I'm going to go help him get them back." As a SEAL, we have been in countless missions like this. Granted the child was being used as a pawn or was a runaway to get Daddy's attention.

"And you're taking Rayne with you?" I had to know what to tell Kennedy. If she would forgive me for what happened, I wanted her beside me.

"Chase's wife is about to have a baby, so Rayne is gonna stay with her and help out."

"What about the rest of the guys, are they willing to join up?" We had four other members of this team, each serving an important purpose. The mission would be damn near impossible without the whole team.

"Havoc is still on active duty, stationed down in Florida until his time is up, but he wants in the second he removes the uniform. Ghost is giving us intel, he's trying to get a job with the Secret Service. Chief is willing to do whatever we need him to while he waits for his girl to get back to the States. Doc is still in Afghanistan, while he waits for his time to be up. He's been working hard on the girl who sent him that package for Christmas, hell of a story there."

I wanted to know more of the stories my guys had going on, but I needed to work on my own relationship first. "Let me see if I can win Kennedy over, smooth this shit out before I give you an answer."

* * *

I tried Kennedy's phone a few more times, each call resulting in a trip to her voicemail. Matt would be leaving the day after tomorrow and I wanted to have an answer for him. As I lay in my bed, the one I'd fantasized about having her in, I tried to come up with a way to get her to listen to me, to see the truth of what happened. As the dawn of a new morning greeted me, I tossed back the covers, determined to get my girl back. Grabbing my cell off the dresser, I scrolled through my contacts until I found his number. "Hello, Mr. Forrester. I'm sorry for the early hour, but I need to speak with you urgently." Kennedy may not want to listen to me, but I knew she damn well would listen to her father.

183

# CHAPTER EIGHTEEN

*Kennedy*

"**K**ENNEDY, YOU HAVE TO CHOOSE." This was the hundredth time my mother had presented this exact same statement to me. In the last few days, I'd become bombarded with my mother's incessant complaints, ever since the not so pleasant conversation she had with my father's attorney.

"He humiliated me, Kennedy. You can't possibly take the side of the man who caused me such public humiliation."

In recent weeks, my father had begun to change; reverting back to the man he was when he first became an attorney. Morals intact, with the drive to be the best he could be and take on the world, making it a better place. His first mission was to set my mother straight and make her see the world by the light he was currently shining.

Dad knew she had a monthly chair meeting at their country club. He chose that particular meeting to send in a deputy, serving her with divorce papers. Reliable sources stated she had tried to hand them back to the man, demanding he admit he made a mistake. A tiny piece of me felt bad when I heard she was left crying and alone in the room she once commanded.

"As I have told you a number of times, I'm not taking anyone's side. This is a matter between you and Daddy." She began to scream at me about how he had taken me away from her, turning me against her. I hoped one day she could come to grips with the truth, though I doubted it would be anytime soon. Especially since Dad had placed the castle he built for her on the market. All of her credit cards had been revoked and she was now living on a stipend set up by the court system. It was a reasonable amount in my opinion, unless you're used to spending money the way she was. Dad assured me she would never be homeless and would have the necessities she required, as long as he was alive.

Dad and I had been spending more time together. His living a few miles from me helped tremendously. He told me after his divorce was final he would be moving in with Leeann. Marriage was not something either of them wanted at the moment, but she made him happy, that much was crystal clear; from the color of his face, to the way he now let a little scruff form on his jaw. He smiled more and he most definitely laughed more. He was the daddy I remembered from my childhood. Leeann didn't try to push a relationship on me, but she gave me an open invitation to come by her home anytime. I told her, and my father, out of respect for my mother I would hold off, at least until the ink dried on the final paperwork. My mother may be an evil woman, with many hidden agendas and venom running through her veins, but she was still the woman who had given birth to me. Without her I wouldn't be here, for that I would show respect.

This morning, my dad called and requested I stop over for dinner. When I arrived, Dad stood in his kitchen, a dishtowel slung over his left shoulder, dressed in a button down shirt and blue jeans—unlike the suit wearing man I grew up with. His hair was a little longer and the smell of his time honored cologne was gone. Another change in my father, he had gone out for the first time ever and chosen cologne for himself. The new smell reminded me of the stuff Zach and Jason wore, which made me miss Zach so much more. I'd avoided him for days, not ready to admit there may be more to his story. Embarrassment and pride kept me from returning his calls.

185

I expected to see empty takeout containers, but when I walked into the kitchen, the room was alive with boiling pots and vegetables waiting to be chopped. Without waiting for an invitation, I took my place, tending to the steaming pot of cooking pasta. Dad had set the stage with the music from long ago. With the Italian menu, Dean Martin sang of love being a kick in the head, it was simple and perfect.

Zach caught my eye across the room, time had not erased the hurt I found last time I saw him. We plated the food and took places around the small kitchen bar. There was no formal dining room table and no dishes so expensive they needed insurance just to make an appearance. Dad was telling Zach about tickets his firm had for an upcoming sports event. He invited him to join him at one of the arenas in the area. Zach thanked him, telling him he would be happy to attend with him.

"Kennedy, it's time to talk about what happened the other night. No more hiding like you did when you were a little girl."

Leaning over, I kiss my dad's cheek. "You're right, I've been acting like a child and it's time we clear the air." Dad took a drink from his beer, a beverage my mother forbade being in her house, stating only commoners drank bottled beer.

"I'd like to go first, if you don't mind?" Zach's deep voice still does strange things to me, turning any rational thought into a puddle of goo.

"I suppose it's only right, since I've shut you out for days."

Zach shot a look at dad and leaned over the island on his forearms, his bottle of beer grasped between his closed hands. "When we went to the courthouse for your restraining order, it didn't sit well with me when Ethan threatened you. With my training, a pot shot like his would have gotten him bent over a table and my fist in his face. But in the society we live in, violence is frowned upon and criminals seem to have more rights than the victims. I couldn't sit back and let another criminal walk out of a hearing with a smile of victory on his face."

My father slid his arm around me, as Zach continued. "Kennedy, when we were corresponding back and forth after I returned your letter, I tried to make you understand how important my team is to me. How they're more like family than a bunch of guys I was stationed with. I told you about Reaper, or Matt his given name, remember? How he was hurt by a guy with a knife, and then by the girl who agreed to marry him. After Ethan's threat, I called my team and asked for help. Matt came running, but he brought a friend."

My breath caught in my throat, a shiver starting up my spine. "Her name is Rayne Winters, and she has single handedly turned a jaded man like Matt into a someone who believes in love again, giving him his smile back."

I'm off my chair and around the island, wrapping my arms around his massive neck. "I'm so, so sorry." I cry into his chest as his arms wrap around me, bringing back the warmth I've lacked the past few days. The smell of his cologne fills my senses, and I can feel my body relax. "She's a beautiful girl." I admit, as it is the truth.

"She isn't you." He assures me. "Babe, there's more." Zach whispers, but I don't care what he has to say. Nothing can change the elation of knowing he didn't cheat on me.

His grip on me lessons as he pulls me back to look into my eyes. "I need you to understand, I had to protect you." Everything about him tells me he is warring with himself as to what to say. "Matt and I went to Ethan's hotel room. What we found, was so much more than a man with a crush on you."

I listened as he told me of the photos they found and what the news would announce the investigators found. He explained how he and Matt gave Ethan a small dose of what the girls must have felt as they took their last breaths.

"Your father and I agree the system is broken." Looking over to my father, I see his head nodding in agreement. "And there are more people in need of help out there."

Looking back and forth between them, I know in my gut what Zach is about to say. "But I won't even consider it, unless I have you by my side." His eyes searching mine, looking for any hint of doubt I may have.

"You'll be with the guys? The ones you served with?"

With his thumb wiping the tears from my face, his smile making an appearance. "We can set up a time for you to meet them. You can ask any question roaming around in your beautiful mind."

I nod my acceptance of his choice, agreeing to meet the men who know a part of him I never will.

"Not to put a damper on things, but Kennedy, what Zach and his men are doing is illegal. If they were to get caught, they could face jail time." My dad and his voice of reason. How Zach managed to get him on his side and look the other way while he took care of Ethan, I'll never know.

"Your father is right, what we will do is illegal, and some would consider immoral. But I can't sit back and let the evil of the world win, time and again." His eyes plead with me to understand his need to make the world better; safer. I cannot find it in me to argue against what he wants to do, or his need to protecting those who need his help, when other resources fail them. I may not be in a position to jump into a mission with him, but I can love him, and be there when he needs me.

"I do have something I want to speak with you about." Setting his beer down and clasping his hands together, Dad turns to face me fully. "The divorce is scheduled to be finalized at the end of the month, so Leeann and I have been talking more about what we want to do. We believe we've come to a final decision." Shifting in his chair, he clears his throat and takes a pull of his beer. "I'm going to be moving into Leeann's condo, but I want you to know this house has always been in your name." I was shocked, I had no idea he had done that.

"You know, with the end of my marriage to your mother comes a new start for me, and my relationship with you." I reached across the granite to take his warm hand in mine. Just like when I was a little girl, his assurance and protection radiates from his touch. I had once believed nothing could ever hurt me, as long as my father was near. "I want to continue to be a presence in your daily life. To be there for you when you need me, even when you don't." His eyes shifted between mine as he motioned for my other hand. "I want you to know, everything I do for you is out of love and the need to always protect you." Something told me his words were more of a confession than anything else. The odds were against me to ever know the truth. Just like Zach, and his involvement with Ethan's decision to end his life, the truth would be buried with the body.

"The house on the lake is Jason's and I've already had this same conversation with him." Dad glanced at Zach, who was preoccupied with shoving spaghetti into his mouth, and then reached into his pants pocket, removing a single key and placing it on the table beside me. "This key opens the front and back doors, you can move in after the fifth. I'll leave all the furniture if you want or you can do whatever you want to the place. It's yours after all."

I looked at the shiny, metal key, the light from the ceiling reflecting its brilliance. I loved this house; the way the entry doors all arched at the top and how the ceiling seemed to touch the sky. There was a tiny courtyard shared between the neighbors on each side. I loved the colors and the smell, I loved it all. "Thank you, Daddy!"

In this house, I was free to act like a ten year old, hugging my father until his face turned blue. Free to cover his cheeks with kisses and no one would chastise or belittle me. I hugged him so tight he began complaining of being choked.

I felt a new level of excitement and also a new level of independence. I could change things about this house, make it more personal. The thoughts kept coming. I looked at Zach, expecting his face to reflect the same joy as mine, only to find a look of disbelief and confusion. I wasn't sure why, this house was so much safer than the apartment over the shop, something he should be happy about. Not to mention the amount of room it has in comparison, so it didn't matter what Zach thought, not really. He owned his own home, a decision I supported fully. This was mine. Zach and I weren't married, nor had we housed the idea of that happening anytime in the immediate future. Not to say I hadn't thought about it or had a vision or two of the day I would wear white for the first and last time.

Zach jumped up and took charge of cleanup. I took him at his word he had it all under control and ventured upstairs to look around. Inspiration ran through my mind like tiny creatures scurrying around the forest floor. The carpet in the bedrooms would have to be removed and replaced, the hardwood floors could use a good sanding and refinishing. A new coat of paint would do wonders, but the bones of the house would stay. Wandering from room to room, I took in places I hadn't been in years; touching doorframes and smiling at the positive memories they held.

"Kennedy?" Zach's silky voice filled my ear, as my eyes were still taking in the small library my father's books currently called home. "You ready to head home?"

"Yes, I'm ready when you are." Leaving my father's house, now that things have changed so dramatically, was difficult. I was free to hug him and tell him over and over how much I loved him. We made plans to have lunch during the week and then the strangest thing happened...my dad hugged Zach. A backslapping, holding back emotions, hug.

As we neared the end of my father's street, it was a left turn to go to my apartment or a right to go to Zach's home. I watched as he turned the wheel in the direction of his house, checking several times to make certain traffic was clear. The streetlights briefly illuminated how his left foot was propped up along the inside of the door rim. His left elbow resting on his erect knee, while his body leaned to his right side, my side. It was the side of him I slept on when I shared a bed with him, the side I tended to walk on as we made our way to wherever we were going.

The soft hum of Zach's car combined with the beat from the radio was a complete contradiction to the angry rock Zach often had playing overhead in his shop. I didn't know the band or understand any of the lyrics, but it wasn't a long drive and it was Zach's vehicle. I did love this particular truck, though. The smell of the leather and whatever cleaning product he used to keep it in good condition. Still the best part of being with Zach was the way he holds my hand. His fingers were rough with calluses, yet he unconsciously left gentle touches on my hand. Sometimes his fingers were still, the connection sufficient, while other times he was fidgety and played with the tips of my fingers. Almost like he was playing whatever song on the radio or inside his head. Tonight, he stroked my fingers, long, soft touches that had goose bumps forming on the skin covering my arm. I wouldn't dream of asking him to stop.

Zach held my hand as he pushed open the door. Standing in the kitchen was the same dark haired beauty, although this time she was dressed and the shocked look was absent from her face.

"You must be Kennedy." She came around the island, her hand extended and a toothy smile giving a hint to her kindness. "I am so terribly sorry about the first time we met. There I was in my borrowed shirt and unmentionables, and you with a look which would make preacher man nervous."

Sitting at the bar was one of the largest men I had ever seen. His dark hair and broad shoulders caused me to slip behind Zach a little further. His face was illuminated by the open laptop in front of him, so as he stood from his seat at the bar, I caught sight of the large scar on the side of his jaw. While it wasn't gruesome, it was large enough to call attention, and perhaps give him an edge of danger.

"I'm Rayne, like the wet stuff which falls from the sky. My momma was sick of all the common names and wanted her daughter to be different. Too bad it became a famous stripper name a few years back."

I wasn't certain if she was kidding or not, but a giggle left my throat and found a room full of friends as everyone else joined me. Getting myself together, I extended my hand out to meet hers. "Forgive me, Rayne. It's a pleasure to meet you. Your name is lovely and certainly original."

Zach stepped around to the side of the island, his hand extended in the large man's direction. "Kennedy, this is Matt, or as I've known him for years, Reaper."

Swallowing the intimidation he created in me, I extended out my hand in his direction. "Matt, or do you prefer Reaper?" Hoping the smile on my face masked the trepidation in my voice and the shaking in my hand.

His hand swallowed mine, even more than Zach's did, with a firm, but not crushing grip. "Matt will work. It's nice to finally meet you, I wasn't certain I would get the chance."

Matt and Zach exchange a look, one filled with tension, leaving me to question how much of our argument he shared.

"Rayne, you managed to grow out of your shyness fairly quickly." Zach startles me with his abrupt subject change and ability to switch direction and attitude. Or maybe it's just the dynamics of their relationship.

191

"I had help," Rayne stood with her hands on her curvy hips. "Thanks to a conversation with a few new friends today." She shoots a side-glance to Matt.

"Zach, are we...?" Matt pointed between myself and Zach, eyebrows raised and voice curious.

"Yeah, man, she knows."

Matt nods his head in understanding, circling back around the island to his computer, his movements fluid, despite his massive size.

"Okay, give me a few minutes to get everyone linked up." Rayne pulls my hand, leading me to one of the empty barstools. Zach moves to stand beside Matt, his eyes fixed on the screen.

"Kennedy, I know this all seems strange and a little scary. Trust me, when Matt told me what they had planned, I questioned my sanity for thinkin' it was a good idea. The more I thought about it, the more it reminded me of the old west and how scores were settled. Don't get me wrong, I'm not okay with cold blooded killing, but sometimes, when the laws of the land seem to benefit the criminal instead of the victims, someone needs to step up and do something."

"You're right." I agreed, lowering my gaze to the pattern of the granite countertop. "I've trusted a few too many people who have only been out for themselves. Killing isn't always the answer, but neither is going to jail and then being released on a technicality."

Zach and my father didn't know I was aware of just how sinister Ethan had become. Yesterday, I happened to stop by my father's office to bring him a cup of coffee and say hello. As I stood in the elevator, I overheard two officers talking about the bodies dug up by park rangers in Colorado and Montana. When they mentioned how the guy who did it was found dead in a local motel, I started connecting the dots. My father wasn't in his office, but Lauren had been moved to a desk outside of William's office. Her name was etched on a brass plate, proudly displayed in the center of her desk, which was unattended, giving me permission to slip into William's office. A few clicks of the mouse later, I was able to see what Zach had saved me from.

"Kennedy, before I show you what you're about to get yourself into, I want you to know how this idiot here mooned over you. I was right

192

beside him when he got your letter and watched the determination on his face when he tried to understand how someone could do such a terrible thing to a beautiful girl like yourself. Most of all, I remember the day he pulled us all aside and told us he was finished with the military and ready to really live. When he didn't like the way Ethan Porter stepped on his territory, he called in a few favors and had the team take a look at him. When we got to his hotel room, and I won't give you any details, suffice it to say in the next several days the media is going to tell you just how bad this man was. What we did to Ethan isn't a tenth of what he deserved."

A lump formed in my throat as I realized how much he cared for me, even before we met in person.

"You are family, Kennedy. And no matter what happens, we take care of our own." Matt never looks away as he turns the computer screen in my direction. The monitor is split into five smaller boxes, each one filled with a different face.

"Ladies and gentlemen, this is Kennedy Forrester, the love of Viper's life. Kennedy, this is the rest of our family." I expected everyone to speak all at once, but everyone remained smiling, but silent.

"Kennedy, when we were in the desert, I was the highest ranking officer, next to Doc." A handsome man on the lower left nodded his head. With his uniform and haircut, he appeared to still be in the military. "Which made me the leader of this group. While we still have a few wrinkles to iron out, we may keep our responsibilities the same." When I failed to say anything, Zach came around the bar to hold me. "No need to be afraid, Kennedy. They wouldn't dare hurt you." He kissed the top of my head, as my attention remained on all the faces looking back at me.

"Kennedy is it?" A female voice severed the tension. "I'm Audrey Morgan. I'm married to this handsome man, Chase, or Diesel as the others call him." She waved her hand at the screen, a tiny baby in her arms with a handsome man wrapped around them both. "Don't you let these guys scare you none, everyone of them would cut their hand off if they even thought they had hurt you. I can tell just by looking at you that we are going to get along just fine." Audrey had a kindness about her and I found it hard not to smile with her words.

"Diesel?"

"Sir?"

"Anything to add or did Miss Audrey cover it?"

Diesel's face broke out into a sly smile as he reached over to rub the face of the tiny baby. He was a handsome man. Hell, all of the faces on the screen would fit on any runway or magazine. "Just that I hope you're doing all right after what happened with Ethan. Audrey had a similar situation not long ago, and it took us a minute or two, to get back to where we are now. I have two brothers, Austin and Dylan, who are busy with an issue here. I'm sure you'll meet them when you come to Charleston."

"Kennedy?" Zach prodded.

"Thank you...Diesel. I'm fine, no sleep lost over a man with issues." Diesel nodded his head and then returned his attention back to his baby.

"Ghost?"

"Sir?"

"You're up."

Ghost has dark hair, with sunglasses sitting on the crown of his head. A scattering of stubble dusted his chin and jaw. From what I could see, he had a few tattoos on his forearms, but his sleeves kept me from being able to see what they were. He looked to be sitting in a park, the Washington Monument in the background.

"Name's Ryan Biggs, or Ghost as these guys know me. Currently, I'm in Washington DC fixing a situation my mouth got me into. But I'll be headed down south soon enough, to help these guys right some wrongs."

"Havoc?"

"Sir?"

An olive skinned, dark haired man, sat up a little straighter. His uniform told me he was still in the military, but the background showed a white-sandy beach, the surf breaking in the distance.

"Hey, Kennedy. My name is Alex Nakos, I'm the good looking one in the group." A rumbling of snickers broke out, with a few "you wishes" thrown in. "These guys all call me Havoc, mostly because I cause a lot of it. Especially when I mix a chemical or two together, just to see what happens. I'm also known for this big Greek family I have, with a mother who won't rest until I'm married with a dozen children." Again the snickers filled the air. "I still have a few months left on my contract, but I'm always available for my brothers."

"Chief?"

"Yes, Sir?"

While the man on the screen looked to be a little older than the rest, he certainly wasn't any less handsome. His hair blonder, eyes a little brighter, but it was his smile I found the most appealing. Where the others had shared their alluring or sexy grins, Chief was all about being genuinely happy.

"I'm the old guy in the group, Aiden Sawyer. My job is to study the area and people we're dealing with. And may I add, Kennedy, keep an eye on that brother-in-law of yours. Your mother isn't the only one with an agenda." I didn't dare ask what he meant, too frightened to know what he would say. I nodded my head. "I will, thank you."

"Last, but certainly not least, Doc?"

"Viper?"

"I haven't heard from you in a while, you okay?" It didn't get past me the lack of 'Sir', as Doc addressed Zach. As hard as I tried to keep the smile on my face, my concern showed through.

"I'm good, but Kennedy, honey, never play poker with me or any of these guys." His index finger circled in the air to include everyone. "The second I didn't say sir, your face contorted. Technically, Zach and I are the same rank, so we don't call one another sir. Asshole maybe, but not sir." This time my laughter joined the rest; I could see the invisible bond these men had formed.

"My name is Logan Forbes. I'm a flight surgeon and the last one of us still stuck in the Middle East. These guys call me Doc. I'm about five months out from the end of my contract. When I leave here, I have orders for Virginia Beach, but after that, who knows?" Doc had darker hair like most of them, but his expressive green eyes stood out against the tan of his skin and the khaki of his uniform. Just like the others, he was pleasing to the eye.

"Well, let us know when you do. I'll try and keep these guys injury free until you get here."

"Heaven help us, if Viper is in charge of medical."

Zach moved around to join Reaper. "This is my team, five men who have put their life on the line, time after time. We've managed to get into some tight situations, but I've never had to question if any one of them has had my back. We may not have been born from the same blood, but our bond is just as strong. Kennedy, Rayne, and Audrey, you have my word as the leader of this team, if you ever need us, no matter what time of day or how severe the reason, I will always be there for you. When you say goodbye to the man you gave your heart to, I swear to do everything in my power to return him in the same condition he left you in." Heads all around the screen nod in affirmation.

"Kennedy, I think I speak for the group, when I say," Doc starts, crossing his arms over his chest. "You couldn't have picked a better man than Zach. He will stand by your side, keep you laughing, and never make a promise he can't keep. But if he ever screws up, give me a call and I'll kick his scrawny ass."

Matt covered his mouth, coughing an oath into his hand. Rayne squeezed my hand, pulling my attention back to her smiling face. "So what do you think, Honey?"

I feel slightly overwhelmed with the brotherhood and respect they have for one another, Zach's pledge to keep his team safe and the unity they all had with what he swore.

"C'mon, Kennedy, what do you have to lose? Hell, I'll have Reaper tell you an Uncle Ray story." Whatever this uncle story was, it had to be plenty exciting as the cheers came for Reaper to tell a particular favorite of each member.

"Tell her the one about the snowstorm and frozen balls!"

"No, the one about the carmel corn and glow sticks!"

Zach slapped his hand on the counter, causing all the shouting to stop, and me to jump with a gasp. "Enough! We want her to agree to stay with me, not run away when she hears about a man freezing his nuts off on a guardrail." His eyes return to mine, a silent plea hidden behind the authority. "As juvenile as we can be at times, we are equally as serious. Right now, I need to have an honest answer from you, before this goes any further."

With All eyes on me, as they awaited my decision to stay with Zach. No matter what kind of allegiance he had formed, my choice had been made the moment I laid eyes on him. I loved him for saving me, for caring enough to let me find my voice and for letting me be silent. For showing me life was so much more than avoiding disappointing people in your life, it was for living it instead.

"I will agree, on one condition." Zach crossed his arms, his brow furrowed. Matt leaned back in his chair, his face unchanged. "I get to hear this story about the man and the guardrail. And why the heck he would be naked in a snow storm."

# CHAPTER NINETEEN

## *Zach*

"JASON, YOU GOT A MINUTE?"

Growing up, I knew what my parents expected of me; try and do the right things, treat people fairly and bring out the good inside yourself. I also knew about honor, not just from my parents, but also from the military. Doing the right thing went beyond returning too much change given back to you at the checkout. It's one of the reasons I was standing with sweat running down my back, asking to speak with Kennedy's brother.

A few weeks ago, I was tattooing the name and picture of a man's late wife on his bicep. He told me how she'd begged him to never place her name, or picture, anywhere on him as she had heard it was bad luck. Now that she had passed, he was making a memorial. He told me of all the good she had done for him, keeping him out of more trouble than he cared to admit and how she loved him, despite his many faults. As he left that afternoon, her high school graduation picture was a permanent reminder of her. Later that night, as Kennedy sat beside me watching a rerun of a popular sitcom, I made the decision to live without regret.

"Um, yeah," Jason answered. "My last client just left and Savannah is busy at her shop. What can I do for you?"

"Well, it's about your sister." My voice cracked like it did when I was twelve. My nervousness was ridiculous. I was a former SEAL, I've taken on more men in combat and come out without a single scratch. It made no sense for me to be sweating bullets about a simple conversation. Jason took my nerves for something else as his eyes took in my shaky appearance.

"Oh, hell no! Tell me you did not get my sister pregnant!" He stood up, fists clenched, his posture resembling a cobra ready to strike.

"No...No! I'm...she...isn't pregnant."

Jason stayed silent for a few seconds, maybe a minute, but either way he eyed me up and down trying to determine whether I was telling the truth. Finally, he sank back down in his seat, relaxing back into the leather of his chair, his posture still guarded.

"So, what's wrong?"

"I'm thinking of asking her to marry me."

"And you're talking with me first? I mean...she does have a father."

Speaking with John had been the easiest part of this equation. Like the gentleman my mother nurtured, I made an appointment, dressed in a suit and showed up on time. I imagined what it was like to be in his shoes, as a virtual stranger swore up and down he would always take care of his little girl. Using blind trust as a guide, testifying no harm would ever come to her and she would never shed a single tear at his hand. All great selling points, but complete fabrications.

I was honest with John. I told him not only in words, but also in bank documents showing I could take care of her financial needs. I swore I would be the first to admit to Kennedy when I was wrong, swallow my pride when it was warranted, and be the best man I could for her. I admitted I was going to mess up, make her cry and have her so mad at me that she could spit nails, but I was determined. She was all I wanted and would work hard to keep her my biggest priority.

John had sat back and commended me on my honesty. He was glad I hadn't sworn from the hilltops I would love her forever and allow him to beat my ass if she was unhappy for a single second. Real life is full of sad moments and promises made before God and man can be broken. John, more than anyone, understood this...he was living it.

*"I've made several changes in my will, including giving Kennedy the brownstone I'm living in now. I know you have your own home and you both may decided to live there, but I need you to let her keep this just for her. She needs to have a place she can do with whatever she wants—sell it, rent it or whatever. Just, please, let her have this piece of independence."*

\* \* \*

With the blessing from both her father and her brother, my plan was set in motion. I was standing inside my bathroom, watching her as she caressed the silver key. For many, it was just a tool used to open locked doors, but to my girl this was the key to her past, to memories that gave her a reason to smile. It would open a place where she could travel and take refuge from the storms of life. While it complicated my desire to have her at my house, I would never make her choose between me and her independence.

"Come with me, please?"

From the first word I received from her all those months ago, I knew she would change not only me, but my entire world. Her dedication to being the best person she can, to making sure everyone around her felt comfortable and relaxed. Treating everyone the same, from the homeless that resided on the streets to the highest paid man in her father's office, everyone received a smile and genuine heartfelt greetings. There wasn't a single fake bone in her precious body.

"Is something wrong?"

Her voice was trembling and I hated that. Hated she was reconsidering her answer, fearing rejection would cause a butterfly effect, ending our relationship and severing the ties that bound us together.

"I have something I need to show you."

I tried my best to reassure her with my words and the warmth of my hand. We rounded the last step and I removed my jacket from where I left it on the banister, sliding my arms into the cold sleeves. Her face was drawn and sad, but she was trying so hard to put a smile on her lips. I could feel the fear emanating from her. She was thinking this was the end, that I was throwing her out.

Social media is full of shared moments, with a nervous young man showing the entire world how he gathered his friends and family while he asks the girl in his life to change her last name by taking his. I could have taken one of those ideas and made this special for her, but I wanted to go back to the way we met. A simple letter given in error and a soldier trying to get it to the right person.

Opening the door that lead to my back yard, the evidence of Reaper's hard work stood proud on the freshly cut grass. Between the two massive oak trees shading the back of the house, stood a military issued khaki colored tent, looking out of place in this suburban desert. White lights hung from the tree branches, illuminating the yard and setting the mood.

Guiding a confused Kennedy into the tent, her body leaned away from me, her apprehension not allowing her to believe something good was about to happen. My grip on her hand tightened, preventing the retreat she most desperately wanted. Ignoring her questions of, 'what is all of this?' and 'what is going on?' I closed the flap behind her. A single cot sat in the center of the tent, a laptop open with the screen as black as the night that surrounded us. I had saved every single letter she had ever sent me, printed off every email, and then placed them all together in a bound book. One single letter, however, was carefully placed in an envelope and sealed with hope and a prayer rested on the forgotten keyboard.

"This isn't anything close to what it was like for me when we first met." My mind's eye replaying my memories so perfectly, I could almost feel the heat from the intense sun. "That morning, all I wanted to do was get the medical convoy going and get the hell out of the heat."

Her bottom lip quivered, whether from fear or something else, I wasn't certain.

"You became so much more than any friend I have ever had. You've shown me true love and compassion are still very much alive in our society." Pulling her closer to the cot, I could feel her body quake with anticipation and worry. "In the first letter, you sought answers to the situation you found yourself in." Her eyes locked on the envelope, alone on the sea of black, random letters adorning the keyboard used to compose the same in such a unique fashion.

"This time, I need you to help me." Her eyes snapped to mine, her brow nearly bent in half with overwhelming confusion. My smile the only offering I could give that everything would be all right. "Read it, please." My words were soft as angel wings, the prayer they contained carried to her ears.

Her hands shook as she slowly retrieved the white paper, turning it over several times, but not a single question left her lips. I watched and waited as my own anxiety increased. Only two possible answers could be given to the words that were scripted on that paper. As a soldier, I've waited on insurgents in some uncomfortable conditions—heat, stagnant water, and dead animal carcasses to name a few. Yet standing here, surrounded by the smell of the tent, the sounds of the cool Atlanta night and the labored breathing of the most beautiful girl in the world, was by far the worst situation I have ever braved. In all of those other times, I had an out, a way to fight to the death or walk away to battle another day. This time, she had the ability to give me the response I had dreamed about for weeks, or shatter my heart into pieces that would never mold together again.

Four words written on the page clenched in her fingers. To anyone else, it would take less than five seconds to read and respond. Yet with an unknown amount of time clicking past, my heart rate increased to immeasurable speeds, as her eyes flicked back and forth over those four words.

As if a ray of light were cast down, sharing its joy by separating the storm clouds and ending the loneliness felt by the pelting rain, her smile filled the tent as her words brought peace to a crumbling man.

"Yes."

# CHAPTER TWENTY

## *Kennedy*

"ONLY DAYS AFTER PROMINENT ATLANTA ATTORNEY, John Forrester, served his wife of nearly twenty five years with divorce papers, a spokesperson for the family announced the engagement of his youngest daughter, Kennedy, to another society mogul, Zachary Michaels, son of Dr. Jonathan and Emma Michaels. No date was given for the young couple's nuptials.

*A trusted source reveals Claudia Forrester was recently escorted out of a high-end boutique when her credit card was declined and Mrs. Forrester became angry. Reports state the Atlanta police were called, however, no arrests have been made at time of this printing.*"

"Yes, Mother. I have seen the paper this morning." My eyes squeezed shut, my index finger massaging my left temple as the pounding of a headache appeared on the horizon.

"How can he do this to me? After all I've done for that man!"

I was able to recall a number of reasons off the top of my head. Claudia Forrester was reaping what she sewed.

"Just you wait! Zachary will find a younger, prettier version and you will end up just like me, a discarded housewife."

Disconnecting, I tossed my phone aside, as the tears made their angry appearance. Turning quickly, I nearly stumble over one of the boxes

Jason still needs to pick up and take to his new home. I had to get out of there, away from the anguish my mother's words had filled me with. How had the happiest of times taken such a downward spiral?

Sitting behind the wheel of my car, I had no a clue as to how I arrived outside Zach's house. Not caring if the car was secure, I flew from the driver's seat and through the back door, the alarm announcing my arrival. I knew where he would be at this late hour. Zach was nothing if not reliable and stable. The sound of the late night news anchor he always watched to wind down for the night filled the hall. I didn't bother to remove my shoes or care where my keys and purse landed as I jumped into his bed, his arms catching and pulling me close.

"She called again didn't she?" He reached over and silenced the television, holding me tighter as the sobs returned. "Let it out, Sweetheart," he instructed, keeping his true remarks to himself.

Zach had a long, heated conversation with his mother and future mother-in-law the last time my mother had upset me. Claudia proclaimed I was an ungrateful child and would suck the Michaels family dry. Her words were venomous and Zach watched in horror as they sank their deadly fangs deep into my heart. His mother, the lady that she is, wrapped her arm around me, whispering she didn't believe for a second what Claudia said. Zach had been too angry to say anything to her as he followed us out of the room.

"I told her to go to hell, Zach." I whispered, nestled against his neck, clinging to him as if my life depended on it. "She said you would stray when you figured out I was useless for much of anything." My words caught his attention and he turned us both, taking my face in his hands, his eyes searching mine.

"You don't need me to tell you how wonderful you are, but since she has planted a seed, I'm going to pour on my own brand of poison and make certain it never grows. You are the most beautiful woman I have ever met. You're kind, even when it is not warranted. You're giving, even when you have nothing left to give. You treat people, even the ones who don't deserve it, with respect and decency. You brighten each and every room you enter, and you make every day I get to spend with you a lot better because you're in it. You give me everything I need and then some."

His eyes stared into mine; reassuring me he was telling me the truth. Zach had the ability to give me the strength to face all my demons. My mother, who had cast me off, and any other obstacle I would ever encounter, I knew he would be by my side. But first, I had something I needed from him, something I had been afraid of.

"Zach—" My voice trembled, not with fear, but with the promise of what I was about to ask. He didn't respond with words, but a soft kiss to my damp cheek. "I—I need you to...”

"Anything, Kennedy. Anything you need from me it's yours."

His words were the key I needed to unlock my courage, freeing myself from the self-imposed prison I had created. I was ready to experience life in it purest form for the first time.

"Make it go away." I pleaded, not only for the hurt my mother had caused, but the doubt Ethan Porter had given me. Doubt in my ability to have a normal relationship with a man like Zach. I knew he didn't need any explanation or further instructions on my request. I also knew I could stop him at any second and he would continue to love me and keep me safe.

With a final search of my eyes and a lick of his lips, Zach dove in. The heat of his breath sent chills down my spine. His hand took a firmer grip on my face, directing my head in the direction he needed it to go. Finally releasing it, he wrapped his arms around my body pulling me tighter to him.

I could feel him, feel his muscles tightening as he caressed my skin. Opening my mouth to his, I wrapped my arms around his neck and pulled him impossibly closer as his tongue met my waiting one. Round and round, back and forth, touches sometimes brief and others long and inducing sounds from me I haven't heard myself make. I tried to pull back slightly, but Zach was unwilling to break the connection and followed me back into the comfort of the mattress, as he continued to explore my mouth with his pointed tongue.

Warm, rough fingers soon make an appearance along my ribcage, traveling at an easy pace in the direction of my satin covered breast, as his pelvis ground into mine. He was taking my request seriously and the reason for my late night visit was slowly starting to vanish.

Open-mouthed kisses lead the way toward the hand holding one of my newly exposed breasts. He pulled back slightly, long enough to remove my shirt and unfasten my bra. Moving me back to the sheets, warmed by our body heat, his mission resumed once again. Wet pressure encircled my left nipple, the sensation causing me to gasp, yet not allowing me to voice my pleasure. Zach was in control and I was along for the ride. A ride that would take me to a place I had only read about, but never visited, even by myself.

His pelvis made deliberate and even paths against my center, each thrust bringing more pleasure than the one prior. Bringing his mouth back to mine, his tongue buried deep in my mouth, my brain was on vacation as his fingers passed over the stitching on the hem of my pants. I felt his hesitation as he closed in on my panty line and, in a bold move, I reached down, directing him past the silk fabric, to the area of my body that wanted him the most.

With his lips attached to my neck, Zach pulled his lower body back enough for me to remove my pants and panties. With the material gone I could feel his erection, and yet I yearned to feel more. While he continues his assault on my neck, I ventured my right hand down his shoulder, passing over his pecks and finally to the soft cloth of his boxers. Refusing to second guess myself, I dipped my hand inside and took his engorged shaft gently in my hand, stroking first with just my fingertips, and then adding more pressure as Zach's moans increased against my neck. I circled my thumb over the head as my remaining digits encircled his shaft. Zach smashed his mouth to mine, pushing his tongue inside; giving me a preview of what I hoped would happen next.

Pulling his cock out of my hand, Zach slowly moved lower, kissing a trail all the way to the junction of my thighs. I should have been trembling, frightened of what was about to happen, but here, in this room, with only the flickering light from the television, I caught sight of the platinum ring he had given me just a short time ago. He had promised forever and placed a sign of that commitment on my finger for the world to see I was the love of his life. With the ring still in my vision, I spread

206

my legs, watching as my future husband locked eyes with me and kissed the tip of my pelvis.

Zach spread me open, as the tongue he had explored my mouth with, discovered hidden treasures. He took his time closing his eyes briefly. I pulled myself up on my elbows to get a better vantage point, watching as his tongue played with my swollen nub, while his fingers disappeared in my opening, bringing about a deep, breathy moan. I could feel his calculated motions as he searched for something deep inside, gasping when I felt the quiver deep inside my pelvis, knowing he found what he was looking for.

I wanted to continue watching his tongue as it pleasured me over and over, but the feeling was too great and the sensations caused me to fall back and close my eyes, my fingers pulling tightly at the sheets. I knew I was close not only by the tidal wave building in my pelvis, but at the wet sounds coming from Zach's tongue and fingers. I had read enough romance novels to know what to expect and had a general idea of what was happening. Nothing could have prepared me for the overwhelming sensations I felt as my entire body jerked and my spirit seem to float above the bed. The utopia of it all explained why men and women craved this act so much. No drug could ever replicate this and I was certain I never wanted to share this with anyone else...ever.

# CHAPTER TWENTY-ONE

*Zach*

THE SOFT PATTERING OF THE SLOWING falling rain against the window, kept time with the rhythm of her breathing. She had come into the shop just before close, wasting little time as she took her place, straddling my hips and taking my lips hostage. Since the blow out between her and her mother, she had become more comfortable with herself. Gone was the young girl killing herself to make everyone around her happy. Now, in her place, was a headstrong, sexier, and confident woman. One who wore my ring with admiration and pride, yet kept the simple life on her compass. A prime example was how she kissed the life out of me, and then turned on all her womanly charms just to get me to take her to the little barbecue place down the street.

She loved to sit down on their wooden benches, eat the free peanuts, and then toss the shells on the floor, laughing as she watched the patrons around her doing the same. It was defying the rules, being a rebel, even if it was expected by the owners. I loved watching her interact with the wait staff, complimenting them on their appearance or how they pronounced their name. She would look to me for advice on ordering her food, knowing I would eat anything she left behind. It was incredibly erotic watching her lick the sauce from her fingers, moaning as the sweet, sticky concoction stimulated her taste buds. I loved listening to her as she commented on each person sitting around us, sometimes making up stories about what they were doing there. Listening to her talk as she drank draft beer until she began to slur her words and holding her tightly against me as we left the restaurant. I was always careful not to let her trip and fall from her alcohol intake, but also to let every swinging dick in the place know that she was mine.

After we returned to my house, a place she found herself most nights—although our level of intimacy had not increased since that fateful evening—she would waltz up to the entertainment center, take out a stack of movies, and announce whichever movie landed face up, was the one we would watch. As she leaned over to pluck the winning title off the floor, I would place my hand over hers, and give my one and only condition. It didn't matter what we watched, as long as it was done from under the covers in my bed.

With the house secured and Kennedy warm from her shower, the movie began to play. Yet my attention was consumed by the perfect creature residing across my chest. Her leg was placed carelessly between mine, the softness of her skin against my much rougher, conditioned exterior. All those years as a SEAL changed more than just my outlook on life. The sweet smell of her freshly washed hair reminded me of the aroma from my mother making fruit pies. I could feel her quiet giggles as the comedy played out on the screen. Kennedy would hug me tighter when the male actor would do something she liked, or in some cases, didn't. But most of all, it was the tiny feather like kisses she would give me at random intervals. As wimpy as it sounds, all of these little things made my heart beat faster.

My decision to marry Kennedy wasn't one that came without question. Although we both grew up in privileged circles, we had vastly different role models. Where my parents didn't go two seconds without the exchange of 'I love you', or loving touches, Kennedy has witnessed nothing but coldness and formality. Her parent's marriage had been one of advantage and convenience, instead of love and honor. My job of showing her everything love has to offer won't be an easy one, something

I'm prepared for. I have prepared myself for many arguments, hurt feelings, and hours of groveling. I'm also prepared for make up sex.

"I have to read the book now." Kennedy said as she adjusted her arm resting between us. I waited patiently as she adjusted herself, getting comfortable.

"Shouldn't you have done that first, *before* watching the movie?"

The best part of Kennedy, the part I craved more than anything, is right before my eyes. Her smile, the one brightened even the darkest corner of the world, on display for me and only me.

"Traditionally yes, but I have to see what happens when the train stops and the next movie in the series isn't out yet." Kennedy scrambled out of my arms and across the room, her soft bare legs gliding across the darkened room. She carried her iPad everywhere she went, it was her constant companion. I watched her slide her finger across the screen, awakening the sleeping tablet. After tapping repeatedly, with a single victorious laugh, she crossed the room and climbed back into my bed. She curled into my side once more and began reading the book she had purchased.

Leaning closer, I read alongside her for several chapters. We found out the couple riding the train to the wall were still together, but running from their own people. My day finally caught up to me as I closed my eyes and fell into dreamland.

I was walking on a skinny pipe, much like the male character in Kennedy's movie, pulling her behind me. Instead of Kennedy helping me escape a shrinking room, she was on her knees pulling my belt from the loops that held it against my jeans, her fingers working quickly to free me from my denim confines. Her mouth was so warm, for a moment I swore it was real and prayed to any God who would listen I didn't wake up covered in my own jizz. Her actions became fumbled and the image blurred. I could hear her talking, chastising herself for her lack of ability to complete the task. I reached out expecting the image to disappear, however I came in contact with the bed sheets covering something hard.

I woke up and looked down, discovering Kennedy hidden under the camouflage of blankets, her warm hand wrapped around my stiff cock, which was still wet from her mouth. I pulled back the covers, getting my first glance at a frustrated Kennedy. Her lips wet and slightly swollen, her eyebrows furrowed in aggravation, and her tiny hand still wrapped around my now weeping cock.

"Baby, not that I'm complaining there is an issue, but what are you doing?" My voice sounded slightly amused. In situations like this when Kennedy would try something new, and then somewhat back herself into a corner, not having a clue what she was doing. It was cute, and it made her all the more special.

"I—I..." Her head lowered as she let out an exasperated breath, a piece of her now dry hair moving from the motion, swaying toward me and back into her face. I never wanted to make her feel small, like she was nothing in my eyes.

"Hey," I spoke softly, reassurance and love my expressed intention. "Look at me." Her body shifted as she slowly and reluctantly raised her head. I gave her time to swallow her nerves, she was growing into such a self-assured person and I don't want anything to deter that.

"I wanted to try it. I figured if I sucked at it, you would just think it was a bad dream and forget about it."

Pulling myself into a seated position, I took her face in my hands. My eyes searched her sad and confused ones. "Baby, first off, what you were doing was amazing. I was having this dream you were doing exactly what you really *were* doing. No guy in their right mind would ever tell his girl that having his dick touched by her is anything other than fantastic." Her hand began to move slowly around the base of my cock, her smile returning.

"And second?" She questioned, her movements not stopping.

"Second, ugh...you've made me forget what I was going to say." Her smile is full throttle, a sight I wanted to see every day.

My eyes never left hers as I placed my hand over hers, giving her silent but encouraging instructions on how to touch me. Her eyes left mine as they studied her hand moving with mine; up and down, twisting slightly at the tip, giving just a slight squeeze as she descended to the base of my shaft.

Finding her confidence once again, she lowered herself back down until she was again eye level with my cock. Her movements alone were causing me to twitch, but thinking about what may come, what I hoped she is about to do made my cock weep. With a smirk on her beautiful face, she opened her mouth wide, her eyes once again locking with mine. I watched as her tongue extended slowly, grazing the head with soft, innocent flicks.

"Take your time, Baby." I lifted my hand to stroke her silky hair, telling her without words she was doing everything right. She descended again, this time taking just the tip between her lips, eyes focused on my face.

"Mmm..." The vibrations from my chest traveled to my balls, spurring her on as she consumed more and more of my cock. Men are visual creatures and I was certainly no different. Watching my girl as she took larger and larger amounts of me into her mouth caused my brain to fall further into a lust filled haze. I decided to let her take complete control and removed my hand from hers before laying back down. I closed my eyes and gave myself over to the pleasure my girl could bring.

The feel of her hot, wet and eager mouth gripping my cock as she hollows out her cheeks with her sucking, and the popping sound of her lips as they pass the head, cause my body to jerk from the pleasure. Her free hand took my aching balls and began playing with them, sending me further into the zone we all love to visit. Kennedy, however, made this visit so much better as she she makes everything better.

She wasn't perfect in her movements and I felt the sting of her teeth several times as they hit the underside of my shaft. She could tell it hurt slightly and she apologized; yet continued. My hands were in her hair in an instinctive reaction to the pleasure she was giving me. I worried my actions would imply something other than how much I loved what she was doing.

"That's it, Baby, suck the head." My instructions were strangled as I was so close and yet ached to be closer.

She followed my instructions and with a quick look at her, I could see her jaw was growing tired. Her down motion was suspended and she was using her hands instead. It didn't matter to me, it all felt incredible. I wanted so badly to shout it out to the world, but that wouldn't happen, this was between us. My climax was imminent and I needed to move her.

212

didn't want to come in her mouth, instead I wanted to kiss her until her lips were swollen and she couldn't breathe. However, in a move that took my breath away, Kennedy took both of my balls into her warm mouth, while her hand continued to stroke my cock. It was unexpected and my complete undoing. I came with a shout of her name and a hard twitch of my body.

The moment, seconds after a release of not only body fluids—but all the chemicals that go with it, where you have barely have enough ability to blink your eyes, much less make words come together in a complete sentence, that's exactly where I am. Kennedy was still resting on her knees, but her bottom lip had begun to tremble. In the quiet of the room, she begins collecting her clothing and what little dignity she can scrape together. My mind is was screaming at me to say something, to explain to her if the house caught fire in this very moment, I would burn up it in. I was desperately trying to get my limp body to do something, anything, to make her stop.

"Kennedy..." I finally managed, my voice laden with exhaustion and contentment, "...wait!"

Her shoulders were hunched until she heard my voice. She slowly turns around, squares her shoulders, and defies the demons who are telling her she failed. Determination lit her face as she finally brought her eyes up meet mine.

"Sweetness," I lifted my left hand and motioned for her to come closer. "C'mere."

She moves slowly, like a child who had been caught doing something wrong, prolonging the punishment certain to follow. Standing tall, yet defeated beside the bed, her expression told me everything. With a small nod of my head, I beckoned her closer. She moves, but with reservation.

"Baby, you've gone and sucked out the last of my brain cells."

With those words, which were as lame as some of those Super Bowl commercials, her smile is back and a giggle fills up the room. Now that, the look currently on her face, the pride and the joy, is my favorite.

# CHAPTER TWENTY-TWO

*Kennedy*

THE ONLY SOUND IN THE ROOM WAS THE TACKY sound of paint being spread on the wall as I pushed the roller up and down. Zach had wanted me to hire a company to paint the house, but I told him I wanted to do it myself. The pain I would likely feel in my arms later may cause me to question my decision, however the feeling of usefulness and pride were my best form of painkillers.

After learning the house, my house, had always been mine in more than just feelings of comfort and security, I began to plan what I wanted to do with each and every corner. What would add to the warm feel it already had? What upgrades would add convenience and value? Zach's proposal caused such immense joy, yet, for a single second, I panicked as to what I would do with this slice of real estate. A single phone call did more than give me a much-needed break from painting the entryway; it gave me the answer to that very issue.

I pulled my phone from my back pocket, not bothering to look at the screen. It could be one of only two people, Zach or my mother. From the formal sound of the deep male voice, I was wrong on both accounts.

"May I speak with Kennedy Forrester, please?" Formality had always caused me to stiffen my spine. The man on the other end caused my muscles to align on their own.

"Yes, this is she. How may I help you?" I tried to sound bored, praying I would get off easy and it would be a salesman or another credit card company offering me a better interest rate.

"Ms. Forrester, this is Officer Frank Simone with the Georgia State Patrol."

My muscles clenched tighter and my heart leapt into my throat. My left hand found the center of my chest as I awaited the dreadful news such a call was sure to deliver. "Yes, Sir. How can I help you?"

"Well, Ma'am, one of our officers responded to a report of suspicious activity in the area around a well known business. When they arrived on the scene, they found a couple engaged in lewd behavior. Both were arrested for the activity they were engaging in since it was in a public place. The female, a Claudia Clarkston, gave my officers quite a fight and she was subsequently charged with resisting arrest."

During divorce proceedings, my father had given my mother every single thing she asked for; her car, one of their vacation homes, and a sizable settlement. He asked for one thing in return, that his name be removed and her maiden name be returned. I closed my eyes tightly, my free hand now flat against my forehead.

"When you say lewd behavior, Sir, do you mean...?" My eyes peeked open slightly, trying to erase the images of what I feared him to confirm.

"Yes, Ma'am. Mrs. Clarkston and Mr. Richard Caldwell, were found in a sexual position, and lacking their clothing." The mental picture his words left me with were enough to cause my heart rate to stop momentarily. "Mrs. Clarkston had a particular, er...part of Mr. Caldwell's anatomy in her mouth."

"I'm sorry, did you say Richard Caldwell?"

"Yes, ma'am. Are you familiar with the gentleman?"

"Sadly, yes," I sigh. "Has his wife been contacted?"

"Yes, ma'am. Mrs. Caldwell came to the station not twenty minutes ago. Mrs. Clarkston asked that you be called instead of her estranged husband, due to the relationship between the two men." *Oh, I bet she did.*

*What in the hell is wrong with my mother, getting caught in a lewd act with her daughter's husband?*

"Officer Simone, how may I assist you with Ms. Clarkston?" It would take many years of therapy and copious amounts of wine to rid me of the mental images now forming in my brain.

"Well, Ms. Forrester, due to the sensitive nature of the crime and the lack of response from the gentleman she was arrested with, we were hoping you would come down and post her bail."

"Wait, what do you mean the response from Mr. Caldwell?"

"Well, when Mrs. Caldwell came to retrieve her husband and found out he was discovered with Mrs. Clarkston..."

"Ms." I corrected, regretting the slip of my tongue immediately.

"I'm sorry?"

"Ms. Clarkston isn't married. She and my father divorced nearly two weeks ago." The silence on the line was uncomfortable. I could hear the rustle of paper and the beginning of chuckling.

"Um...well, when Mrs. Caldwell found out who her husband was arrested with..." The unease in his voice was no match for the way my skin was crawling as I processed the information. "She informed her husband he could kiss his bid for the Senate goodbye."

It took everything I had to keep my laughter inside. Apparently my sister couldn't turn a blind eye to everything her husband did outside of their marital bed. I thanked the officer, right after asking what would be considered an odd question. "Sir, does the jail have business hours?"

Zach arrived just after I had cleaned the last of my paintbrushes. He molded his body around mine, encasing my tiny form in his larger, stronger one. "I missed you today." His words finding my ear, as his lips found my neck, nipping and caressing the tender flesh.

"I missed you too, Baby." The edge in my voice telling him it had been a bad day. I covered my face with my hand as my body sagged with fatigue.

Zach being the super star fiancée he was, presented me with a bottle of cold iced tea. The smile on my face was more than any word of thanks I could ever utter. However, he also noticed the pain at the edges of my eyes, pain that came from more than just a hard day's work.

"Talk to me, Kennedy." He hugged me closer, for his comfort as well as my own. "Tell me what happened."

I refused to let this moment go and allow the harshness of the outside world fill it with negativity. Instead, I removed the cap from the bottle of tea and, in the most unlady like fashion, began to gulp it. Between Zach's warmth and the chill from the dripping condensation, two worlds provided me comfort in completely different arenas. The only noise in the room was provided by a group of passing children, singing a song both of us had heard many times. I turned in Zach's direction and placed the now empty bottle on the side table. I found strength in his eyes, his strong fingers, and his gentle smile. All were features I prayed our children would inherit.

"I need to cancel dinner with you." My fingers fumbled with the hem of his shirt, where the ink of his most recent tattoo peeked out. I was told it was a Latin proverb.

"All right," Zach conceded, releasing me and crossing his arms, making his massive biceps bulge. "What are we doing instead of eating? Because you're crazy if you think you're taking care of whatever is bothering you on your own."

So I told him, every detail I had been given. How I couldn't believe my mother could treat my father and my sister this way. She had betrayed her daughter, the one who followed her at every turn.

"Kennedy, you do know who your dad was seeing, correct?" His fingers touched the tip of my chin, bringing my face up to align with his, his eyes searching mine.

"That's different, he wasn't..." I didn't get to finish as Zach placed a firm kiss to my lips, his arms stopping any body movement, and my rambling as well.

"It doesn't matter." His breath brushed against my lips, calming me to the core. "What are you going to do about helping her?"

While sitting on the floor of the room I had been painting that afternoon—surrounded by paint cans and drop cloths, pizza from a delivery guy and beer left behind after my father had moved out—I told Zach about the internal war going on inside me. I felt this sense of duty to do everything to protect my mother, and yet, felt my mother needed to solve her own issues. Zach gave his attorney a call, insisting every man deserved their day in court, regardless of how guilty they may be. They both agreed a night in jail may be a good reality check for Claudia.

* * *

It was nearly seven the next morning when Zach held my hand as he drove me to the address I was given to post bail for my mother. The single story, brick building held nothing special in its appearance. Patrol cars were parked in neat vertical lines as Zach pulled his truck into a space just outside the main doors. With my hand firmly encased in his, he opened the door to the station and we made our way to the information desk. Once we had spoken with the polite woman who was manning the desk, we were asked to have a seat while the paperwork was gathered for Claudia's release.

While we waited in the plastic chairs, we listened to the sounds of phones ringing in the distance, fax machines sending information, and various conversations going on around us. It was one particular conversation, between the man standing at the end of the elongated desk and the receptionist, captured my attention. His uniform gave me the impression that he was a firefighter. I couldn't help but overhear his conversation with the kind woman who had taken our information earlier.

"So how soon before you have to be out?"

"Less than a month, and the wedding is next weekend." The fireman responded. He went on to say the news was not easy to deliver to his future bride. It seemed she had lost her mother last year in a car accident and they already had to postpone the wedding due to the funeral. Now it appeared the apartment they had been living in was sold and the new owners weren't interested in keeping the current tenants. I heard his confession of having no place to live and no hopes of finding one, as all of their funds were tied up in their wedding and honeymoon.

I placed three quick taps to Zach's thigh; causing him to release my shoulders he had been holding while sitting beside me and rose from the chair. With a deep breath and a tiny prayer, I approached the man.

"I'm terribly sorry to have been eavesdropping, but your conversation was carrying over to where I was sitting." I pointed over my shoulder to where Zach remained seated. "My name is Kennedy Forrester." Extending my hand, I placed a smile on my face, hoping it would be returned by the man before me. "I think I can help with your housing situation."

For the next thirty minutes, the fireman, whose name is Cole, and I discussed how I was willing to rent my childhood home to him and his future wife, Melanie, in exchange for the remaining repairs being completed. I would have my father write up an agreement for the couple to lease the house for the next twelve months, any work done to the house would be deducted from the monthly rent payment.

Before we finalized the agreement, a commotion arose from the back. I quickly excused myself, but not before Cole apologized to Zach as he hugged me in a gesture of thanks.

"Sorry, man, you have yourself an angel." Cole's voice was full of grateful emotion. The hug was pure gratitude as was the handshake he shared with a laughing Zach.

"It's about goddamn time you got here!" A disheveled Claudia stood rubbing her wrists. Her hair looked like she had gone a few rounds with a rabid squirrel. Given the events of the last few months, Claudia's words did not surprise me, or Zach for that matter. What was surprising however, was the fifty dollars I took from my back pocket and placed on the counter in front of my mother.

"Take a cab, catch a city bus or hitch hike, I don't care! You have earned nothing and I feel sorry for you. If you don't wise up real quick and change who you are, you're going to wake up one morning with nothing and no one in your life."

I didn't wait for a response as I shook Cole's hand one last time and confirmed the meeting time to sign the lease. I took Zach's hand and exited through same door I had entered, Claudia yelling my name and other choice words as the door closed behind me.

As Zach revved the engine, he placed his hand on my inner thigh and squeezed the jean-covered skin with a wink. "That was fucking hot, Baby."

"Oh, yeah? Just wait until we get home."

* * *

"Let me." His voice was ragged with want, as he crossed over to me, replacing my hands with his own. "You're driving me crazy over here."

I allowed my hands to fall away, groaning as his callused fingers resumed what mine had started. Our eyes met and I could see the fire growing behind his dark orbs. Full of the passion I created and couldn't wait to unleash, appreciate, and enjoy.

"Come here." Zach took over, his hands leaving my nipples to wrap around my naked back, lowering me to the softness the cushions provided. His mouth was warm and eager, his tongue commanding my lips and taking my tongue by surprise. I wanted this, I wanted it so bad. To be free and choose for myself, to give this to him on my terms and not when it's socially acceptable to do so.

His lips moved to my throat, but not for long before he rapidly descended to my navel, causing my breath to catch in my throat and my eyes to shoot open. This wasn't the first time he had explored that area, the place my grandmother told me to keep boys away from. But Zach isn't a boy, he is a full grown man. A man who has just ripped away the last piece of clothing separating my core from him. His thumb is already buried knuckle deep inside me as his teeth hold my clit prisoner.

He plays my body like a fiddle, knowing exactly where to touch and the quickest way to make me come. Several nips later his goal is achieved and my body is jerking from the overwhelming sensations. He doesn't stop though, as his tongue replaced his thumb, his hands finding my breasts once again. Zach's large hands engulf them, squeezing them as his tongue darts inside me over and over. I should have felt embarrassed, as my fingers thread into his hair holding him as my orgasm draws closer, but I don't. I will never feel anything but love when I'm with Zach.

"We can stop here." He looks up at me, his chin is wet from my orgasm, and his eyes pitch black with desire.

Pulling him up to me, I cover his lips with my own, silencing him and answering his unspoken question. My tongue finds his and I taste myself on him; it's tangy but not horrible. He never questions me when I don't

220

object after each time we have done this. It's not enough to stop me from doing what I want more than anything.

There is nothing between us, no layer of latex or fear of repercussions. Zach had to be tested recently for a life insurance policy his lawyer told him to take out. With my limited number of partners, there was no need. I gasped slightly as I lower myself over him, pressing the head of his cock past my exterior lips. Zach was a big man, bigger than any other man I had seen. I knew I was ready for him, ready to take this step, as I continued to lower myself, reveling in the feeling of fullness.

I stop briefly, but Zach never pushed, not moving or trying to move me. He's patient and understanding. I lower myself a little more, moaning as the pressure increases. A throaty sound comes from deep within Zach's chest, he feels this, enjoys it.

I placed my second hand around his neck and continue my tortuous descent over his shaft. Zach's face never falters, but I can see his eyes dilate as I descend further and further. Two things happen when I have him fully inside me. First, I can feel his pelvis against my clit, it's a nice feeling, creating a stirring in my belly. Second, Zach's fingers digging into the sides of my hips, stopping me, holding me in place.

Zach turns us over, his cock never leaving me. His rhythm is slow at first—in and out, in and out. I watched as his eyes close and he changes his strokes, adding a sweep that rubs my clit with each downward motion. I can't stop the moans coming out of me, causing Zach's eyes to open and his thrusts to increase. I can feel the head of his cock getting bigger, slicker with the lubrication my arousal is producing.

I want to come, to cry out his name and live the Hollywood fantasy where our bodies are slick with sweat and we finish together. But we are far from a movie couple, this is real. This is the man who will see me at my worst and, thank God, my absolute best. It's that realization and serenity which causes the tingling in my pelvis to rise to the top. With quicker thrusts from my end, my back arches and my breath quickens. This is so much more than a physical act, more than a move toward independence. This is our pledge that when things are good, and even when they're bad, we can come together and share the intimacy and pleasure we bring one another.

# CHAPTER TWENTY-THREE

*Zach*

KENNEDY WAS DUE HOME ANY MINUTE. She had been invited by her father's office manager to a baby shower for Lauren, one of the partner's daughters, who found herself pregnant. The father of the baby, William Vale, a beady-eyed geek who Claudia tried to push her into marrying. According to Kennedy, this Vale guy was somehow related to the presidential family she was named after. Following a series of bad investments, which landed his family in debt, he had been selling off most of the inherited possessions. When John and Claudia divorced, he had a historical curator come in and take all of the furnishings his ex-wife had purchased from the Vales, giving them to several museums. Claudia had not been happy.

I'd promised my girl I'd make her favorite meal for dinner, with a bottle of wine chilled and ready when she got home. With the steaks sitting in a homemade marinade, I cracked open a beer, and waited for her to arrive.

Sliding onto a bar stool with the remote for the television in my right hand, I'm just about to hit the power button when the computer on my left comes to life. Turning the screen to face me, I enter my password to open the program. With everything we went through with Virginia

Greyson and Ethan Porter, all of our electronics had iron clad firewalls and resetting passwords.

Doc's somber face greets me as I click on the icon. My heart falls to my stomach as I take in his face. "Doc?"

"Viper let me get everyone on before I tell you what has happened." Nodding in understanding, I take a pull of my beer as we wait for the rest of the team to login. This can't be good, and I hope whatever it is, has nothing to do with my team. The sound of the back door opening filters through to the kitchen before Kennedy's tired face comes around the edge of the door.

"Hey," she calls out, eyes going wide as she notices the computer and Doc's tired face. "Sorry, I'll just go upstairs." She whispers, pointing to the ceiling. Having Kennedy living with me has been a double-edged sword. While I loved having her around, sex on the couch being an added bonus, the proverb of not knowing someone until you live with them, is incredibly true. Kennedy has a head full of long, beautiful hair, which clogs up the sink and shower...all the fucking time.

"No, Kennedy," pulling out the barstool beside me, I motion her over. "I want you here to listen to what Doc has to tell us." When she met the guys, and chose to stay by my side, she also became a part of the team. While her part will consist of keeping the home fires burning, it is a vital role in my world.

"Hey, Kennedy. How are you doing?" Claire Morgan, Diesel's sister-in-law, and Kennedy have spoken several times over the past few weeks. They discovered similarities in their childhoods, forming a similar bond to the one I have with my team.

Kennedy tells her about the events of the office baby shower, including the uninvited guest who claims her baby was also fathered by William and is due within days of Lauren. While no fight broke out, John Forrester was called into the office to have a talk with William Vale.

"I thank God everyday I found a good guy in Dylan."

A smile forms on my girl's face as she turns to grab my chin. "I know what you mean, Zach is my personal hero." Her eyes gleam, colored in the truth of what she is saying.

223

"Ladies, as much as I'd love to hear about how you are the luckiest women on the planet, I do have some sad news to pass." Doc's voice pulled us both back to the screen, the faces of my team sectioned off into squares.

"Ramsey was stabbed to death on patrol last night. Captain said he had been playing with a scorpion, trying to get it to attack him when the lady came out of the shadows. She managed to stab him more than ten times before they got her off him."

The memory of the lady who did the damage to my arm came rushing back. Ramsey had wanted to see some action, experience real combat, I doubt he imagined it would be in the form of a female and the sharp end of her blade.

"Ramsey's only relative is his younger brother who is currently a guest in the Arkansas State prison system. The Red Cross got in touch with him, but his brother still has several years to serve out of his sentence and wouldn't be allowed to attend his brother's funeral."

A silence fell across us; the miles apart meant nothing at the moment "Kevin Ramsey will be buried in Arlington, by men and women he didn't know. No girlfriend will stand alone and cry for her loss, no mother is left behind to remember her son as one of the fallen."

Mentally, I'm packing my bag and calling the airlines to book a flight. I look to Kennedy, who has her phone out, sending a text message to my aunt of a family emergency.

"I've gotten new orders and will come to Arlington to attend his funeral and house hunt." Doc added the last in a reverent whisper. "Viper, I know you found Ramsey to be a pain in your ass, but you should know, his orders to go to Coronado came this morning." Ramsey would never know he had gotten his chance to become one of us.

"You're right, Doc. He deserves a proper funeral. I'll book my flight and meet you in Washington." My heart felt heavy, sadness gripping me like a vice. Based on the man I knew Ramsey to be, he wouldn't have lasted beyond the first day of training, but he had passed everything else required to get in. I owed him, as his mentor and friend, to give him a SEAL's funeral.

"Lindsey has an interview with CNN this week, I had planned on surprising her, do a little celebrating." Ghost mentioned as I watched Kennedy booking flights from Atlanta to DC. "I can join you two and give her time to finish up." Lindsey Jennings, one of the country's up and coming journalists, was as beautiful as she was smart. She and Ryan had met during an interview gone wrong. Lindsey came to the Korengal Valley to talk with the locals on their views of how the military interfered with their poppy harvests. She assumed since she was a beautiful female, the locals would respond with open arms. She was wrong.

When the shit hit the fan, Ghost came out of the shadows, scooped her up and got her to safety. For him, it was love at first sight. For her, in my opinion, it was an opportunity to launch herself to stardom. And it worked. She went from weekend reporter to co-anchor of a national station in the blink of an eye. He has caught her many times, with numerous news executives, always with an excuse and night of incredible sex. No matter what we tell him, he is convinced she is the one for him. We are all waiting for the right girl to fall into his lap.

"Count me in," Chief's voice full of reverence, his eyes fixed on his folded hands. "I'll see if Rachel can come with me." He didn't say much about the nurse he had been seeing. Long distance relationships can be difficult, especially as a SEAL, where you can go for months and not be able to tell anyone where you are.

"Rayne and I will be there," Reaper's deep voice added, his eyes blank with sadness. He was a hard man, but deep inside was a heart bigger than his body. Kennedy and Rayne had kept in touch, she shared how Matt continued to surprise her in the gentleness he showed her, despite his massive size.

"My brothers and I would like to join. While they didn't know Ramsey, they want to express their condolences as a part of this team." Diesel sat beside two other men, their matching blue eyes sharing the brotherly bond they had developed over the years.

"I'll be there too. It will get me out of meeting yet another girl my mother wants to set me up with." Despite the seriousness of the moment, laughter filled the room. Havoc's mother would never rest until she had him married with ten kids.

225

\* \* \*

Bright sunshine rested in the center of the clear blue sky. A slight breeze tickled the blades of green grass, creating a symphony of sounds as it billowed through the leaves of the maple trees, reflecting the somberness of the day. Seven Honor Guard Marines stood in formation, the infamous gold stripe vertical down their legs, rifles in their white-gloved hands.

The six of us stood at attention, waiting for the twenty-one-gun salute to begin. As guns were raised and with the sounds of my medals clicking as the wind danced around them, I chance a glance at Kennedy. This morning, as I donned my uniform, she commented on how her reaction to me would have been different if I had shown up in my dress whites, instead of the camo's I'd worn home on the plane. When I sat my cover on the top of my head, she tucked her lip between her teeth, letting me know I affected her just as she did me every time I looked at her.

The sound of the first seven shots echoed through the trees, signaling the beginning of the end of the funeral and causing her to flinch. The Honor Guard lowered their guns, feet still spread apart as the command for the next seven shots was given. A lone tear trailed down Kennedy's face, heartfelt emotion for a man she had never met. She would have made an incredible military wife and she will kick ass at what is in store for her.

"Ready, aim, fire."

The second set of seven split the silence, the bangs echoing off in the distance. Dylan, Diesel's brother reached over, pulling Kennedy into his arms, encouraging her to cling to him as her sadness took over. What I knew from Chase about his brother was Dylan had been a crass, asshole who made no apologies for how he treated women, until he met his match in Claire, his beautiful wife.

"Ready, aim, fire."

The third and final set of seven rang out as the chilling sound of the bugler, filled the air with the sound of *Taps*. Kennedy giving way to the sobs racking her body as Dylan pulled her closer, kissing the crown of her head.

Ramsey had no family to attend, as the remaining Honor Guard folded the flag that draped his coffin, the Chaplain laid the triangle in the center of the polished wood. Reaper was the first to break formation, kneeling at the head of Ramsey's coffin. Pulling the glove off his right hand, the white material falling at Havoc's polished shoes behind him. With the naked hand, Reaper reaches for his Trident pin, ripping it from his uniform jacket and placing the sharp tacks against the wood, slamming his hand hard on the metal, "Oorah," spilled from his lips, emotion coloring the battle cry of the SEALs.

Havoc followed, his Trident joining Reaper's, both men remaining on one knee as we each took the coveted gold shield from our jackets, paying honor to the man who died.

The Chaplain and Honor Guard waited patiently to show their respect, each young and hopeful face addressing me as "Sir," followed by how sorry they were for my loss. I know they mean well, whether out of obligation or respect, they've taken the time to say something.

Diesel bends over, taking the folded flag into his gloved hand, turning it over several times. The ladies, who chose to come with us, stand in a huddle just past being able to hear what he is about to say.

"This started out with one man's need to protect the girl he loves." His eyes flash to Dylan, who nods his head, but remains silent. "We continue for the innocent who can't find their voice, for the tired and the afraid. For the ones we love, and the strangers we're destined to meet. We do it together, with no regrets."

Looking down at Ramsey's coffin, six Trident shields glisten in the sunlight. Everything we did was accomplished as a unit, no one more important than the other. What we wanted to continue would require more bravery, and perhaps stupidity, to make it successful.

"We do this as brothers, just as we've always done." Diesel looks to each member of the team, making certain they understood what this meant. Austin and Dylan had always been civilians, but I felt confident Chase could mold them into productive members of the team.

Bending down to touch the shield I had placed on Ramsay's coffin, I recall the history lesson he had given over what the symbol meant, the sacrifices we all made to wear the shield.

"The Trident Brotherhood."

The end

# THE OFFER

Join my mailing list and I will send you a FREE eBook.
Visit my webpage CaycePoponea.com.

# OTHER WORK BY
*Cayce Poponea*

## SHAMROCKS AND SECRETS
*Book One*

Event planning, dealing with demanding clients and defusing situations before they get out of hand are all in a days work for Christi O'Rourke. But when a mystery man seems to appear at every turn will she have the ability to handle him as well?

Power and wealth are staples in the world of Patrick Malloy. But when family obligations dictate his future, a future involving a certain spirited young woman, will Patrick have what it takes to win her heart or will his lifestyle place her in more danger than he ever dreamed of?

. . .

## CLADDAGH AND CHAOS
*Book Two*

Shamrocks left us with Patrick posing an intriguing question. What exactly happened during those twenty-five years? We know that they got their happily ever after, but how did Patrick and Christi get there? Could love have a shelf life?

. . .

# STOLEN SECRETS
*Book Three*

Arianna Covington's world is turned upside down after the tragic death of her fiancé. Her friends watch as she tries to put the pieces of her life back together, only to fall further into the depression and seclusion her loneliness creates. To them, a trip to New Orleans for Mardi Gras will somehow make the demons, which haunt her, vanish into the sweltering heat of the night.

What they don't know is, Arianna has been living a lie, a spider web of secrets she keeps in order to stay alive. Using the city's reputation for lost inhibitions and excessive celebration, she vanishes into the sea of spectators. She emerges with a new look and endless choices, leaving behind the secrets and lies she never wanted or earned. How can one night of burying your past, turn into a war with Dominick Santos? A man even the devil himself fears.

\* \* \*

# SOUTHERN JUSTICE TRILOGY

## ABSOLUTE POWER
*Book One*

Dylan Morgan has it all; a prestigious career as a Detective for the city of Charleston, devilish good looks and a selection of girls whenever he chooses. Southern born and raised, he lives by the pearls his Granddaddy imparted to him. But when he questions his worth to the citizens of Charleston, his fears are realized when someone close to him is in danger. Does he follow the letter of the law as his position dictates, or does he follow his conscience, which will cause him to straddle a fine line? Can Dylan overcome the demons he creates for himself? Or will he toss everything away in a moment of reckoning?

Claire Stuart has fought hard her whole life not to fall into the same trap as her mother. She refuses to allow men to use her and toss her away. Needing to escape the hardship her family creates, she seeks education over acceptance and uproots herself from the backwoods of Kentucky to the charm of Charleston. She knows all about Dylan Morgan and his choice to bed every woman he comes across, yet she finds herself unable to listen to the warnings her mind and friends give her. Can Claire ignore Dylan's past and allow herself to let someone in? Someone who could shatter her very soul

. . .

# ABSOLUTE CORRUPTION
*Book Two*

"Hold a door open for your girl, not because it's expected of you, but because it gives you a moment to appreciate her as she walks ahead of you."

Austin Morgan left the safety of his home in Charleston, accepting a position in New York City to make a name for himself. He wanted to earn his reputation through hard work, inventive ideas, dedication, and not by the legacy or influence of his family's name. His dedication to work leaves little time for a social life or the promises forgotten, creating the perfect opportunity for deception to reach its greedy hand out and grab ahold of this Southern born gentlemen. What will happen when he has to make an unexpected trip home and rediscovers what is really important? Will his eyes finally be opened to the deceit and misplaced trust of those around him?

"Never let the fear of falling keep you from learning how to fly."

Lainie Perry has never backed down from a challenge her entire life. She has come to count on her wits and stamina in achieving her goals. She has left her fears and those who would prey upon them in the dust. What happens, though, when her latest adversary exists only in her mind? Can she win the battle when the imagined enemy is already dead? Or will she need to seek help for this struggle?

Can these two find the help they need in each other?

. . .

# ABSOLUTE VALOR
## Book Three

Chase Morgan said goodbye to the Marines, believing by removing his uniform, the hero persona would go with it. But when he meets the girl who shows him how the hero lives in the heart of the man and not in the clothes he wears. Will he be able to ignore the demons of his past, which plague him with reminders of cruel intentions? Or can he let true love move in and take residence in his heart.

Audrey Helms describes herself as a bad country song, complete with a boyfriend who treats her badly and more baggage than a Kardashian. Can this timid southern girl be the one to mend the bonds of brotherhood? Or will the sins of her past be too big to forgive? Will Audrey and Chase learn the meaning of true love, and how to live with no regrets and absolute valor?

* * *

# CRAIN'S LANDING

When life threw her a curveball, Natalie Reid adjusted her stance and hit a home run. With her life packed neatly into the back of her SUV, she bids goodbye to her college life and steers toward adulthood. With the help of her father, she has been given the opportunity of a lifetime. Will she be able to win the hearts of the sleepy southern town. Or will it's hidden secrets be more than what she bargained for? How long will she be able to resist the persistent Grant Crain?

Grant Crain is well acquainted with the joys of living in the south. All his life he's known that when Ms. Connie makes her famous pecan pie, you better hurry and get a slice. That when the fireflies dance in the dusk, it seems to make the heat of the summer day a little more bearable. He had decided long ago this town would always be home to him. He never expected that a tiny, Yankee girl would turn his comfortable and carefree world upside down. Or that a ghost from his past will do more than come back to haunt him.

\* \* \*

# DEDICATION

To every man and woman who have served with our Army, Navy, Air Force, Marine, and Coast Guard. My personal gratitude to the elite members of Special Operations around the world.

# COMING SOON

**SECRET ATONEMENT**
*(Book Five Of Code Of Silence)*

**BURIED SECRETS**
*(Book Six In Code Of Silence)*

**OPERATION SEAL**
*(Book Two Of Trident Brotherhood)*

**A SEALS REGRET**
*(Book Three Of Trident Brotherhood)*

**A SEALS HEART**
*(Book Four Of Trident Brotherhood)*

**A SEALS MISSION**
*(Book Five Of Trident Brotherhood)*

**LOVE OF A SEAL**
*(Book Six Of Trident Brotherhood)*

# ABOUT THE AUTHOR

Cayce Poponea is the bestselling author of Absolute Power.

A true romantic at heart, she writes the type of fiction she loves to read. With strong female characters who are not easily swayed by the devilishly good looks and charisma of the male leads. All served with a twist you may never see coming. While Cayce believes falling in love is a hearts desire, she also feels men should capture our souls as well as turn our heads.

From the Mafia men who take charge, to the military men who are there to save the damsel in distress, her characters capture your heart and imagination. She encourages you to place your real life on hold and escape to a world where the laundry is all done, the bills are all paid and the men are a perfect as you allow them to be.
Cayce lives her own love story in Georgia with her husband of eighteen years and her three dogs. Leave your cares behind and settle in with the stories she creates just for you.

# AFTERWORD

Follow me on my webpage, Twitter, Goodreads, Pinterest, and Facebook for information on future works of fiction.

## Caycepoponea.com

Twitter @CPoponea

Made in the USA
Middletown, DE
24 February 2017